AILSA KAY

Under Budapest

A NOVEL

GOOSE LANE

Edited by Bethany Gibson.
Cover image "Smoking in the Light" © 2009, Soós Bertalan, www.soosbertalan.com.
Cover and page design by Julie Scriver.
Printed in Canada.
10 9 8 7 6 5 4 3 2 1

Library and Archives Canada Cataloguing in Publication
Kay, Ailsa
Under Budapest / Ailsa Kay.

Also issued in electronic format.
ISBN 978-0-86492-681-4
1. Budapest (Hungary)—Fiction. I. Title.
PS8621.A78U54 2013   C813'.6   C2012-907141-2

Goose Lane Editions acknowledges the financial support of the Canada Council for the Arts, the Government of Canada through the Canada Book Fund (CBF), and the Government of New Brunswick through the Department of Tourism, Heritage, and Culture.

Goose Lane Editions
500 Beaverbrook Court, Suite 330
Fredericton, New Brunswick
CANADA E3B 5X4
www.gooselane.com

This book is dedicated to my husband, Todd Fullwood:
your love makes everything possible.

And to my family,
Maureen and Bev, Laird and Raymond.

Budapest Night

So me and Csaba, we're walking down Szent Istvan Korut toward Margit Hid. It's late. Hardly anyone on the street. And it's fucking cold out, so we're walking extra fast, heads down. We're talking the way we always talk. Meaning, I'm doing most of the talking because I'm eloquent that way.

"Here's a perfect idea. Where can tourists go to get real authentic Magyar?" This is what I ask Csaba, my best Hungarian friend since we were ten.

Csaba only wipes his nose with the sleeve of his coat, so I keep going.

"In the summer, Budapest is crawling with tourists, right? Thousands, maybe a million even. And what do they see? Just the usual *turista* shit—Vaci Utca, the market, Castle Hegy, whatever. Churches. Maybe they buy a painting of the Duna. Maybe they eat cake in a superior Budapest café. But they don't see the real Budapest because what they see is fake. They get nothing truly Hungarian. No authentic Magyar."

"Tourists don't get authentic nothing," says Csaba. "Except maybe authentic girls. Tourists definitely get them."

"True. Sometimes American men, and even European men, get lucky with Hungarian girls because they have money."

"So you want to offer authentic girls for money? Bro, that's not original."

"No, I'm not saying we sell the girls. That's not what I'm saying. I'm saying we give tourists the real deal, Hungary like Hungary truly is. Veritable Hungarian families, like yours, for example, make dinner for tourists and talk about Hungarian life for real. Maybe they talk about communism. Americans love communist shit. Stalin and gulags and shit. What do you think? Take the tourists into a truly shitty communist *panel* apartment, serve them a nice goulash, and tell them veritable Hungarian stories. This is what I call a premium opportunity."

Sometimes Csaba doesn't get my ideas. He has minimal imagination. So I say, "You could tell the one about your Trabant."

"Ha. To make that Trabant start, I had to strap my mom to it, tell *her* to go." Csaba's laugh always makes me laugh. His voice goes high like a girl's, then gets stuck in his teeth like *ts–tsts–tsts*.

"See. That's what I'm talking about."

"Yeah. Hulyes drug addict took my car. Should've stolen my mom. Woulda got away faster." *Ts–tsts–tsts*.

"TRUE Hungary—all one word. Some shit like that. Package tours, bro."

He's getting it now, nodding his head, grinning that skinny grin.

"We just need a couple investors, some advertising. Fortunately for ourselves, money's no problem. I know the veritably richest Hungarian family in Canada. Have you ever seen a true

Ferrari? This one dude owns three of them. He lives out in the country, and he let me drive one once. I accelerated it from zero to two hundred in under five seconds. Unbe*liev*able. I thought I was gonna fly. Dude said he never seen anyone drive his Ferrari that fast. I'm a premium natural when it comes to Ferraris. When you visit me in Toronto, I'll take you to meet this guy, and I'll drive you in his Ferrari. I know this guy. For sure, he will love our idea." I always say it's "our" idea even when it's usually mine. I learned that in leadership class for delinquents at the Toronto Y: share the glory, build team loyalty. "He'll give us the money for our plan for sure. He always tells me, 'Janos, you remind me of me. You don't stay under any frog's ass for long.' That's what he says. Also, he says, 'You're a man of opportunity.' What a guy. You'd love him. He's a crazy fucker. Mega-rich. I do him favours sometimes. I'll call him tomorrow. He'll do me a favour, no problem."

Csaba says, "What model Ferrari?"

Csaba always asks me so many questions about Canada. He says he'd never leave Hungary because he loves his country. I know what he's saying because I love this shithole too. My family left because it used to be communist and oppressive, but in 2010 it's not. I been back to my homeland twice before this time, and every time it gets better. But still, I think Csaba would come to Toronto if he could. If he had the money. If our business venture works, maybe by next year he'll have money. That's the point. We have so many ventures, for sure one of them will work. I got exactly one year here to make it work, and two months is already vanished with doing nothing except thinking of ventures.

We stop at the bank at the corner of Margit Hid and go

inside to the bank machine. I slip my card in the slot. Since Csaba lost two of his shitty jobs last week, I'm paying for everything. I don't mind. I'm generous. It's my nature. Plus, Dad deposits money in my account every month for me and my grandma—for groceries and rent and shit—just until I stand on my own feet, he says. We're not rich, but compared to Hungarians we're Kardashians. My family owns one of the best restaurants in Toronto. Once, Cher ate there. For real. We got her picture on the wall next to my mom when she was prettier, before my dad left her. Me, I don't want to run a restaurant, but I could own a bar. I did bartending for a few weeks at high school parties, and honest to God, I did flair like nobody ever seen. Like everyone was coming up to me, and asking for my cocktails, saying I'm like Tom Cruise in that old movie. In fact, if you go to YouTube, you'll see videos of me and my best Toronto friend Marco doing cocktails in my dad's basement. We got so many hits, and we got so popular all over the Internet, we were going to start our own private course. But I came here to Budapest instead because this is the land of fucking opportunity.

The bank machine spits out the cash. I split the wad and pass half to Csaba. Csaba looks at me like he's thinking he should say no, but he doesn't think long. He takes the cash and he stuffs it into the pocket of his nigger-hoodie. That's what he calls it. Well, it's what I taught him to call it, but it sounds hulyes when he says it—stupid. I don't know why. Maybe because they don't really have niggers in Hungary.

"Thanks for the loan, bro," he says. As if it's a loan. How's he gonna pay me back? Guy earns shit. No, worse: he earns forints.

"Whatever. Pay me back in dogwalking. Been looking for someone to pick up Csenge's shit."

Joke. Nobody picks up dog shit in Budapest.

We're going down the ramp to the Margit Hid underpass. It smells like a fucking urinal down here. Not just tonight—every day. Which raises a question: how many dudes piss under this bridge? New idea: if we dress like security, we can catch the piss-for-brains who piss down here and fine their asses. Ha! A thousand forints each. We'd be immediately rich.

But Csaba stops, takes the wad out of his pocket, and he smacks it into my chest. His face goes all proud, like the way he gets in his uniform. He thinks he's a real Magyar fighter in that uniform. He says he's defending the real Hungary. I never know from what, but skinny fuckers like Csaba sometimes need to talk big.

"Fuck you," he says.

"Bro, I was joking." And I laugh to show him no hard feelings.

I try to push the money back on him, and just then this fucking gypsy comes up to me. He comes right up to my face. "Cigarette? Telephone card?" The guy stinks and he's wearing this long, filthy old winter coat, and he's got a kid with him, and the kid's not wearing any hat or any mitts, and he's looking at me with those pathetic beggar eyes and his nose is running. Disgusting. They think I'm a tourist, think this'll work on me same as it works on hundreds of other stupid foreigners.

The gypsy grabs my elbow. "Cigarette?" Kid hangs back, looks hungry.

"Fuck you." I shake him off.

The floor of the underpass is wet and greasy. I didn't mean to drop him, but the guy loses his balance, lands on Csaba.

"Fuck." Csaba shoves the gypsy back at me. I push him off again.

Csaba pushes him harder this time and I jump out of the way. The guy lands on his ass. Csaba laughs. *Ts–tsts–tsts*. It is kinda funny, I have to say.

Gypsy tries to stand up, Csaba kicks him back down. "Sit, dog-fucker."

Honest to God, all I want is to get to where we're going, score the dope, find a party. Fuck, but I can tell by Csaba's voice, he's getting the way he gets sometimes because Csaba's God-given talent is losing his shit.

The gypsy can tell. He shimmies backward on his ass. Leaves an ass-sized trail in the greasy wet.

"Come on," Csaba says. "Beg, gypsy. Beg the nice Canadian. He'll give you money. He gives everybody money."

I'm just standing there, not aiding or abetting, but the gypsy looks at me like I'm gonna save him.

"Beg." Csaba kicks the gypsy in the face. Blood spews out the guy's nose. "Beg. You pathetic dog-fucker."

And Csaba laughs — *ts–tsts–tsts* — and then I'm laughing because why is he calling him dog-fucker, first of all. And second, I laugh when I'm nervous, and when Csaba goes off like this, I get nervous.

Csaba's twirling and dancing around the guy like some kind of crazy folk dancer in boots. Bam. He kicks the gypsy in the kidney. Guy screams. Like really screams. Like a girl.

Csaba stops dancing. Looks at me. "You not gonna give him money?"

The guy's on the ground not even moving.

"Come on, turista. You love to see people beg."

Turista? "Fuck you."

"You want to fuck me?" Csaba shouts in my face. "Turista wants to fuck a real, authentic, veritable Magyar now? Wants a TrueMagyar 'all-one-word' prick up his Canadian asshole?"

He shoves me. I'm bigger, so it doesn't do much, but for a second I think he's gonna come at me for real, lose his shit on my ass. I'm his best friend, for fuck sake. My grandmother bakes him pogacsa. I see the gypsy slithering away. I don't even think. I stomp on the fucker's ankle and he yells out. I yell back: "You think we let you go now?"

"Yeah!" says Csaba. And we're on the same team again, like it should be.

"Go home, you dog-fucker," and he kicks the gypsy in the head, and then the guy's truly fucked. He's on his back, and no way can he fight back, but Csaba goes apeshit on him. He kicks at him with those fucking boots, and the whole time the gypsy is saying, "Stop" and "Please," which is useless, and I don't understand why he doesn't just see it's useless and shut the fuck up.

Finally, Csaba falls back, worn out. Gypsy's a bloody shit sack on the floor, looks like roadkill. Csaba's sweating and breathing out hard white puffs, specks of blood on his face, but you can tell now he's satisfied. Like he's put something right. Then I hear something move behind me. Dumb-eyed kid. Totally forgot about him. Soon as I turn, he runs. Fast little fuck on fast little legs. Through the underpass and out the other side. Me and Csaba just look at each other. We don't even have to say a word. Telepathic is what we are. We take off after that little fucker. Up the stairs and out into night. Down Balassi, asphalt sidewalks and cobble streets. We bang past parked cars and that touristy csarda. He's a fast little fucker, that gypsy kid. And I don't even know why we're going after him, just to get away from Csaba's fucking mess in the underpass, just to run. Maybe we're gonna beat up the kid, but I'm not thinking about that. I'm just thinking, Go. Kid dekes onto Hold. I nearly knock over a girl holding on to her boyfriend's arm when I take the corner. Csaba's behind me. I can hear him. Gypsy kid flies super-fast and everything's like a movie. You kinda want a soundtrack for a chase scene, but nobody's playing one. Just our feet, pounding. We're hunters and it feels like fucking. Like power-driving the ass of the most beautiful girl who's ever shot you down, just letting her have it. Fuck, yeah. Past the parliament, past huge apartment houses and the trees on the side and the coffee-hut in the middle of Szabadsag Ter and I am on the little fucker's heels, maybe five metres behind, and he runs right into the middle of that fountain that comes up from the ground like a room made of water. I follow him into it, but he's gone. No joke. Like a fucking ghost. Four walls of water around me and no gypsy boy. "Fuck." I step toward one wall to make the water stop and it does. I walk through it like I'm fucking Moses and there's Csaba. Bent over and breathing so hard he's almost puking.

"Buli." I smack his back.

He wheezes out a laugh. He gives me the sign, our sign: "Party."

We pick up the dope, same as usual. Not a lot. Just enough for us. That's one business venture we've never even tried to plan.

Fucking Vietnamese have it all sewn up these days. Nothing against the Vietnamese, but I'm not their culture. And besides, I'm a man of opportunity, not an idiot. We duck down a side street and share a joint. Fuck, it's cold. Thank God for my Eminem hat. It's wool, keeps my ears warm. Chicks love it.

"Where to next, boss?" I call him that sometimes. Joke. I mean, partly joke and partly I like to build him up a bit.

Csaba takes a big inhale. Holds it. "Buli in Obuda. The dockyard."

You're kidding me. "No way, man. Too far. Gotta be some party happening around here."

He waves the joint in my face. "You think I killed that gyp?"

"Nah." In fact, I'm a little worried about this exact thing, but all I really want tonight is to be high, have fun, maybe meet a girl, and have sex in her car or in a park. Can't take her back to my apartment because I'm sleeping on my grandma's couch. Temporary. Just until me and Csaba get our business venture off the ground. Point is, gypsy is not my problem. A real, premium Budapest night, that's what I want. Get high, get laid.

"Fuckin' taught him a lesson, though." Csaba laughs. "Oh my God, and that kid. That was the funniest. You chasing after the little kid. How'd he get away?"

Man, the weed's wet. Keeps going out. I pull out my lighter again. Fingers are so cold they're like somebody else's. "I dunno. There's got to be something happening this end of town."

"I bet you let him go on purpose."

"Suck your daddy."

"You girl! You couldn't even kick the gypsy dog." Csaba's laughing, getting in my face.

Csaba never gets laid. That's why he's like this. When we

go out to a club, the girls stick to me like honey. They love how I talk. They say, "You talk Hungarian like my grandpa," and I say, "Dirty, dirty old man," and they think that's funny. I guess in Toronto we talk old-fashioned Hungarian, which is maybe why I'm so eloquent. But the point is, Hungarian chicks love me, and sometimes I tell them how great Csaba is, and then maybe he gets lucky. But he's not so good-looking and he doesn't know how to talk to women.

"Let's just go to the Seventh District. There's always something happening around there."

"Obuda," he says. "Way better party. I'll call Abel. Maybe he's driving." He reaches into his pocket for his phone. "Fuck!"

I know it before he says it.

"Fuckin' gypsy took my phone. Fucker!"

He's mad, but he's kinda happy too. Makes everything make sense, you know. For a guy like Csaba.

"Gypsies stealing fucking everything from us and then our fucking government tries to shut *us* down. Tells us *we're* the problem. We're trying to *solve* the problem: ciganybunozes."

"Fuckers," I say. Just to be on his side.

I offer him the last wheeze. He butts it. Then we're walking; floating, I should say. My phone rings. It's Csaba's brother, Laci. Weird. Why's he calling *me*?

"Bro," I say. I call him that sometimes.

"Hey. Csaba with you?"

I pass the phone to Csaba. Csaba says, "What," listens, and passes it back to me, looking pissed off.

I give Csaba a shrug. "My man," I say to Laci.

"You been smoking?"

"Nope. You offering?"

"How fast can you get to Blaha?" Meaning, Blaha Lujza Ter. Meaning, he's partying.

"Pretty fast."

"Good. Meet me at the romkocsma on Akacfa. Don't bring Csaba."

Csaba's looking at me like he knows something's up. He fucking hates Laci. Sibling rivalry.

"A favour, Jani. I'm counting on you."

Awesome. Laci Bekes is counting on *me*. This night is definitely improving. Really, I'm not so surprised that Laci called me. I've been cultivating my relationship with him ever since Csaba told me what a big deal his brother is now. I mean, I know Csaba and Laci from way back. They live next to my grandma, so I knew him when I was a kid and visiting. But now, it's different. Laci's a businessman, and I'm an entrepreneur in a new situation. I have to network and cultivate business relationships. Fortunately, I'm good at that. I totally impressed Laci, except that I'm friends with Csaba, who he thinks is an idiot. I told Laci about my BuliZone idea. That was an awesome business venture: the movable party. The idea was, we supply the music and the vibe and maybe some good-looking girls, and we just find a new location every weekend and advertise it online as *BuliZone!* (all one word). And we charge admission and sell beer and make a shitload. And the sweet thing? The smartest thing? The location costs us exactly zero. We move into one of those old vacant apartment buildings. They're all over the city, just sitting there, totally empty. Government's going to tear them down one day, except there's no money to tear them down. Some of these places are even in the best parts, the really cool parts of town. Unbelievably great business venture, right? Except Laci told me, "It's been done." No *way*. But it's true. Now that I been here for a couple months, I know at least five party houses. They're called romkocsma and they're totally cool. *Exactly* what I planned. So he didn't invest in my venture, but he did say, "You seem like a normal guy. Why're you hanging out with Csaba?" Can you believe a guy would talk that way about his brother?

We're walking, and Csaba's mad. I can tell. He's kicking frozen turds and his boots sound like he's marching in some army parade. It's all about that Magyar Garda. He says gyps and Jews and immigrants are fucking up Hungary, weakening it, destroying our traditions. Me, I figure if the Jews really have all the money, we should be friends with them. Maybe some Jews can invest in our company. We could have a company especially for Jews. Serious. We could have a company that trains Jews how to be TrueMagyar (all one word). Even though they never will be, really, because they're not Hungarian blood like me and Csaba, but they could learn to be *more* Hungarian. Because they have to adapt to their environment, right? Survival of the fittest. Cockroaches will be the only living thing left after nuclear war. I read that once. So here's a question: "Why would cockroaches survive nuclear war? I mean, wouldn't they burn up same as everyone else?" I ask Csaba.

We're going down into the subway. Hey, no ticket guys at the gate. Sweet. Csaba gives me the fist bump I taught him. Maybe he's not mad anymore.

He says, "If there's a nuclear war, I'll come down here. Deep enough. No radiation could get me."

"Then what? Then it's you and the cockroaches. Everything else is toast. Radiated toast."

"Then I go to the country where I did my training. Start from scratch. Me and Ildiko."

Ildiko's the girl he met at this training camp. He showed me a picture of her posing in uniform with her rifle. She's cute. But there was no picture of the two of them together, just Ildiko shooting, or eating a bowl of soup, or Ildiko with her arms around two other girl soldiers, like some kind of TrueMagyar *Charlie's Angels*. He says him and Ildiko were hot, but they couldn't get it on because of military rules. *As if.* (I just think that, though. I don't say it out loud because why shoot the guy down, right? I'm his friend.)

"What about a training camp for tourists. Same as the Garda, but expensive, for foreigners. I bet there's guys in London or Sweden who never held a gun in their lives, never learned hand-to-hand combat. What're they gonna do if it comes to protecting themselves? They gotta be prepared. We could call it MagyarWarrior, all one word."

He's always saying we have to be prepared to protect the true Hungarians. From what, dude? Ciganybunozes, he says. Gypsy crime. I don't totally believe him, but maybe if you're Csaba and you don't get laid and you don't have a job and you live with your mom and dad and you don't even have your own bedroom because you sleep in the living room, you gotta blame someone.

The romkocsma on Akacfa is *hopping*. Wall-to-wall cool people. Super-hot babes on every floor, no joke. And there's three floors. And the DJ is spinning and some people are sitting and some dancing and some drinking, but everybody's cool and not the way people in Toronto are cool. I tried to explain this to Csaba once, the difference in cool. I don't think he got it. The thing is, Toronto babes laugh a lot, and they wear expensive, tight clothes, and their hair is shiny, and they say things like, "You're so cute," but they're just fake, is what I'm saying. Hungarian babes are cool but real. They are real Magyar babes. They're totally different. And tonight, they're *all* partying here. Jesus. It's like someone put the invitation out to hotties only. And this romkocsma, man, it's unbelievable. Must have been a super-rich apartment building in the old days before communism, but now there's just us cool people hanging out on old sofas and grandma chairs. In a couple weeks, everyone will know about this place and then maybe the cops will close it down or maybe they won't.

"Awesome," I shout over the music at Csaba.

He just gives me the sign: "Fuck, yeah."

We find Laci on the second floor in a room that's totally red—everything painted, walls, ceiling, furniture, floor, like a vampire room or something. There are some girls talking to him. They're hot, but Laci seems like he doesn't even notice how hot they are. He's looking out for us is why. He's a man of opportunity too. That's why he likes me. We got that in common, see.

"Dude." He does the fist bump. That's not usual, but tonight's different. Tonight, I'm in with Laci Bekes and we're tight. He talks English to me a little. "I told you not to bring the donkey." Why he calls his brother *donkey*, I don't know. I'm a little impressed he knows the English word.

"He can be helpful," I say. In English. Csaba doesn't understand. And I keep my eyes on Laci so Csaba doesn't know we're talking about him.

Laci gives me a look. He's the businessman, not me. That's

what the look says. It also says, I have no time for this bullshit.
"I got a serious proposition."

I light up a smoke. "How much?" I mean, we both know I'm
gonna do it, no question. But it's business, right? I'm not stupid.

Laci gives me that superior look. "One million."

Get. The fuck. Out. I figured Laci would pay well, but this
is unbelievable. I mean, one million forints. Not dollars, but still.

"All *right*."

"Yeah," Csaba says. He gets the gist, I guess.

"Good." Laci switches to Hungarian. "We don't have a lot
of time, so I can't explain everything. You're just gonna have
to trust me on this."

"Sure, bro." Fist bump. Yeah. More hot girls walk in. They
give us the eye. The room's crowded. I'm feeling hot, but I don't
want to show my hat head so I just take off my coat. It's an
awesome coat, a Maple Leafs leather bomber. When I wear this
coat here in Budapest, girls come up to me right away because
they want to practise their English. Well, that's what they say.
Really, they just want to talk to me. But no time for play tonight.
I ignore them. We're businessmen here, talking business.

"I'm supposed to meet these two guys tonight. Here. Talk
some business."

"Right."

"Right, so problem is I have to be somewhere else. I got this
really important thing over at Csepel tonight. I can't reschedule.
And I can't let these dudes think I'm too busy to talk to them.
They're not the kinda guys you reschedule."

"Right."

"So I was thinking. How can I be two places at once?"

"Right. Impossible."

"So then I figured, if *you* could be here..."

"Absolutely. I'm your man in Pest."

"Great, bro. I knew I could count on you. But here's the thing. They have to think you're me."

Huh?

"Don't worry. It's dark in here. They don't know me, really. I mean, they know me but not well."

"You want *me* to be *you*?"

"That's what I'm saying."

"Cool."

"You have to give them a message. That's all."

"But not a message *from* you because *I'm* you."

He looks worried. He thinks I'm gonna fuck it up.

"All you say is, 'Tell your boss, I'm not jerking him around. I just lost it and now I'll find it. No disrespect intended."

"Honestly. I lost it. No disrespect. Wait. What'd you lose?"

"You don't need to know."

"But if I'm you, I should know, right? It's my back story." Actors always say that. Cool.

He thinks for, like, a second. "Okay, a letter. Say, I didn't mean to lose the letter. Try it again."

"I can't find the letter. Honest. I mean you no disrespect."

Laci's frowning, looking even more worried. "Good. Fine. Maybe remind them that you—that is that I—am a businessman. I know who my friends are, and I like to keep it that way."

"I know who my friends are. Do I look like an idiot?"

"Okay, stop. Don't ad lib like that. I would never say, 'Do I look like an idiot?' Just stick to the script."

"Cool." God, Laci's so nervous he's making me nervous.

Maybe he's a micro-manager. I heard about people like that. Managers like that are no good because they waste time on small details that should be done by the smaller nobodies in the company. So I say to him, to make him feel better: "Trust me. I can handle the details."

Csaba's just watching all this. He's pissed off, but he wants to be part of it. Laci always does this, treats him like he's retarded. And, I mean, Csaba's not always smart, but he's got his talents. Laci should recognize his talents now and then. Be a lot better for their sibling rivalry.

"I mean it, bro. This is serious business. Don't mess around. And take that stupid bank robber hat off your head. Here's my coat. Gimme yours." We do the switch. He checks me out. "Jeans, okay. Sweater, whatever. Shoes, man."

He takes off his black leather shoes, slides them over.

"My Nikes? Seriously?" He just looks at me. I take them off, put his on. "They don't fit."

"Not like you're going anywhere. Just stay exactly here. Have a good time — on me. I'll be back in a while."

"Right. When you're done your meeting."

"And, Csaba, your job is to fuck right off."

"Truly?" Csaba thunks himself down on the sofa, throws his boots onto the coffee table. Laci lets that slide for exactly a nanosecond. Then he hauls his little brother by the coat, shoves his head under his arm, and walks him out. Fuck. I feel bad. I feel like a bad friend. But I can't follow Csaba because this could be my chance, the big chance. I mean, Laci Bekes? I don't even know half of how Laci made his money, but he has it figured out. Luxury developments, real-estate trading, and now he's in on the construction of the M6 — providing concrete or something. I don't know construction, but the way Laci does it, it ain't swinging hammers.

So here I am being Laci in a smokin' hot vampire party room. How cool is this? I light a smoke, lean back in Laci's rich-dude leather coat. When I finish the smoke, I stump it out on the table. Why not, right? Not my table. Probably some old neni's once upon a time, with little lace whatchicallits on it. Not anymore. I set my feet up. Laci's shoes. Pretty nice. What's Laci got in his pocket? Wallet? Fuck, he's gonna be mad when he figures that out. Keys to his SUV. What do you know? Right on. I am Laci Bekes. I got a SUV and a house in Rozsadomb, and a hot little wife and a girlfriend on the side, and I do business with *you*. That's right. I'm the business. I am *business*. Construction, right. But deeper. You want multi-million-American-dollar luxury condos—I'll build them. I'll do that. You invest in my company, I'll turn it around faster than a bitch, make you rich. Wait a second. How's he getting to Csepel without his car? Fuck. Do I go after him? But he said wait here. He said exactly here. Fuck.

"Laci."

I look over to the door. Two guys. They look pissed and they're big. Bigger than me, even, and I'm pretty big. Fuck. Laci didn't tell me their names.

"Dude," I say. Guy Number One doesn't do the fist bump. Number Two neither.

"You fucked over the wrong guy, Laci Bekes."

Fuck me. "I meant no disrespect. I just lost it. I lost the letter."

"You think we care?"

Guy's pushing his chest into my face.

"What I'm saying is, I just can't find it at this moment. But I will. I'm a businessman."

"Janos, you backstabbing shithead sonuvabitch twat." Punch to the side of the head, not fake this time, and I'm laid out flat, sprawling. Csaba. What the *fuck*. Guys are looking down at me. I get up.

Guy Number Two turns on Csaba. "You called him Janos? This isn't Laci Bekes?"

"Laci Bekes?" Csaba laughs. Csaba, man, you gotta work on that laugh. That stupid sonuvabitch laugh.

You know that smile, that smile that says, "Not funny. Not fucking funny, you hulyes fucking idiot." That's what both dudes are giving me.

"Thanks, little man," says Guy Number Two. He takes Csaba by the arm, shows him the door. Csaba gives me one last look, and there he goes. Now it's just me. And I'm not feeling so good.

"Okay, you know what? Time's up, Laci or Janos or whoever you are. You're an artificer and I don't care for artificers."

Artificer? I don't even know what that means. Neither does the other dude, I figure, by the look on his face.

"Yeah, well, it's complicated. Laci asked me—"

Other guy opens his jacket. FUCKI'MGONNADIE. Do I put my hands up? Oh, they're already up. Weird. Holy fuck, I've never even seen a gun like that—not in real life. I'm just some guy. I don't even really live here. Is anybody seeing this?

"Okay, dudes? I'm *not* Laci. Serious. Whatever he's into, it's got nothing to do with me."

"Put your hands down."

Right. Chicks at the bar over there turn their back on me. Bartender's leaning into them. Room full of cool people and no one sees what's going on.

"Walk ahead of me. Everything's normal. Nobody's looking at you."

Right. Walking. Nobody looking. Down a flight of stairs and into what used to be a courtyard. Still kinda is, except it's grooving, and maybe people see me and maybe they don't. Everybody just hanging out, looking hot, and no one knows who I am. My dad is gonna *shit*. I can hear him now: "How do you get in these *situations*, Janos?"

Past the bouncer. What does this dude care? If I were *really* Laci, he'd care. Fucking right, he would. But I'm just me. Janos Hagy. Entrepreneur. Nobody.

Dude. Mercedes-fucking-Benz, dude. Are you shitting me?

"Get in."

"My friends, I'm not Laci. I don't know what Laci did, but I swear to God, I got nothing to do with it. I'm Janos Hagy. I don't know who you are. I promise I won't report you. Please let me go. I'm only here for my gap year. Next year I gotta go to college. I swear, I won't—"

"Shut the fuck up." Guy slams my head into the car roof. "Get in."

Fuck. I'm in, dude. I'm shutting up. Not a word. No. I'm gonna be fine. I'm Janos fucking Hagy, man of opportunity. You'll see. You'll see what I am.

Whoa.

You never know how quiet inside a car can be till you're in a Benz going over a bridge in Budapest in the middle of the night with two guys not talking and one serious fucking gun.

What We Deserve

Tibor Roland unbuttons his blue shirt and hangs it on the hook. He eases off his stiff Campers and his cotton socks and places them inside the locker, socks stuffed into shoes. He drops his khakis and his Joe Boxers and hangs them on the other hook. For a moment, he stands in the deserted change room entirely naked. He breathes deeply of the humid, chlorinated air and he feels the spongy padding beneath his feet, the draft on his legs, the slight chill emanating from the metal lockers. At thirty-five, he knows he's in reasonably good shape. Though not what anyone would call "cut," he enjoys, in a simple way, the solidity of his thighs, the straightness of his spine, his lightly haired chest. In this naked interval, free of rumpled clothes, he is a living, breathing entity made up of hundreds of thousands of sensations, and he can feel every single one of them. Then he pulls on his trunks, knots the string at the waist, snaps a bathing cap on his head, slips feet into flip-flops, locks his locker, and flip-flops out to the pool.

The hotel has a decent pool, he's pleased to see —not Olympic but at least ten metres long. No waterslides or multi-coloured pool noodles. Windows the length of one wall look out over Montreal. Exactly right, except. Except someone has beaten him here. He pauses, towel in hand, and feels his moment decay just a little.

Never mind, he tells himself as he places towel over plastic lounger, licks his goggles for suction, snugs them over his eyes, and steps out of his flip-flops. This is still good. In violation of the sign-posted rule, he dives in.

They pass each other as they do their laps, the woman at a steady breaststroke and Tibor front-crawling. At least she understands the concept of lengths, doesn't paddle around in circles like some hotel swimmers, their chins beatifically raised. The swimmers ignore each other as they pass. He could almost forget he isn't alone. After about twenty minutes, he stops at the end of the pool to catch his breath. The woman is still breaststroking, which she does with ease, dipping her head under and knifing forward. She pauses at the other end to catch her breath, fastening her gaze on the clock. Maybe she's timing her breaks. She wears a red one-piece and a bathing cap. Tibor Roland, from his end, his elbows on the edge of the pool, sees how she frowns at the clock and how her chest moves with her breathing. In and out.

Then she starts again.

Tibor, too, starts into his third set. When he makes his turn, the woman has stopped swimming and is sitting on the ledge at the opposite end of the pool, massaging her foot. When he reaches her end, he stops. It's a narrow pool. They are close.

The most obvious thing about her face, from this angle at least, is her chin and the set of her mouth. She has a strong chin, a single shallow dimple at its centre, and she bites her lower lip hard, as if biting down a pain. And it is maybe this combination, of the strong chin and the serious frown when she looks at the clock, together with the bitten lip that makes Tibor want to talk to her even though, for all he knows, she speaks no English.

He does another lap and then emerges beside her. "Cramp?"

She half laughs, more like a sniff, embarrassed. "I always get them." American, he guesses. Probably also here for the conference. Academics occupy the entire hotel — geographers, historians, political scientists, legal theorists all here in Montreal, Quebec, to discuss the meaning and future of post-Soviet Central Europe.

"You have to walk it off."

Holding her foot more tightly, she nods. "I'm sure it'll go away in a minute."

And Tibor, in a moment of what he would later consider remarkable insight, realizes that she is likely reluctant to struggle clumsily to an undignified stand and hobble away.

"Let me get your towel."

"Oh. Thanks." And she points to where it lies folded on one of the plastic lounge chairs.

He drapes the towel over her shoulders. "Can I give you a hand up or would you like to sit for a bit?"

"I'll just sit it out, I think."

"All right then. Well. I'm done for the day." Tibor grabs his own towel and flip-flops back to the change room.

Warming in the sauna, he congratulates himself for being both perceptive and generous. He could have swum for another half-hour at least but instead had done the gracious thing, leaving the woman to deal with her affliction without spectators. He hopes she'd recognized how perceptive he'd been. He hopes he'll see her again before the conference ends.

. . .

They nod when they see each other in the pool again the next morning. And then that afternoon she attends his paper on the twenty-first-century reverberations of early twentieth-century Hungarian nationalism, and she stays to ask him a question after the talk. Her stiffly collared shirt makes him long for the red one-piece, but he is undistracted by the freckled cleavage the shirt coyly hides as he explains the Hungarian emotional attachment to territories long-since lost.

There's not much mystery to Tibor Roland. He knows this. He would like to be more intriguing. He'd like to have more layers, but he doesn't. Mostly, he's made his peace with this because, he figures, it's what made him a historian. History gives him mysteries to solve, stories to tell. He'd chosen to specialize in Hungarian history both because this was his mother's birthplace and because she refused to talk about it. So maybe his mother has layers that he doesn't. In any case, Rafaela, clearly, is interested. On the last evening of the conference, over glasses of cheap Australian Shiraz, as limp, savoury pastries circulate in a newly carpeted room without chairs, they talk. The plastic square that dangles from her neck identifies her as an "independent scholar." That is, unemployed. She'd completed a Ph.D. in regional studies, specializing in Russia, at Harvard six years ago, but she is based in Toronto now. She moved there with her husband when he got a job at Queen's Park. No, not a politician but a policy analyst.

There are not too many women named Rafaela, certainly not more than one married to a provincial policy analyst. It is a coincidence, but there it is. Daniel had never introduced Tibor Roland to his wife.

"Daniel loves it," she continues. "I can't imagine anything

more boring. Provincial politics — it's all health care and education, wait times and dropout rates. Makes me want to stick a fork in my eye." Rafaela grins. "Which I've never done, by the way. I'm really a paragon of self-restraint." She lifts her wineglass to her lips and sips, somehow without shifting her laughing gaze from his.

Is she flirting with him? Has she mentioned her husband to make the boundaries clear? He expects her to say next: "I think you know my husband. Didn't you go to school together?" But she doesn't. And her tone is a ball tossed ever so gently. It says, How flimsy — no, how arbitrary and scalable — a boundary is a husband.

"Self-restraint's all right if it saves your eye, I suppose, but I'd hate to think you'd adopted it as a defining virtue."

"Really? I thought you Canadians were all about self-restraint. I've been trying to master it ever since I moved here, but I don't think I've got it yet. I can tell by the way people stiffen." She bares her teeth in aghast-Torontonian rictus. "Sort of the way you looked when you first saw me in the pool that day."

Tibor feels himself blush. "I like to have the pool to myself." He shrugs.

Mouth twitches. "Ah, Tibor. It's hard to share, isn't it?"

Rafaela's breasts are perfectly pendant, barely supported, and they stretch the cotton dress she wears. Tibor thinks he would like to hold them, one in each hand, as he penetrates her from behind.

"I wanted to ask you yesterday," she says, "about why Hungary seems to have become more nationalist, with more fascist leanings, than, say, Poland or the Czech Republic."

They regain the ground of ordinary academic conversation, now pleasurably heightened by their confidence in their own attractiveness, the increasing likelihood of sex, their distance from her husband, Daniel, who has apparently never told his wife about his old friend, Tibor Roland. Tibor decides he's hurt by this omission. Around them, the poorly ventilated room fills with the brittle polite laughter of academic networking. They go to the bar for more wine. Later, they sit together at dinner and when she turns to talk with the man to her right, Tibor feels abandoned and ridiculous. When she turns back, he is confident and witty again.

She has chocolate cake for dessert. He has pecan pie. They both have coffee. The less lucky drift away from the tables and back to their solitary rooms, leaving white napkins and crumbs of pastry.

"I'd like to see you again," he says.

Tibor bites the inside of his upper lip but keeps his eyes on her face. He's chosen the phrase carefully, not to offend, leaving it open for her to decide. Her reaction seems inordinately delayed, and for a moment he wonders if he's misjudged, if she takes her marriage seriously and their conversation had been empty flirtation, not invitation. She is parsing the question, considering. God. She is going to tell him to fuck off. And then she's going to go home and tell her husband that his old buddy, Tibor Roland, hit on her. But then, reprieve. Vibrant pink begonias blooming from her cleavage, all the way to her forehead.

"In my room?" she says finally. Daniel's wife says, all red.

⊕

"I'm making eggs. You want eggs?"

"What kind of eggs?"

"Scrambled?"

"Scrambled is good."

Daniel had his own place, a room in a shared house just off College Street. Tibor often slept on the couch on Thursday night after pub, unable or unwilling to return to his cheaper but much less exciting room north of Dupont. No one lived north of Dupont, but Tibor had found a basement in a house owned by lesbian filmmakers who grew vegetables in their front yard and charged him almost nothing in rent in return for his walking their dog and shovelling their walk in the winter.

This morning he remembers was fourteen years ago.

Tibor wandered into the kitchen in his bare feet, rubbing his eyes. "Tea?" he asked.

"Sure."

Daniel whipped eggs as Tibor filled the kettle, his face stretched in its rounded chrome surface flecked with brown and orange spatters where grease had dried. There were four years of spattered grease on this kettle, and Tibor remembered when it was new and he'd only just met Daniel and he'd come to Daniel's apartment to cram for the Russian midterm and Daniel had made tea, boiling the water in his brand-new, just-moved-out-of-home kettle. This kettle had seen four years of their friendship. Four years of Thursday nights and Friday mornings just like this one. Four years of sharing the pains and victories of academic life.

This kettle had witnessed the first nomination to dean's list (both of them), the first C- (Daniel's for a paper he'd written too quickly and, in retrospect he had to admit, too polemically), the first piece published in the student newspaper (also Daniel's, an editorial, also polemical), the first suggestion from a professor to apply to graduate school (Tibor's, from a history professor). Other momentous events: Tibor's passion for the Japanese Visa student in his cultural geography class. It had lasted for the entire year, unrequited. Daniel's joining the campus communist party and growing his hair long. Then meeting Juliette and cutting it all off and considering a career in law. Tibor's confession that he had also been in love with Juliette. Both of them deciding together that being a socialist was more ethical than being a lawyer and then realizing that was the dumbest conclusion they had ever reached when Tibor, stoked on Solzhenitsyn and his first-ever reading of Foucault, reminded Daniel that any system has its disciplinary apparatus whether panopticon prison or gulag. Fight the power; want nothing.

Tibor loved the layers of grease on chrome. It was history in the making, tangible and unclean. Hardened volcanic streams of orange and brown also covered the gas stove—on its once-pristine white enamel surface, years of sausages and bacon and fried egg and canned beans. There was a satisfying feeling, in the house, of unperturbed masculinity, of the accumulated effort of boys becoming men.

Tibor's mouth tasted ugly and he smelled of cigarettes and sweaty sleep and beery farts under flat polyester quilts but this, too, was a Friday morning joy, the stink and muzz of hangover. They ate on the futon couch that Tibor had slept on, holding plates mounded with eggs and toast close to their chins. Famished. They fed their bellies. They slaked their thirst with huge gulps of sweet hot tea from mugs purloined from family cabinets, evidence of the roommates' pre-independence histories.

Daniel's firmly declaimed *OPSEU: Your union* while Tibor sipped from someone's chipped homemade pottery.

"Aaah." Daniel leaned back, hoisted his feet onto the milk crate that served as a coffee table as he lit a cigarette. "Good breakfast."

Tibor leaned back beside him. "Great breakfast."

In the kitchen, two of Daniel's roommates talked in morning monosyllables. Tibor heard cornflakes hitting a bowl. How is it you always recognize it's cornflakes? The sound of it, dry and husky. The cornflake sound.

"I got into Harvard."

Daniel said it between drags, still holding his inhale so the sentence came out tight. Foreshortened. He exhaled, and the smoke plumed about his head.

Tibor's chest tightened. He didn't even know Daniel had applied to Harvard. Harvard. Who the fuck applied to Harvard?

"I didn't want to say it out loud. I mean, it's Harvard, you know."

Tibor slapped Daniel on the shoulder—somewhat clumsily because they sat too closely together on the couch to manage a sincere, manly clap on the back but well intentioned. "Well, way to go, man. Harvard."

Daniel's face, as Tibor sneaked a sideways glance at it, seemed to shine. He was trying to hold back the shine, but he couldn't. That face shone with the most arrogant son-of-a-bitch shine on the planet. It shone with worldliness, with the love of the world itself. The world *loved* Daniel and he knew it. He'd always known it and now he had proof. Sun-shining-out-of-his-ass proof. Fucker.

"Well, I should get going." Tibor bent to find his socks

somewhere under the coffee table. "Gotta get to the library. I'm so behind in Soviet politics."

He fumbled his socks on. They smelled of his feet.

"Really good news about Harvard," he said, standing. "Really. Amazing news." And he patted his shirt pocket for his cigarettes, his pants pockets for his wallet. "Sorry to run like this. We'll celebrate next Thursday?"

"Sorry, Rolly. Can't next Thursday. I'm cramming." Daniel always called him by his last name, Roland, Rolly for short. It used to make Tibor feel like he was part of a club. Now he hated the familiarity, the presumption. How had he never noticed the advantage it gave Daniel—the right of the namer to name.

"Right. Of course. Harvard man must cram." Tibor heard his voice and didn't like the sound of it. Better to just leave. Envy was a fist-sized bolus of undigested egg, lodged just above his sternum.

"See you later then," he said, smiling widely at Daniel, who still sat on the sleep-rumpled futon, basking in his own glory.

In the grey linoleum hallway just the other side of the door, Tibor shoved his feet into cold shoes, grabbed the satchel he'd dropped there on the floor the night before, and fled.

The once-stylish Palmerston Boulevard, where Daniel lived, was just regaining its elegance in the early 1990s, but the eras were still rubbing shoulders: working-class immigrants who'd bought in the early 1970s and made vegetable gardens of their backyards, single men in tiny rooms with hotplates and bar fridges, students in similar tiny rooms, or shared apartments with hardwood floors newly exposed. Rents weren't cheap in this neighbourhood. In summer evenings, up and down College, gorgeous young women with nonchalant hair laughed and swallowed red wine in great gulps and ate mussels with bread or sharply seasoned pizza, and young unshaven men with more wit than Tibor made them laugh and shared their wine and debated O.J.'s guilt, or Clinton's charisma, or art funding in Canada.

When he first visited Daniel on Palmerston (when Daniel first made him tea with the brand-new kettle), Tibor felt he'd finally entered the heaving, bubbling pool where life itself was formed. This, right here, was the organic mess from which ideas, history itself, would emerge. You could feel the surge of it. You could walk along College and feel the sidewalk cracking, the old storefronts heaving, the streets blowing with futurity. And if you were here, you were part of it. Simple as that. Living cheek by jowl with the great and the potentially great, you could be poor, be artists, be scientists and writers and intellectuals, and you could whip this world. This was what it meant to be off College. It was not Tibor's world. Tibor lived in a basement north of Dupont, a land barren of pretty girls and Italian coffees, and as he walked north, he knew that mattered.

Tibor had applied to Toronto, McGill, and Queen's. He'd yet to receive an answer from any of them. He was reasonably certain that Toronto would accept him into its master's program, but he was hoping for a federal scholarship, enough money that he could move to a new place, maybe a smaller place, more compact, where he could thrive and grow into the proportion he felt was rightly his. But an American school? He should have expected it from Daniel. And to keep it a secret too.

Tibor propelled himself northward, legs and arms pumping past the apartment balconies where he'd rather be, furious with his own passivity, furious with the fucking Tibor Rolandness of him that he hadn't had the temerity to imagine Harvard for himself.

⊕

Three weeks pass before Rafaela calls. June. For the first week, he checked his answering machine regularly and his heart jumped when the phone rang. But then nothing, and he figured that she'd gotten home and given her head a shake, realized that she was married and what had she been thinking. She seemed a practical kind of woman, one not likely to succumb to fantasy.

So when she calls and says, "Hello, this is Rafaela," she is answered, at first, by the blank silence of surprise.

"Rafaela," he says finally. "How are you?"

"I'm good, thanks, and you?"

"Well, I can't complain." Did he really say that? He cringes, knocks a fist to his forehead.

"Great, great. I'm just calling to…" And here she, too, stumbles, uncertain of the tone and language required to set up a meeting where obviously the purpose is sex but where, just as obviously, the purpose couldn't be overtly stated. "Are you free this Thursday afternoon?"

Tibor does a quick mental run through his schedule. Empty, basically. Why pretend? "Thursday? Thursday's fine. Where would you, ah…"

"How about… There's a Second Cup on King, near Jarvis. Say twelve-thirty?"

"King and Jarvis," he repeats, writing it down on the back of an envelope as though he might forget it otherwise. "I'll see you there."

King Street is nowhere close to his home, or his work,

thank goodness. Also far from the University of Toronto student ghetto. Not much chance he'd bump into anyone he knew, students or faculty. King and Jarvis, where the business and bank towers peter out, and where, just a thin block away, furniture stores and condos are shouldering aside homeless shelters, pawnshops, and prostitutes. The Second Cup—bland and in between, the perfect setting for an illicit rendezvous. An *affair*.

Sometime not far into his cappuccino, he stutters to a stop. How absurd to be sitting—no, to be sunk—in a brown leather armchair with his knees uncomfortably high under posters of lavishly frothed milk, trading observations about Toronto in the summer—too humid, bad air quality, but there's nothing like the pleasure of a beer on a street-side patio—and doesn't it all look so *utilitarian* after Montreal's pretty streets. It is so absurd that it almost entirely obliterates any sexual desire. The steam of latte, the brainless chatter of glossy-haired girls, the fucking endless grind and whirr of machines: it's enough to flatten the most illicit of passions. And Rafaela. She is, after all, a quite ordinary woman with crow's feet at her eyes and chapped lips. He watches her suck her frappuccino through a straw, eyes focused on the street outside, and he tries to hold on to the freckles and the wet red suit and the pink begonias, but they are fading fast.

He's about to make up an excuse about a forgotten appointment or a diseased testicle when she fastens her blue eyes on him and says, "If you think you feel stupid, imagine what it's like for me."

There are things that he could say, but thankfully he does

not say them. Without another word, they stand and leave their quasi-coffees on the table. They walk out and across the street into St. James Park under a blue sky pulled impossibly tight. They stroll out and ahead of their self-awareness. They *stroll*— slowly, closely. The heat feels good with that city humidity pushing down, flowers pushing up, and the dark still-cool lake at their backs. Junkies drowse, indolent under trees, and dogwalkers stoop to pick up after their pets while under the cover of the Victorian gazebo a tourist levels his camera. By the time they reach the end of the short park, Tibor is beginning, but just beginning, to remember the colour of Rafaela's nipples.

Thank God the hotel is close. If they had to travel, it wouldn't work. Imagine the two of them in her little Toyota on their way to an illicit hotel rendezvous. What radio station would they listen to? Classic rock? Country? It's too painful to imagine. As it is, the hotel appears at the other end of the park, at the end of their walk, as though they have summoned it.

They don't speak in the elevator. They don't speak when they get to their room on the seventeenth floor looking out to the north of the city. As she had in Montreal, Rafaela goes into the bathroom, leaving the door ajar as she takes her clothes off, turns the shower on. "Tibor. Aren't you coming?"

Metal slide of the shower curtain rings on their rod, grate of thin plastic curtain against his arm and thigh. She stands, eyes closed, head back under the streaming water. Begonias bloom through clouds of steam.

. . .

After this encounter, they agree to meet next at Tibor's apartment.

Tibor lives on the second floor of a multiply divided Victorian mansion on a leafy street south of Dupont. South is better than north of Dupont, and it's still an easy commute to suburban York University, where he teaches.

Upstairs is a graduate student in physics at University of Toronto, in and out at all times of the day. Downstairs is a writer—not the literary but the technical type and she is almost always home. He doesn't really know either of these neighbours, and they don't really know him and probably wouldn't notice who made their way up the shared walkway lined with bushes that needed clipping. But even so, Tibor feels self-conscious. Sex in the middle of the day. The floor creaks and sound travels via radiators and God knows what other conduits. Plus, there's one elderly Portuguese lady, across the street, still dressed in mourning though no doubt her husband has been gone for years, maybe decades. And she's always on her front veranda, not reading, not doing anything, just sitting and watching the street. She would now know this about him. That he is having sex. And so what? For once his self-consciousness doesn't impinge because at the thought of Rafaela Tibor feels, just barely, at the base of his throat, the very edge of happiness, paper thin and hopeful.

⊕

Four years ago, Tibor and Daniel were still friends and somehow they'd both landed back in Toronto. Tibor hadn't left the province, had gone to Queen's for his master's degree, and then returned to the University of Toronto for the Ph.D. He was just finishing his dissertation on nationalism and modernism in post-war Hungary, a study of treaties and boundaries, the politics of geographic and territorial identity. Daniel hadn't completed the Ph.D. in political economy and government at Harvard, but as he explained over a tumbler of Jameson's, he'd never really wanted to be a scholar. He wanted the real world, all its messy, ego-driven scrapping, its material stakes. And Toronto. He'd had enough of America, frankly. He'd brought his fiancée home with him, a woman he'd met in Boston, and they were expecting a child. Life. Tibor would like her, an academic type, just like him. Rafaela. Yes, great name.

In the over-warm bar, all gleaming wood and glass, Daniel talked with the same confidence as always, dismissing anything that clearly didn't count. And Tibor, as always and against his own will, believed him. It wasn't just the timbre of Daniel's voice that pulled him in, nor his casual name-dropping—he'd had drinks with men whose books were described as "seminal"—it was simply and undeniably Daniel's *intelligence*. With Daniel, it was as though everything accelerated: the heat of whisky in the throat, the throb of the crowded room, the flash of the waitress's belly ring, the clamour of dishes from the kitchen, the snow outside that pressed against the glass, the bar humid and dark. Between them, conversation rapid-fire, not tumultuous or aggressive, but seeking, sparking, connecting in new and unpredictable combinations. It made Tibor's heart race, and not figuratively. Pounding excitement. Whether the topic was Argentinian economic policy or *Big Brother*, Daniel formulated. He fulminated. Ideas shot to the surface and scattered, phosphorescent. Talk was crucial. It was *urgent*, and important things hinged on *words* traded just like this, over a varnished table in the steam-pressure of a clamorous bar on a winter night between intellectuals of similar, if not identical, left-leaning political stripe.

As they left, Daniel, feeling for the keys in the pocket of his expensive-looking grey parka, turned to Tibor: "Dissertation sounds really good, man. Really interesting. I'd like to hear more about it sometime."

It was just after midnight, and the snow was rushing down, tumbling under streetlights, pulsing in dark. They paused, face to face, shoulders hunched. And Tibor knew that his best friend was lying. Daniel didn't want to hear more about the dissertation. Daniel didn't give a shit about post-war Hungary. Daniel was being polite.

So then why, given that, did Tibor respond as if he'd detected nothing. "Great, great. Well, why don't we grab a drink next Thursday?"

Daniel, keys in hand, had already taken one step away. He sucked his breath through his teeth, grimaced. "Oh. Well, I'm not sure about next Thursday. But sometime soon, for sure." And then he took one step back toward Tibor to clasp him in a firm, manly hug. "Really good seeing you again."

"You too." Tibor clapped his friend's back. "Good to have you back."

They separated with a "See you soon," and Tibor pulled his toque out of his pocket, snugged it over his head, and trudged the twenty minutes home through five-centimetre drifts, feeling like he'd just been shit on.

Yet, two weeks later, Tibor held a tiny plastic birdie upended over his racket and inhaled, focusing. He pulled his racket back gently and swung it forward: *tap*. The trick is to contain the energy in the swing, contain it and release it in the tap, which ought to be unhesitating, direct. Only a small surface of the racket meets hard red rubber. All the energy of the elbow and shoulder, all the packed tension of the poised legs, the slight gravity of the falling bird must be concentrated exactly there in the racket's *tap*.

He'd sent Daniel an email: "Up for a game?" No risk, no pressure in that kind of invitation. They used to play tennis together, back in the day. Badminton was almost as good and easier to get court time. At first, Daniel had demurred—Badminton? Really?—but with a bit of cajoling, he'd agreed. For old time's sake.

Now the two men faced each other on the badminton court, Daniel in baggy blue athletic shorts and a faded red T, Tibor in dandyish white from top to bottom. Daniel, bouncing on the balls of his feet, launched the first verbal challenge, swaying in a parody of a sportsman on the ready: "Show me what you got, Rolly." Still pals. Still boys. The years apart meant nothing between old friends.

Tibor served. Daniel caught the shuttle on the edge of his racket, belted it back. Tibor tapped. Daniel crashed to the other end of the court, went wide, and missed completely.

In badminton, to Daniel's disadvantage, the technique is different than tennis. The whole game, in fact, is different—the psychology as well as the physical technique. He managed to return at least half of Tibor's serves, sometimes managed to smash one by him, but it was obvious this was Tibor's game.

Tibor, as the experienced player, kept score. He called it out with every point. Four–One. Five–Two. Seven–Two. Eight–Four.

Daniel stomped. He sprawled a second too late every time, every actual contact the result of heroic leap and flail. There was no plan, no attempt at navigation, just dash and smash, smash and dash. But Tibor felt the quivering flight of the shuttle in his own sternum. He flew with it. He was winning. He felt the win in his abdomen, a glowing absolute. He was unbeatable. He was victory, personified, *the* victor.

Daniel chased after the bird that Tibor sent high curving over the net, arm extended ahead of him. His shoes pounded the floorboards. He caught the white plastic tail of the thing and managed to knock it back into the air. It snagged in the net.

Nine–Four.

Tibor served again and Daniel watched it. The bird flew low and even this time, just barely over the net, straight for him. Not so fast, really. Not so fast he couldn't reach it, smash it, pound it into the net or back into Tibor's smug grin. But fast enough that his brain couldn't decide: left or right, backhand or forward? Defensively, half knowing this was about to go wrong, he crimped left, right arm moving into backhand. Not fast enough. The bird smashed into his forehead.

"Fuck." He bellowed. "Fuck." His hand to his head. He'd already sent his racket flying, skittering across the varnished wood floor. "What the fuck was that for?"

Daniel's face was purple, almost, with exercise and fury, staring at him. Tibor approached the net, his racket dangling loosely from his right hand. "What did I do?"

"Whatever." Breathing hard, Daniel bent, hands on his knees. And Tibor felt it in his throat first, the fizz of laughter, a nervous involuntary reaction. A tickling all the way to the back of his eyes. Tibor thought the last thing he must do now is laugh. He told himself sternly the last thing he should do is laugh. He. Must. Not. Laugh.

Daniel must have heard the sniff, first, a larger snuffle. Then a noise like a hiccup. Still in a half-crouch, Daniel slowly turned his head toward Tibor.

Tibor just the other side of the net held his hand clamped over his mouth, but suddenly unable to contain it, he loosed a breathy, high-octave wail of laughter. Tibor held his stomach and staggered backward. "I'm sorry." He gasped, waving his hand in either apology or denial, trying to distance himself from his own behaviour. "I'm sorry."

Daniel straightened. Other players around them were looking now, their attention caught by Tibor. They exchanged querying looks. They shrugged. It was a joke nobody got except Tibor, who had just seen his old friend unmanned for the very first time. For the first time in their whole friendship, he'd won. And the laughter wasn't because Daniel looked like a sore loser, a boy who'd lost his ball, but because of the sheer ungodly delight of being better.

"Okay, you know what? Fuck you." Daniel turned and left Tibor standing there, still laughing.

Months later, Tibor heard about the wedding. He'd considered calling to wish his old friend congratulations. He'd even gone so far as to dial the number and let it ring. But then he decided the call would only draw attention to their drifting apart. And to the fact that Tibor hadn't been invited to the event. Better to let it go. Let him call first. He didn't. So fuck him.

⊕

Why does she come to him? Almost every week for four months, she arrives with hair dishevelled or tidy, satchel slung over her shoulder, sometimes bearing a baguette and cups of takeout coffee, sometimes a bottle of wine, once a half a joint. She is usually on her way to or from the university library, just four blocks from his place. She might not have an academic position, but she refuses, she says, to let go of her research. He once joked that if he lived anywhere else in the city, she'd have lost interest in him long ago. As the realtors say, "Location, location, location."

She'd chortled with that full-throated, unchaste giggle. But hadn't denied it.

It is amazing, being with her. Maybe the most amazing experience of his life. So Tibor tries not to ask himself questions like Why did she come? Or What about Daniel? Daniel is irrelevant. The fact that they are both in some way attached to Daniel, well, that's just coincidence. Happenstance. No, Daniel is random. But Tibor and Rafaela—*Tibor* and Rafaela—together in these enclosed and perfect hours, they are what matter. Hours outside of history, he tells himself. An entirely separate place and time. And though he knows it is completely delusional, that's how it feels.

"Okay, your top ten dictators."

She rolls onto her back. "As a believer in democracy, I have to call your question invalid. Illogical. Immoral even."

"So top one. Come on. Everyone has a favourite dictator."

"Stalin."

"Why?"

"He invented the five-year plan, a phrase now used unironically by every major and rinky-dink business in America, never mind life coaches and *Oprah* addicts. He created a nation of surveillance, the most insidious and powerful form of governance deployed by government, also the basis of great reality TV. And even now, he survives as both revered dead leader and kitschy collectible."

"Good answer."

"Who's yours?"

"Oh, I hate them all equally. I believe in individual liberty."

"I hate you."

"Really? But I fuck so superbly."

"*God*, you sound like Daniel sometimes."

Blam. Doors and windows slam in sudden vacuum. World goes cold as Siberia. They both feel it.

"I'm sorry. I shouldn't have said that."

Tibor shakes his head. "It's okay. I mean, I know you're married. If anything, it's kind of strange you never talk about him. Or your daughter."

"No," Rafaela says, her hands curled into fists, holding the sheet to her chin. "It's *separate*. It's the only way it works."

He loves her more. He loves her more and more.

One day, as they sit side by side in Tibor's queen-sized bed, sharing a sandwich, Rafaela chews, swallows, and then tries to answer his question. "I love my life with my husband. I love my family. Do I still love *him*? The man I supposedly fell in love with — though I hate that phrase — the man I found so fascinating four years ago that I couldn't bear the thought of him not finding me equally fascinating? I don't even know if the question makes sense. The love isn't about him, anymore, but what we have, and who we are together." She looks at him. "I'm not going to leave him, if that's what you're asking."

It is October already. The leaves have turned and the old locust outside his bedroom pixillates yellow, tossing light against the walls and making the air glow. Maybe that *is* what he is asking. And he thinks, I love you. I love you so much I can hardly bear being with you, but he says, "So why do you come here and make love to me every Thursday?" And he tries very hard not to sound petulant, or insecure, or wounded.

She wipes the crumbs from her mouth with a napkin. "I love your calm," she says.

"A sexy, passionate calm?"

"I know how that sounds, but it's praise, believe me." Rafaela pauses. She pauses for a long time, long enough for Tibor to finish half of his sandwich.

"I feel clear when I'm with you," she says. "I can be just who I am, just ordinary and uncomplicated and unattached. The way I remember being, before Daniel and Evie." She'd been staring out the window as she talked. Now she looks at him. "Well, and you're irresistibly sexy." She adds this last bit matter-of-factly, as though stating an obvious truth; but Tibor is conscious, sitting up in bed and eating the other half-sandwich, that his stomach has two very slight, soft rolls and that he is likely getting crumbs in the creases.

It has nothing to do with him. That's what she is saying. The best thing about Tibor is that he isn't Daniel. Isn't complicated or passionate or dizzying or infuriating or larger than life. Tibor has no mystery.

Rafaela stands. With two rapid actions of wrist and fingers

that Tibor can never quite catch, she pulls her hair into its scrunchie. This is the signal that their time is over.

"The traffic was unbelievable today. I don't know why I drive." She leans over to kiss him goodbye. "See you next week."

⊕

It was bound to happen, and so it does. Saturday afternoon, he sees Daniel at the Summerhill LCBO. He spots him among the New World Wines, under the vaulted, church-like ceilings of the converted train station, now racked and gleaming with bottles, elegantly lit. The sight of his once best friend, so unexpected and so present, stops him dead. He isn't prepared. He'd prepared for it every day for a while, and then stopped. Now there he is. Daniel holds on to his daughter's hand, his left shoulder stooped to reach her. What is her name? Evie. Father and daughter face the wall of bottles together. She wears a purple corduroy dress with striped wool tights, her straight hair tied up in two pigtails, and as her father browses the Argentinian selections, Evie turns her face in Tibor's direction. She chews on the foot of a blond Barbie, drooling over her hand and into the sodden pink ruffle of Barbie's dress. She stares at Tibor with small, squinted blue eyes that make him think: mongoloid. The kid has Down syndrome?

They stand like that for what feels like minutes, staring at each other, the retarded girl and Tibor. And Tibor thinks, So that's why. That's why Rafaela comes to him. And then he thinks, Maybe Daniel got what he deserved. And then he just thinks, Jesus, I didn't know.

She breaks the stare, butts her head against her father's hip. Daniel holds a bottle in front of her: "What do you think,

Malbec or Cabernet?" She guffaws like it's the best joke in the world and he smiles. "All right, then. Malbec it is." Bottle in his right hand, holding fast to his daughter with his left, Daniel manoeuvres the two of them delicately, doggedly sideways down the aisle just as Rafaela emerges from behind the cheese display with a bottle of white, smiling at her family.

"Good timing," Daniel greets her.

Clutching his own bottle to his chest, Tibor turns to avoid them. Too late. Daniel's voice: "Rolly? My God, it's been ages."

Gellert Hegy
Gellert Hegy

Long before the revolution of October 1956, the rumours were that the Soviets were tunnelling. Their tunnels spread with the speed of rhizomes, under the surface of Budapest. The rumours spread the same way, sprouting and multiplying, their source untraceable.

When the revolutionaries stormed Communist Party Headquarters in Koztarsasag Ter on October 30, they found half-cooked palacsinta—far more than would be required to feed the number of prisoners found in the building's cellar prisons. Frantic, searchers fanned out into every dank hallway, looking for secret doors, knocking index knuckles on walls that looked solid, testing for hollow. There were so few prisoners in the building. Where were the hundreds who'd vanished? Someone had heard shouting from below. Someone else had heard a number: one hundred and forty prisoners. Where were they? They had no food, no water. Time was running out. General Bela Kiraly, the commander of the Revolutionary National Guard, gave the order to drill.

Three boring masters were ordered to the city from the Oroszlany coalmines. Drill! From the National Geophysics

Institute came one cathode-ray oscilloscope, four Soviet-made geophones, one anode-battery with necessary cables. Drill! Twenty metres down and not far enough. Drill! Heavy machines, the same used to excavate the city's extraordinarily deep subway tunnels, were put to revolutionary service, much of Budapest's Sewage Company too, with their ropes, their pickaxes, their Soviet labourer muscle. Drill! Searchers spread into the sewers. They dug out the cellars in the houses surrounding the square. Hundreds of people gathered with shovels and pickaxes. They dug and they scraped and they listened, desperately, for the voices of the interred. The search ended early morning November 4 when Soviet tanks thundered into the city. The revolution was suppressed. The prisoners in the tunnels remained buried.

In 1993, the search began again. This time, a film crew hired the National Geophysical Institute to find the tunnels. Anomalies in the soil structure were found. An oil drill with a diamond bit was ordered. The drill hit something four metres below the surface, a hard substance that ate up the diamond. And another, and another. Three diamond bits were wasted on that impenetrable substance below the square.

It doesn't matter that the tunnels were never proven. Everyone knows they exist. They must. It's the only possible explanation.

1.

Tibor wakes to the battering *rat-a-tat* of a cement drill to realize he's hot and unbearably itchy under a hotel comforter of prickling fibreglass. It's 11:13 a.m. He throws off the comforter to find the crinkly burst plastic of the airplane snack that somehow landed in his bed when he did. Cracker crumbs in his chest hair. Hauling himself upright, he teeters to the window and yanks the curtain cord. Light pours in. Ah.

Across the Duna, the parliament gleams, white spiring the complete blue of sky. Budapest, finally: the salve his poor, love-damaged soul needs. Salvation. He'd been dreaming of this moment for months. Granted, they had been some of the worst months of his life. After the devastation of losing Rafaela, he retracted. The way he described it — to himself, that is; he'd never say so out loud — was that his soul had beat a retreat, had shrunk up and back inside itself like a penis, coldly plunged.

The reason he can't stop thinking about what happened, he thinks, is that they didn't have final words. He didn't get to tell her that he loved her, that he's sorry he never told her that he knew Daniel, that he didn't intend to make life difficult for her, that he wishes things could have been different — that she'd had a normal child, that he hadn't fallen for her, that they'd both been truthful from the beginning, that he'd never bumped into them like that in the liquor store. He'd never forget her face as, foundering, she put things together.

"Rafa, this is my old friend Rolly. Back in undergrad, we were inseparable."

Rafaela extends her hand. "Hi. Nice to meet you."

"And this is our daughter, Evie. Evie, say hi."

Slobbering child opens her mouth and caws.

How did Daniel not see what was happening? His wife every shade of crimson and fury and his friend stiffly grinning.

He'd half expected her to call to yell at him, call him names, accuse him. And he'd considered calling her — to apologize, to explain, to confess his love. He is still every day in his mind composing the words that would salvage something from the disaster, but sometimes, there's just no salvage. He lost her. It feels impossibly bad.

A bit self-consciously at first, he named this bad feeling grief. "Grief," he said out loud. But even that potent word could do nothing to tame the writhing vermicular mass of loss and abandonment or fortify the queasy state of "being loser" that having lost implies.

Tibor wrestles his attention back to the spires, the Carpathian blue sky. He's here now. At home, it's reading week. Here, it's the day before the conference begins. He's made it. He'd made the decision in January. A bit last minute. Peter, a friend of his, was putting together this conference and had first contacted him back in October, at the very centre of the maelstrom called Rafaela. When one of the participants dropped out, he emailed Tibor again, and for some reason, the proposition struck Tibor as exactly the right cure. A conference. He'd always excelled at conferences. He likes the showmanship of it — the off-the-cuff opening, the studied pause, the sly aside — and his research, he likes to think, lends itself to performance. He would have his argument sewn up, solid, and he would dismantle any attempt at critique. A conference was exactly what he needed. And in *Budapest*. He hasn't been here since his post-doc days eight years ago.

And now, the city awaits. He turns. The bedside clock radio glares: 11:15.

Which means his mother has been waiting for him in the lobby — showered and dressed — since ten.

His mother.

She'd ambushed him over a plate of turkey fillet in paprikas cream sauce.

"You what?" he gabbled, mouth full, fork hovering. "I mean, have you booked a hotel? A flight? You can't just do these things last minute, you know."

She spooned more sauce on his plate, beaming pinkly. "You'd be proud of your old mother; I even did a web booking." She said *web booking*, not *veb booking*. Her *w* was perfectly Canadian and *now*, now of all times, she'd decided to go home. Tibor cursed the Internet and the amiable North York travel agent who apparently had no problem sending a seventy-eight-year-old woman on an arduous journey across the world to a potentially volatile post-communist state. "I never would have done it on my own, but since you were going. Well, I thought it might be my last chance." She didn't say, Before I die. She didn't say, I am old and alone. But he heard it. He heard it and he wanted to cry.

Sure enough, in the hotel's ground-floor, near-empty restaurant his mother sits by herself at a window seat, a ringed espresso cup in front of her, a heavy paperback balanced against the table's edge. The awkward, upward tilt of the head keeps her glasses from sliding off her nose. It also makes her thin neck as vulnerable as a downy gosling's. Pecking her on the cheek, he slides into the chair opposite. "You should have called. I was fast asleep."

She closes her book. "I didn't want to wake you. But the menu is *so* expensive here, Tibor, so I didn't order lunch."

"No problem. The Angelika's just around the corner. Not cheap, by Hungarian standards, but good food, great atmosphere."

"The young lady at the desk tells me there's a palacsinta house just five minutes away. I would *love* a mazsolas-turos palacsinta."

"I'm sure they have palacsinta at the Angelika."

"She says this place is very good. And inexpensive. When I was a girl, I thought I could live only on palacsinta. Hortobagyi husos and mazsolas-turos palacsinta was all I wanted to eat."

"Mom. I'm sure we can afford lunch at a decent restaurant."

"Persze, Tibor, persze." *Persze.* Such a harmless, conciliatory word, with multiple, micro-sonar nuances as yet untabulated. Of course, Tibor, of course. As she tucks her book into her bottomless handbag.

"It's a great restaurant, Mom. You'll love it."

"Good. You know it's been hours since that airplane snack."

The Angelika doesn't serve palacsinta and it doesn't suit her. A renovated old convent, its floor is at least four feet below street level, and stained-glass windows look out onto pedestrian feet. High-ceilinged, white-walled, and pristine, with his mother here in front of him, it suddenly seems pretentious.

She orders a soup, the cheapest item on the menu. "Salty," she concludes but finishes it. She's so hungry, she'd eat grass right now. She asks for a chamomile tea. They're sold out. She orders a cup of hot water instead, which earns her a stiffly polite nod.

"My aunt and uncle lived not far from here. After the war."

"Is that right." Eager to recover from his error, he tilts too far toward enthusiasm. She doesn't seem to notice.

"It was only one small room. My uncle put their bed up on stilts to make room for a table."

He says, "My friend Peter and his wife had exactly the same arrangement in their flat. It works surprisingly well. Like a loft."

She blows to cool her water and tentatively sips.

Tibor settles his coffee cup in his saucer. "So, it's men's day at the Kiraly today and I thought I'd take advantage, go to the baths this afternoon, Mom, if you think you can manage by yourself for a while."

"Persze, Tibor. You go ahead. Relax. You have a big day tomorrow." A pause, and Tibor braces himself for the *but*. "I think I'll go to the cemetery. I asked the girl at the desk and she tells me it's quite easy to get there by subway, just a ten-minute walk from the Keleti train station. I'm sure it's not too complicated. She gave me a map."

"You're okay on your own?"

"Persze."

She gazes out the window that offers no view. She seems all right. Or is she pretending? She rides the subway all the time in Toronto, but that's Toronto. It's different here, as she'd discover. Some underground stations house whole villages of homeless, aggressive panhandlers, pickpockets, beggars, particularly near the train stations. People selling puppies and stolen cameras and cigarettes. In her tidy American boots and all-weather coat, she'd be a walking target.

"Are you sure?"

"Yes, thank you, Tibor. They've been dead a long time. Almost twenty years now, hard to believe. I just want to pay my respects. I'm sure I'll be fine."

At dinner, she'd tell him how hard it was to get there, how rude were the gypsies. She'd call them gypsies. She'd say nothing about sadness or grief or the funerals she'd missed. She'd detail the unkemptness of the paths, the graffiti. How nothing was the same, nothing respected.

"You don't want some company?"

"No, no. Really. You don't have time. I know your presentation is tomorrow. You should prepare, practise."

She probably assumes he's the main event at this international conference — her son, the star. And Tibor feels suddenly both abashed and fond, and under the tidal insistence of such fondness, his plans erode.

At Batthyany Ter, the escalator descends about a hundred metres at warp speed at a nearly vertical angle through a tight red-and-white metal tunnel. Tibor supports his mother's elbow as they take the step together and are borne vertiginously down, handrail jiggering.

"So this wouldn't have been nearly complete by the time you left," he says. "Work on the metro halted in … 1953, I think. It was this massive, hubristic exercise in Soviet symbolism. The deepest metro in the world, vertically superior to any other subway. I wish I knew who thought of the idea first. What chaos. Thousands of workers shipped in from the country to dig with shovels and pickaxes at fourteen different locations."

"It's true, I —"

"The dig under Rakoczi Ut was apparently the deepest. That's the remarkable thing: there was absolutely no structural or engineering reason to tunnel so deep. Of course, in the absence of reason, one Soviet science journal claimed that tunnelling would expose the buried secrets of Budapest's prehistoric past, bringing them to the surface for the enlightenment of all workers."

His mother seems surprisingly unworried by the dizzying, speedy descent, the look on her face almost seraphic. When they get to the bottom, she steps unhesitatingly as harried people push past.

They sit side by side on the cold vinyl bench, and the train carries them under the Duna. His mother grips a bouquet of flowers — calla lilies, ferns, three yellow roses, some pink carnations — wrapped in stiff, crinkly green paper. With one gloved hand, she fiddles with the paper.

"The Soviet propaganda said that commuting via subway would save workers nine million working hours annually. Can you imagine? One newspaper declared that meant millions of Hungarian people could watch more than four and a half million movies. Right, Soviet movies, exactly. But then after Imre Nagy came in as prime minister — the first time, I mean, not for those few revolutionary days — the Soviet leadership ordered it all to stop. All the workers went home. They'd decided the workers needed apartments more than they needed transit. So they started building up instead of down."

The subway grinds to a halt. An electronic voice announces that the doors are opening. People pour in. The voice warns, "Careful. The doors are closing."

"They built it so deep so the top party officials and their families could be kept safe in case of a nuclear attack," she said. "That's why they went so far down."

"Well, that was the rumour circulating, yes."

"There were stores of food down there when the rest of us had nothing. "

"It must have seemed that way."

"They were preparing for war. Many people died building those tunnels. Country people. We learned that later."

She always did this, corrected him, as if to remind him that no matter how much history he studied, his knowledge could never match her real-life experience. She ambushed him with her past. In a grade six geography class, he learned about borders. Distraught, he confronted his mother after school: "Hungary is part of the Soviet Union?"

She looked at him, confused. She was peeling potatoes into the sink and when she turned, one pink-rubber-gloved hand held the peeler, the other the potato. "What are you talking about?"

"Why didn't you tell me?"

"Well, where did you think it was?"

He was at a loss. He felt how hot his face was, how sweaty because he'd walked so quickly all the way home just to ask her this. "But people are poor there. And you can be arrested just for speaking your mind. It's like a prison, and there's an iron curtain all the way around it."

"That's true. Now aren't you happy you are Canadian?" She went back to peeling potatoes. "Na. What did you learn in French class?"

Now she fiddles with the crinkly paper of the bouquet. "My mother was only sixty-three when she died. I'm more than a decade older than my own mother. Can you imagine?"

The subway jostles. "She was probably about forty when I left. She seemed so old. Old and angry. My God, always angry. We couldn't do anything right. Zsofi and I, we used to go out at night just the two of us, sit in the courtyard, or wander up and down Szent Istvan Korut, just to be free of her."

As his mother rambles, Tibor turns his mind to the coffee

house near Ferenciek Ter—its elegant round tables and soaring ceilings—and the reading he'd brought with him. If they spent thirty minutes in the cemetery, an hour even, he could still salvage the late afternoon. She'd need a rest and he could get away, finish his paper, join his friend Peter later for a drink, as planned. Tibor wanted to talk to him about this paper he was working on, about the tunnels and the creation of fear, fear and far-right paranoia. He and his mother ride the rest of the way without talking.

"Here we are." His mother pats his thigh. Grasping the rail, she stands while the train is still moving. It shudders to a stop and she sways, finding her balance.

Forty minutes later, Agnes picks her way along the rough stone paths of the old graveyard, map in hand. The map is drawn in blue ballpoint on a sheet of paper torn from the kind of little notepad only old ladies carry in their purses. It's getting soggy in the rain.

"Mom, can I just take a look at that?"

She hadn't asked him to come. She hadn't asked for a lecture on Soviet architecture or his solicitous hand at her elbow. She doesn't need his help reading the map, though he's already twice reached out his hand for it. "I am fully capable of reading a map, Tibor," she's said each time, but she doesn't want to seem secretive or raise his suspicion. He'd never believe her, for a start. He has his own ideas about history. That's fine. Historians tend to miss the point.

"I don't think we're going in the right direction, Mom. Could you just let me see the map?"

The rain had started almost as soon as they'd exited the

subway. A cold, thick winter rain. She'd worn waterproof boots, in expectation of slush. Tibor had not, and his suede walking shoes were getting soaked through. She says nothing about his impractical shoes or the slush or the creeping cold. Neither does he, though they've been wandering in circles for more than an hour.

Agnes looks around. Nothing is quite as it should be. The paths veer left where they ought to be straight. Trees obscure what she'd been assured were obvious markers: the sculpture of a couple, dressed in 1950s workers' garb. A tall angel, wings spread. The rain is creeping under the collar of her jacket, and her umbrella is next to useless. A fool's errand, made worse by her son's immaculately contained seething.

The map is from a Hungarian woman she'd met in Toronto at a funeral. It was funny, the way it happened. So coincidental, she couldn't help but think it must mean something. The service was over and Agnes was downstairs in the church basement, eating a sandwich. The Hungarian accent was the first thing she noticed.

"We were four women to a cell. There was me, Klara Lengyel, Marta Horvath, and Zsofi… Zsofi Perec? No. Zsofi *Teglas*. You see, I tell you their names because—"

"Zsofi Teglas?" Agnes shouldered someone aside, grabbed the woman's wrist. "Did you say Zsofi Teglas?"

There were crumbs on the woman's black dress, a half-eaten egg sandwich in her left hand, a half-smile on her face.

"I'm Agnes Teglas. Zsofi was my sister."

"Zsofi's sister? No."

"She was with you in prison? In 1956?"

"She was," the woman declared. "And in Vienna, spring of 1957."

"Vienna?"

"That's right. Zsofi and I escaped together. Through the tunnels."

"Mom. We're not going to find it this way. Look, there's the street. I'm going to see if I can call us a cab."

But hold on. There's the angel. There, the honoured workers. And there, where two paths meet, the white mausoleum.

"Persze, Tibor. You're probably right." Agnes places herself squarely in the archway of the mausoleum's door. Shelter, she points. "I'll just wait here for you."

He gives her a patient smile, meant to show her how nobly he endures, and jogs off, shoes squelching.

The woman's story was preposterous: she and Zsofi, digging, then a friendly prison guard, directing them into a hidden passageway. An entirely unbelievable story, yet here, exactly where she'd said it would be, exactly as the map specified, here was the exit of the tunnel through which Zsofi and this woman, Dorottya, had escaped.

Agnes pushes at the door. Pushes with everything she's got. Then sees the chain and the massive padlock securing it. It's futile, she knows, but she yanks at the padlock. It leaves rust all over her new grey gloves, but it doesn't give. She nearly cries with frustration—to come all this way, to be so close, and still so far from the truth. Then she realizes: why would anyone lock up the dead? If there is nothing in here but bones, there is no reason for security.

So, she doesn't have evidence of a tunnel, exactly, but then again, she doesn't see the absence of tunnel either. It isn't proof, nor is it proof to the contrary.

The existence of the tunnels and underground prisons has never been proven. Searchers just didn't know where to look, Dorottya insisted. "I don't know how many tunnels there were. Endless tunnels. Miles of them. We lived in darkness. We saw light twice a day, at mealtimes. The guards carried lanterns. We all turned into moles. The light hurt our eyes. I stopped believing in my own hand; I couldn't see it. There's no darkness like it, the darkness of the earth. We talked to stay sane, but some people lost their minds, thought they were buried alive, in their graves. I still can't stand the dark. But then, I don't know what happened, some of us were conscripted to dig. The digging was awful, painful and hard, but at least we had light. At least we knew we were alive."

A guard helped them escape, escorting them through an underground maze to this exit. Here. Here, Dorottya and Zsofi emerged, close to the southern train station and close also to Koztarsasag Ter, Communist Party Headquarters, where the tunnels were believed to begin. The moonlight seemed like day to their eyes. They scrubbed their faces with snow. They melted snow in their cupped palms and drank it. Then they caught a train to Sopron, jumping off before the station to run through the fields and the forest to the border.

Agnes hears the car pulling up behind her and shoves stained gloves into her pockets.

"I'm sorry we didn't find the grave, Mom," Tibor says. He's being tender, and she feels sorry this brief and uncharacteristic moment of empathy has been evoked by a lie.

"Do you see the communist martyrs' circle?" she says. "Martyrs," she scoffs. It's a clumsy change of subject, but it does the job. Tibor always has something to say about monuments. The cab leaves the cemetery, swerving through hard, wet traffic. When she tires of her son's monologue, she can listen to the taxi's two-way, a woman's voice crackling with addresses: "Visegradi utca huszonkilenc a tizenharmadikban, ötödik kerület Oktober 6 utca tizennégy, Liliom utca negyvenegy a kilencedik kerületben." The guard who helped them said there were other exits. That's what Dorottya told her. An exit somewhere in the city park, near the Szechenyi bath. And one on Gellert, a natural chasm in the rock, another somewhere up on Rozsadomb. Dorottya didn't have maps for those.

Windshield wipers shush. Tires kiss the pavement. Agnes listens to the scrolling addresses and the rain as her son patters on.

2.

"Egesegedre." Peter raises his glass. "What took you so long?"

"Good fucking question."

He'd left his mother in her hotel room with a blanket over her knees and a bowl of soup ordered from the restaurant on her table. She was fine. She'd be fine. This is his night. Eight years since Tibor had last been here, on a research grant. At the time, Peter was doing his Ph.D. at the Central European University and working part-time at the Open Society Archives associated with the university. Now, Peter's still a teenager in a faded green concert T-shirt, jeans that seem rarely washed. And yet he's married and he's got a five-year-old boy. "You still in that one-room place near the university?"

"No. Moved to a panel apartment out in the Eleventh District."

Tibor winces.

"It's not so bad. More space than downtown. But what about you? What happened to that woman you told me about, with the name?"

"Rafaela."

"Rafaellaaaa."

"Tragi-comedy. She found out I was her husband's best friend. The end."

Peter slams the table with his beer and guffaws. It is kind of funny, when you think about it. Why doesn't he have friends like Peter in Toronto?

Peter is fun. He knows all the places to go. He leads Tibor down deserted black streets that Tibor will never remember, and doesn't try to, into clubs that aren't really clubs but condemned apartment houses turned into parties. Courtyards become tented lounges. Apartments are smashed open, graffitied, paint slopped on parquet floors. In one, a bathroom has been made up to be its own museum exhibit, glass-fronted, decorated with pages from communist-era textbooks. Tibor feels counterculture and cool. In another, the woman they call the veces neni (the washroom auntie) has a sign in twenty-six languages. She says hello, and here's your toilet paper, and two hundred forints please, in *twenty-six languages*. Her Russian is sullen. Her English perfect. Her Japanese about as good as Tibor's.

"Stop." Peter puts his hand in front of Tibor's camera. "You can't do that."

"Why?"

"Because you look like a tourist."

"So?"

Tibor takes a picture of the veces neni and of Peter, frowning, of a girl leaning over a balcony, smoking. The smoke hangs so heavy in the air, it looks like someone's barbecuing. Of a room full of laughing faces. Of feet on coffee tables. Of hands around steaming mugs of tea. A bartender's haircut. A video screen showing a bikinied lady with a huge, bouncing balance ball.

Peter is the best friend ever. He invited him to this conference that would save Tibor's soul, and now he's reminding him how great life can be in a decaying post-communist, economically bereft, precariously employed nation. "My soul is Hungarian," Tibor declares over waves of reggae.

"Your soul's a stupid loser?"

"Precisely."

"And that's why you chose to specialize in our irrelevant history?"

"Exactly. Because Hungary is the guy who never gets the girl."

Peter is sardonic and depressive and hilariously fun. Spontaneous and sincere and worn out. "I hate that Hungarian-loser rhetoric," Peter says.

"Because it's true?"

"Because it breeds monsters like Jobbik and the Magyar Garda."

"You know what I hate? I hate that I'm on vacation with my mother."

"You really are Hungarian."

Tibor feels younger by the minute, but it's their fourth romkocsma, his sixth beer, and it must be getting late. He checks his watch: only eleven-thirty. "Fuckit. Jet lag."

"I'll call you a cab," says Peter.

It's 4:12 a.m. The room hums. His comforter itches. He scratches his ankles, his rib cage. Fibreglass? Crackers.

Christ.

Tibor sits. Heaves one leg after the other over the side of the bed.

In the bathroom, he flicks on the light, sheltering his eyes (too late) from the glare. Bleary-eyed, he fills the tumbler with water and drinks with his eyes closed. He fills it again, trying not to see himself in the very large mirror. When did he get that sag above his hipbone? My God, it's not just the hip either. It starts from his spine, then overflows. Putting down his water glass, Tibor grabs his rolls, one in each fist. Holy Christ. How could he ever have believed that Rafaela might have loved this? This pale, wistfully slack waist. These insufficient arms.

Tibor turns his back on the mirror and stands over the toilet, watching his urine hit the glossy toilet bowl and pool.

He could try to go back to sleep, but he knows from experience that trying to go back to sleep is the worst thing to do. He'd just lie there rehearsing his talk and audience reactions to his talk. He'd get nervous. He kept the anxiety at bay all yesterday, and all yesterday evening with Peter. I am not worried, he says, sternly. I've always excelled at conference papers.

The street at 4:25 a.m. is empty. Streetlights, strung from overhead wires between buildings, cast watery, meagre light on ice-frosted asphalt. He steps out. Enjoys the first slap of cold on his face, in his lungs, and heads off toward Gellert. Eight years ago, he ran Gellert Hegy twice a week. He could jog all the way to the top and over, without stopping. He isn't as fit as he was then, but he could try. And if he could get there by sunrise, he'd get some great photos. He carries his Canon digital in his jacket pocket.

At the foot of the hill, Tibor checks his watch: 5:00 a.m. and still no dawn, no stars either. The clouds and the city lights together conspire to turn the sky an even purplish blue. He jogs on the spot, to keep his heart rate up, looks up the stairs that lead to the paths through the wooded hill. Poorly lit. Deserted.

So what are you afraid of?

Tibor feels the rush of adrenalin. A flood of endorphins. Exactly: what am I afraid of? A lonely hill? Bad guys lurking in caves? Those are just phantasms, irrational night terrors, as are all fears when it comes down to it. It's all in your head. It can be mastered. Yes, mastered. Master it, Tibor. Master your fear. Run up that ancient hill, and show your fears who's boss. Who will deliver a resoundingly perfect paper? Who will soon publish an article that will revise dominant thinking about post-communist Hungary? Who kicks ass? And with that thought, Tibor leaps up Szent Gellert's stairs, three at a time.

He stops not quite halfway. Above him, the statue of Hungary's first Christian, Szent Gellert, floodlit and white. He pulls the camera from the pocket of his windbreaker. He loves this camera—the size of a cigarette case but also capable of shooting video. Also gives him an excuse to catch his breath, which plumes in gusts. To be fair, he used to run the hill from the other side where the slope was less steep. He hears a loud creak. Likely just a tree in the wind. No reason to linger, though. At the top of the stairs, a gravel path. His thighs are burning.

His calves too. His breath is louder than anything else, fighting to catch up with the arrhythmia of his stomping step. He is whipping this fear. He is kicking it.

Where the path splits, Tibor chooses the second, the path less trodden — always the choice of the fearless — which curves round the front of the cliff face. What is that smell that comes out of the brush at night? Even when the ground is mostly frozen there's an alteration in the air, some kind of nighttime exhalation. The bushes are brambles of dry twigs. They chatter dryly in the wind. The few, sparse evergreens shudder. Below him, the Danube coils darkly. The black road follows it. Along the black road, the occasional car flies, headlights bright. *Zoom.* As it takes the curve. Tibor slows, the footing precarious with protruding roots, jutting rocks and to his left a drop steep and sudden and unforgiving. Puny guardrails keep him safe and he feels the delicious, tautening effort of awareness. His skin, his eyes, his ears, even his hair is sentient. His soul stirs. I'm coming back from the dead, thinks Tibor. I am Tibor Roland, master of Gellert.

He's past the halfway point where the hill juts out hard into the curve of the river, the wind picking up, when his self-congratulation is broken by a sudden ruckus of sliding gravel close above him, a muffled cry. Tibor freezes.

"Nice try, idiot. Where d'you think you're going?"

"No. No, please," a voice blubbers. "Please, I'm not Laci."

"So you say."

There are three Hungarians up there, up above him somewhere under the trees, on a different path, two frighteningly steady and calm, one younger and terrified. Tibor hugs the curve of the cliff wall. If he shouted, would the bullies back off or would they come for him? Jesus Christ. Jesus Christ, I am not a hero.

"Please," says the one voice in thick sobs. "I didn't do anything wrong. I didn't do anything."

"That might be true, but for me, I don't care. I do my job. I get my pay."

A heavy, butcher-counter sound of flesh being hammered, bones cracked.

"Where's the letter?"

"I'm not Laci."

Thunk.

"Where's the letter?"

"I don't know."

Crack. A muffled scream.

"Where's the letter?"

"Laci lost it."

Two voices move away. The young, broken man must be lying not five metres above him. Are they leaving? Tibor hears the electronic ping of a cellphone being dialled. The one man must be speaking into the phone. "Look, he looks like the photo in the driver's licence, but he's got another wallet in his pants pocket and he keeps saying he's not Laci. I'm starting to believe him."

Closer to Tibor, the injured man is starting to move. Brush crackles and scatters against hard ground.

Still speaking into the phone: "A risk? Maybe."

A pause.

"Done."

One dull thud, the movement stops.

Tibor has stopped breathing.

"Jesus. What the fuck?"

"He said take care of it."

"He's the wrong fucking guy."

"True."

"Jesus, fuck. And you had to do it here? What're we gonna do with this? The car's like a kilometre back."

"Yeah, well. Gimme the fuckin' axe."

"Here?"

"You'll see."

Tibor hears a dull crack.

"Ugh. Christ."

"You fucking buzi."

Another thunk. Then five more dull crunches. Tibor counts them.

"All right, gimme a hand."

Crush of branches as they walk but not far.

"Watch this."

Scrape of something heavy, moved. A pause.

"What the hell? How deep is it?"

"I don't know. Deep enough. Trust me, no one will ever find him down here."

Less than two minutes of activity and then underbrush crackling, twigs snapping, as something rolls, bounces, downward and right over Tibor's head, coming to a halt somewhere in front of him.

"Fuck," the men shout in unison.

Silence.

"Oh, man," says the one. "Oh shit, shit, shit."

"Shit, do we look for it?"

"Down there? Fuck, man, for all we know it's halfway to the highway."

"So what do we tell Gombas?"

"Tell him it committed suicide." High, breathless, juvenile laughter.

"It's a jumper."

The laughter spins itself thin and stops.

"Fuck."

"Yeah."

Tibor hears their footsteps trudge up the hill. He's dropped to a crouch, and now he sinks, legs giving way entirely. Maybe he'll never get off this hill. As the sky pales, tree branches seem to separate, differentiating themselves from night. Lights go out. The river turns grey. Far below, and through the trees, Tibor can see the old church by the bridge, the rows of headlights as people start out for work. Normal life is down there. But directly opposite Tibor, caught in the prickly undergrowth not two metres below, a head, looking up at him, eyes open. A young blond head. A kid, without his body.

In the lecture hall, Tibor's audience waits. Someone coughs. Feet shuffle on low-pile carpet. Here and there paper rustles as notebooks open. Tibor looks down at his paper. His right hand is shaking. Yet he doesn't *feel* nervous. His feet in their Doc Martens—not the iconic counterculture boot but the sturdy, thick-soled shoe—feel grounded. He breathes in through his nose and out through his mouth: he learned this from the yoga classes he took a couple of years ago, precisely to get him through situations like this. With each breath, he feels his substance reasserting itself. He presses his trembling palm flat on the podium. He begins.

"Long before the revolution of October 1956, the word was that the Soviets were tunnelling. Their tunnels spread with the speed of rhizomes..."

He couldn't say how he'd found his way down the other side of the hill to the Hotel Gellert, where he grabbed a cab. Back in his room, he dumped his clothes in a huddle and stepped straight into the shower, where he stayed for a good twenty minutes, leaning his head back into the pummelling water. After calling his mother to wish her a good morning and excuse himself from breakfast, he ate a bread roll and cheese in his hotel room, got on the subway, and emerged here.

His audience seems to be listening. One man nods approvingly at a critical juncture. A woman in front of him squints, then jots in her notebook, clearly stimulated by what she's heard. Good. Now he's established his context and the urgent question that his research will answer, now he can just let it happen. The magic. Taking his hand from his pocket, he elaborates a planned aside and turns back to the words on the page.

The type blurs. He blinks, rubs his eyes. The ideas seem strangely foreign, the sentence structures impossible to anticipate. Where does he pause? When does he breathe? When he looks up, the faces in the front row are frowning. Do they think he's wrong or just stupid? Are they impatient with his argument, his hand-in-the pocket posturing? His heart pounds and his chest tightens.

Page two. Keep going. "As many of you are perhaps aware, the Historical Archives of the Hungarian State Security was opened in 2003. This signified an end to secrecy—and perhaps the end to rumours of tunnels. Security documents are housed there, but they can't be accessed by just anyone. If you were one of the many 'observed' by state security informants, you can read your own files, and know the names of those who observed you, arrested you, or tortured you. If you were, yourself, an informer, agent, or torturer, you can be assured that only your victims can know this about you."

Tibor prickles with sweat, his chest so tight he can hardly lift his arm to turn the page. Fear is all in the head. Master your fear. "This creates a curious quandary. In a state where complicity was demanded and rewarded, where so many ordinary and otherwise decent people turned information on others for the sake of their own safety, the archive must not be vengeful."

He's breathing too fast. So fast, he can't catch his breath. The room is breathing, its walls swelling and shrinking, and swelling. Tibor staggers away from the podium, pushing through the heavy side door, gasping for air. Outside the classroom, he sinks onto a bench in the hall. He leans forward, presses his right hand to his heart. Just breathe. But it hurts to breathe with a three-pronged fork stuck in his lung. Maybe he's dying. Dying of cowardice—is that possible? A woman with a neat ponytail and turtleneck, one of the conference organizers, has followed him out. Ilona. That's her name. Ilona crouches worriedly at his side and puts a hand on his back. "Are you all right?"

He sees his academic career, his entire future, crumbling. From fear. From bad timing and bad luck. "Food poisoning." He grimaces.

Kind Ilona calls him a cab. Passively, he takes her arm as she leads him to the door. She puts him in the cab and gives the driver the name of his hotel, pays his fare. Huddled into the backseat, breathing like an asthmatic, Tibor screws his eyes shut, trying to block out the humiliation.

"I don't understand. There was a mugging at the conference?"

Tibor's mother hasn't left the hotel yet. Dressed and coiffed, she'd just finished her breakfast—delivered by room service; apparently, she was getting the hang of this hotel lifestyle—and was in her room, watching TV, when he knocked. He meant to sound competently unperturbed, and he concealed the actual, horrifying event for her sake, but obviously he's not being clear. He has decided to report it. Tell someone about it, get it off his chest. It is the only way to get over the shakes that assaulted him this morning.

"Not at the conference, Mom. When I went for a run this morning."

"So you witnessed a mugging *before* you went to the conference?"

"That's right."

"Thank God it wasn't you, Tibor, out there before dawn by yourself. This isn't Toronto. You know they found a head on Gellert Hegy this morning? Just a head. It was on the news. But where was the mugging? Was anybody hurt?"

"Oh, not far from here. It was just a little scuffle."

"Not far from here? Did you tell the people at the front desk? Maybe we should change hotels."

"No, no. I mean, it wasn't that close. And you're right, it was stupid of me to be out jogging in the dark."

His mother's eyes have gone back to the TV: an advertisement for the new right-wing political party, Jobbik. "Hungary for Hungarians" is the party line. Twenty years after the end of Soviet communism and somehow this rhetoric is gaining traction. It's the economic downturn, after a too-short period of optimism. It's knowing that the too-high taxes, which more than 70 per cent of the population avoids by working at an official minimum wage and receiving the rest under the table, end up in the pockets of corrupt politicians. The story has just broken: money that was supposed to pay to modernize Budapest's transit system, its buses and its highways, had landed in someone's pocket. This has nothing to do with Jews or with the Roma, but Jobbik's propaganda suggests that they are the ones ruining Hungary.

"They think it was an organized crime, the head on Gellert."

Not *an* organized crime, Mom.

"But they don't know who it belongs to. His poor family." She tsks. "But I suppose if it's an organized crime he was probably a murderer too, or a drug dealer."

"Probably."

"So. He got what he deserved." Decisively, she changes the channel.

Tibor feels a cautious relief. If they've found the head already, then he is off the hook, isn't he? It's too late to save the boy, after all. And he has no need to play the hero. No, his first impulse was the right one: stay out of it. So, maybe he'll go back to the conference this afternoon. *Or* he could use his food poisoning as a reasonable excuse to take the day off, go to the baths, as he planned to do yesterday. Today would be men's day at the Rudas. But the Rudas is at the foot of Gellert. There would be police. Reporters. But why should he worry? No one knew he was up there, witnessing. A long, hot steam followed by a cold plunge, a soak. His mother is still talking.

"...meeting him for coffee. But if you want to come along, I'm sure he'd love to meet you."

"No, no, thank you. I'll just head back to the conference. After I speak with the police, I mean."

"I don't know how we'll recognize each other. After fifty-three years. I told him I'd wear a maple leaf pin on my lapel. But did you get a good look at the man? Even in the dark? All right then, have a good time at your conference. And I'm glad your presentation went well. You've always been so good at public speaking."

He's backing out the door as she talks, her eyes again fixed on the TV. The door clicks behind him, and he's free. Two more minutes and his gym bag is packed—toiletries, a hotel towel, flip-flops. The wind's picking up, gusting along the river, blowing dust up each narrow street. Who else, on his holiday, has the implausible misfortune to witness a hit. A hit? It was the vocabulary of American cop shows, not his. He hops on the streetcar.

The swarms of police he'd expected at the foot of Gellert are not there. There's no yellow tape either, at least not at the bottom of the stairs to the white saint. Maybe the investigation is complete. Maybe they found the rest of the body. At the Rudas, he pays his entrance fee to a surly cashier in the booth, proceeds into the change room, which is mostly empty. A good time of day to be here. He breathes deeply of the humid, sulphur-misted air and feels softly, amply justified. What if the police needed him to identify a criminal? Or testify? He'd spend his entire trip sitting in stuffy police stations, giving evidence. Witnessing the murder was an accident, not his fault, and certainly not his responsibility. Drug deals go wrong every day, according to the news and TV police dramas. They'd have suspects in cells by nightfall. This is not some British murder mystery, just ordinary life among a criminal underclass.

The water in the central octagonal pool is 24 degrees Celsius. Naked, he sinks into it. Four large men on the other side of the pool chat in low voices. Their bellies rise, an archipelago above the water. Mumbles amplify and resound under the stone dome. Sinking deeper, Tibor rests the back of his head against the stone lip. He lets his arms go soft. They float. His legs bend, his penis happily coddled. He looks up at the fist-sized holes in the dome through which light beams in. Too bad they don't allow cameras in here.

He straightens. Waves crest the lip.

My camera.

He had it in his hand, then he put it in his pocket after the statue. But did it come down the hill with him? There was no reason to think it hadn't. But what *if.* What if it was still there? What if his slim-as-a-cigarette-case Canon camera was still up on Gellert under the butting rock where he'd squatted? An ordinary person's camera—with its innocent pictures of frozen waterfalls, fall colour, wildlife, of his mother on her seventy-sixth birthday, of Rafaela's orgasm (she didn't know about that), of the party houses with Peter. The camera might be still up there.

Holy. Fuck. FuckFuckFuck.

"The nearest police station?" The front desk clerk handily withdraws a map from the stack on the counter. He marks the location on the map and then painfully slowly, he traces the route in ballpoint from the hotel to the *X.* "I hope everything is all right, sir." He pushes the map across the counter. Tibor speaks fluent Hungarian, but the clerk speaks English back to him.

"Fine, thank you"—Tibor glances at the man's nametag—"Gabor. No worries." He taps the map on the counter, the way confident men do. He's halfway out the door before he realizes he's still got his gym bag. He can't report a murder while carrying a hotel towel and flip-flops. Maybe the inquisitive Gabor will hold it for him. He turns back to the desk.

"Tibor. What perfect timing."

His mother is crossing the lobby, towing behind her an elderly gentleman in an expensive-looking overcoat, a wool fedora in his hand.

"Tibor, this is Uncle Gyula. You remember I told you about Gyula. We're just on our way out for a little coffee."

Not for the life of him. "Yes, yes, of course." Tibor extends his hand to the old man. Tall and distinguished. Thick head of grey hair. Was he some kind of cousin? "Very good to finally meet you, Uncle Gyula."

"What did the police say?"

Right. He'd forgotten. He's holding his gym bag on the counter, in the other hand, the map, the X clearly marked. Beside him, Gabor-the-clerk pretends to be checking something on the computer.

"I haven't got there yet."

"Gyula says it's becoming more and more common. And you absolutely should not be running around by yourself at all hours of the night."

"It's true. There are many thefts these days, sir," Gabor-the-clerk tunes in—in English, despite having now overheard the entire party speaking Hungarian. "We tell all our guests to lock their valuables in the safe provided in your room."

"Thank you, Gabor," Tibor says tightly. "But I was not robbed."

"No, thank God," his mother jumps in. "But he witnessed a mugging."

Gabor frowns at this news, as if now even more worried for Tibor's safety. "I'm sorry to hear that, sir. Where was this?"

"He said it wasn't very far from here."

Tibor feels a snapping inside his head—the minute popping of blood vessels. "But not in the immediate vicinity," he reassures the anxious Gabor. Then, clapping a hand on the bag assertively: "Could you please hold this for me until I get back?"

"Certainly, sir. And, sir, at night, the underpasses are to be avoided at all costs."

Avoided at all costs? Who says that?

"Tibor, you're not taking that to the conference are you? It looks like an old gym bag."

"It *is* an old gym bag, Mom. I went to the Rudas."

"That's good, Tibor. You need to relax. I'm sure Gyula would be happy to come with you to the police station, if you'd like."

The quiet man seems as embarrassed as Tibor, but he nevertheless politely repeats the offer. "If you'd like my help, of course. But I was telling your mother that, by the sounds of it, what you witnessed was a fairly commonplace theft. The police probably won't be interested in your statement."

And what does Gabor have to say to that? Nothing, apparently. But perhaps only because his head is below the counter, stowing the bag.

"Here's my number, in any case." Uncle Gyula scrawls it on the back of a hotel card.

"Great. Thanks. Nice meeting you." And before anyone can open their mouths again, he steps into the revolving door.

The police station on Pauler Utca is both intimidating and dull. Winter coats smell of cigarettes and salami and slush. Complainants press at the desk, and officers loll back in rolling chairs, stupefied. Tired. No one has clean boots. Boots leak melting water onto the floor. Ceilings leak. Pipes rattle and radiators fail. Tibor notices these commonplace things and he thinks, It's all so ordinary. People are robbed, kids are stabbed with kitchen knives, apples are wrinkled and potatoes rot, and politicians steal your last bite. Better not to expect too much. That's what the faces say. When he asks where he might report a murder, the woman at the desk looks at him like she's not prepared to believe anything. She frowns. She points him back with the end of her pen.

The officer seems unimpressed with Tibor's account. "No," Tibor corrects him, "I didn't discover it. I was there, I witnessed... I overheard the murder. No, I'm not exactly sure about the time. Around five this morning. I was jogging."

The police officer, young and smooth-faced, gives Tibor his hardest look. "It's now" — he checks his watch — "nearly four. You waited for some reason?"

"I know it looks bad, but I was booked to make a presentation first thing this morning." This was true. "And I was terrified, quite frankly. I heard a man being murdered, for God's sake."

The officer nods, maybe sympathetically, but it's hard to tell. Maybe he doesn't believe a word Tibor says. Maybe he's jealous. Wishes it was him. Knows he'd have done the braver thing and beat the shit out of those murdering cowards.

"Where exactly were you jogging?"

"I took the path to the left, the one that goes along the face of the hill, overlooking the river."

"Why?"

"Why?"

"Yes, why? The paths are not safe. Why would you go up there?"

The police officer, whose name is Ferenc, strokes the front of his immaculate blue shirt. His mother likely pressed it for him this morning while he was jacking off in the shower. You get what you deserve—this is what Ferenc's look tells Tibor.

Tibor pushes on. He'd come here to give information, and so he would. "I went for a jog to get over the jet lag. I had not quite rounded the point when I heard voices. I stopped and hid because…well, I don't know why I hid. Instinct, I guess."

"Go on."

"The kid kept insisting he knew nothing. Then they killed him. Well, one guy killed him. The other one seemed surprised. They didn't seem very professional. They dropped the head."

"They dropped it?"

"Yes. It got away on them. They joked about that. He's a jumper, something like that."

Ferenc seems too young to be handling this kind of an investigation, but then maybe there are multiple officers on the case and this kid is only one of them. Still, shouldn't there be a greater sense of urgency in the air, a driven, ambitious push and scramble? But Ferenc is a serious officer, and he writes down what Tibor tells him.

"Okay, okay. Start from the beginning. You heard voices."

It's as though he's telling a story. And telling the story makes him feel like he's doing something right. Not like a hero — not extraordinary or central — but like a good man, a man who knows that the truth is important, a man who does the thing that needs to be done if the good guys are going to win the day. Tibor tells Ferenc, as precisely as he can remember it, the morning's exact sequence of events. He'll have to wait for the right moment to raise the question of the camera.

"Gombas? You're sure that's the name?"

"Sure I'm sure. I mean, it's not one you'd forget — Mr. Fungus Infection."

"Wait here, please."

Smooth-shirted Ferenc hurries off. Finally, a hurry. And he hasn't even got to the part about how they dropped the body parts into a very deep hole. They'd want to know that, to locate the body.

Tibor stands, stretches. The day is catching up with him, and the jet lag. He checks his watch: 4:45 p.m. There are no windows in this room where he's waiting and it's airless, fluorescent lit, paint flaking from walls no doubt poisoning everyone with lead. Outside, it would be getting dark.

"My wife keeps saying we have to get rid of the dog. Because it shits in the house sometimes, you know. I tell her if she walked it instead of waiting for me to get home, it would stop shitting in the house, but she's too lazy. Rather sell my fucking dog than put her coat on and walk it around the block."

The speaker's standing just on the other side of the door — a police officer, presumably, with nothing to do on the day of a mafia murder investigation.

"Power struggles, buddy. That's what marriage is all about. Power fucking struggles."

At the sound of the second man's voice, Tibor starts. A reedy voice, stumbly and nasally congested.

"Don't give in. He's a beautiful dog. You don't see dogs like that every day. And you raised him from a pup, trained him. No, a dog is like a friend. You don't sell your friend."

"Sure, I trained him. And he's smart. Not his fault he can't hold it for twelve hours. I mean, what does she expect? But I swear I'm gonna get home from work one day and he'll be gone."

"So if she sells your dog, you sell her clothes. Bet she's got some nice clothes, right, maybe her mother's jewellery, sentimental stuff. That's what you tell her. Tell her she better start walking that dog."

The door swings wide, and the men step inside.

"I understand you have some information on the Gellert head," says the murderer.

Agnes hadn't expected the streets to be so disorienting. New houses and structures fill places that used to be empty or replace buildings she remembers. It is the same city, with a new city laid over top of it. Street names have changed, and not a word of Russian to be seen. Gyula is proud. He drives her around in his luxury car, shows her the restored opera house, takes her past the Unicum factory to the new performing arts centre. He speaks as if it's his own personal property, what it cost, how perfect the acoustics. Well, in a way, it is his. She's not sure she understands the details, but it's clear his company built part of it. He has three children, all still in Budapest. The eldest is just thirty-five. So his wife must be much younger, she thinks, a baby in 1956. She doesn't ask. He says, "I lost my Judit two years ago. Cancer." She thinks how similar and different he is, the new Gyula laid over top the old. This new Gyula doesn't seem to notice her. As polite and charming as he is, the perfect tour guide, he doesn't look at her. She doesn't expect the looks they used to share, but there's an odd vacuity as if he's only just barely there.

The cake is sweeter, eggier than any she remembers from her childhood. The bitter coffee is done in a swallow. Waitresses offer minimal smiles, giving nothing away for free. This is the same. As are the low, private voices. She's forgotten how loud Canadians had seemed when she first landed. Here, all conversation, including her own, is traded intimately, conscious of listeners. Maybe this is generational. Maybe the children born after 1989 are as loud as tourists.

He's explaining something about the restoration of the café, the attention to period detail. His fingernails are chipped, dirty. Odd, for a man who surely pays others to do his labour. Under the table, his knee jitters. She remembers the jittering—always too much energy to sit still for long. Surprising, in an old man. Around them, the staff hustles, discreetly silent.

"You've done well for yourself, Gyula."

"I've done all right." Gives her a prepared smile. "Construction's a lucrative business."

Enough already. She doesn't need the tour guide, the businessman. They're not on a date, and she's not a girl to impress and there are things they need to say. She looks straight at him. "I'm sorry I never replied to your letter."

This businessman Gyula shrugs it off, as if it was nothing

more than a slight inconvenience, as if she was being sentimental. "It was a long time ago."

"I was married, pregnant with Tibor."

"It doesn't matter. Please. How's the coffee? Like you
remember?"

That letter, in 1963, nearly made her vomit. It was the shock.
He'd asked nothing except, "How are you?" In the fewest words,
as if he had to pay for each one, the letter described where he'd
been: After November 4, the day the Russian tanks shot the
hell out of their revolution, he'd been caught, arrested, and
imprisoned first with others and then by himself in a windowless
solitary cell for what he estimates was a period of three years.
He was released along with dozens of other revolutionaries in
a sudden amnesty. She sat there at her kitchen table, aware of
the nail polish on her fingers, the Formica under her hands,
the refrigerator humming behind her, the very ease of all her
surfaces. After she'd read it through, this letter on rough,
unbleached paper, in clotting blue ink, she put it back in its
envelope, and for a while she kept it on top of her dresser,
believing one day she'd answer it.

After leaving Hungary, she'd first made a living sewing
and cleaning. She learned English. She started working at a
preschool, not quite teaching but almost. Then she'd married
a Canadian, James, who taught math at a high school, and
they bought this house, and now they were having this baby.
Budapest was a different world, and the Hungarian Agi a
different person than this new Canadian Agnes, who spoke
English with only the slightest Hungarian accent and who
never, ever turned a w into a v. In his letter, Gyula had said

very little of Zsofi. He'd seen her at the student housing that day the Russians stormed back into the city, and he hadn't heard from her since his release. He'd stopped in to visit Agi's parents. They were fine. They'd had no news of Zsofi either, and they complained that Agi never wrote. *Your mother is angry with you,* he'd written. And then, *Some things never change.* She read it through once and then propped it against the mirror on her dresser and never opened it again. Eventually, she tidied it into a drawer and let herself forget.

Gyula has finished his coffee. His cake is virtually untouched. He shifts in his chair. He folds and refolds his napkin. Used to be she was the nervous one and he was never nervous enough.

"It was hard for me to face it. So. That's it. I'm sorry."

"Your bad luck. Until ten years ago, I still had my looks."

She laughs more from relief than the joke — finally, the old Gyula. The laughter feels good. Yes. This was the feeling. This is it exactly.

"Isn't this strange," she says. "Being old."

"It's certainly a surprise."

Yes, that's her Gyula. Look at him. She puts her hand on his because it feels right. Because they are still the kids they were, and here they are. "Gyula, Zsofi escaped."

The look on his face.

"Escaped? That's why you didn't write?" He seems almost defensive, as if she's accused him of something.

Next to them, a family of tourists marvels in English at the ceiling, the cakes, the everything. They're too loud, and they don't know it.

"No. Why would I not tell you that? I only found out two months ago."

As he pulls his focus back to Agnes, in front of him, she thinks madly, momentarily, that he is going to hit her.

"*What* did you find out?"

"She was arrested. And she escaped."

"When." He doesn't question but demands.

"I met someone who says she was with Zsofi in prison and they escaped. In the winter of 1957."

He takes a moment to absorb this information. Then he leans back as if released. "What? Through the underground tunnels? Secret passages from jail to freedom? Is that what you heard?"

Yes.

"Christ. Agi."

She refuses to feel stupid.

But the pantyhose she'd pulled on underneath her trousers squeezes her stomach and her sweater is too heavy for this warm café. She'd remembered every place as cold. How much warmer the city is now, how much brighter.

"You didn't hear anything from her after 1956? Nothing?" she asks.

"You think Zsofi escaped, and then what? Came back to liberate me?" He's both superior and irritated.

"I just want to know, Gyula. I'm just trying to understand."

"You haven't heard from her since you left. You think she's alive? She's not."

The waiter picks up their coffee cups and Agnes's plate. She focuses on this, this meticulous tidying, careful brushing of crumbs. She will not cry.

. . .

The sun is sinking as they leave the café. He parked the car just around the corner. An expensive car. Leather interior. Better than any she's ever owned. Gyula drives her back to the hotel. All the storefronts along Jozsef Korut are lit up like little stages, a train of stages, flashing by.

"She stayed because of you. Because she was in love with you," Agnes says.

They stop at the lights. He stares straight ahead, angry and hard. That's what she thinks. He wants to be rid of her. The lights turn. The car surges, pinning her to her seat.

Election posters banner the lampposts. A streetcar clatters past, and she'd like to be in it, inside the bright, swaying, clattering noise of it, hanging to a strap the way she used to, unperturbed and agile.

"Detective Tamas Sarkady." The detective extends his right hand.

"Detective Number Two," says the other. Not really, but Tibor forgets his name immediately.

Tamas Sarkady takes Ferenc's seat. Number Two pulls up a second chair. Neither is uniformed. They wear their badges clipped to their belts. And they don't look like murderers but like ordinary, constipated guys who fight with their plain wives and eat supper in front of the TV knowing life should have treated them better. They're good guys. Normal guys, understanding of other, normal guys.

Tibor looks Tamas Sarkady in the eye. He sees that Tamas Sarkady knows that he knows that this is not interrogation but intimidation. Tamas Sarkady is not bothered by the fact that Tibor sees this. Because he's a good guy, a normal guy. Just play along, his look says. Be cool.

"So you were going for a jog," Tamas Sarkady prompts.

"I was, yes. You know, I should probably leave a message at the hotel. I'm travelling with my mother. She'll worry if I'm late for dinner."

"Mothers," says Number Two.

But neither offers a telephone.

"This won't take long. You were jogging on Gellert Hegy in the middle of the night."

As he repeats his story, they take some notes. They ask a few questions. When he gets to the part of the story where the one guy names Gombas, Sarkady interrupts.

"Are you sure that's the name you heard?"

That's what he *says*, but his look says I'd really like to help you out here. It says, We can help each other.

"I *think* so," says Tibor. "I mean, I suppose I could be wrong."

"So you're not absolutely sure?"

"Not absolutely, no."

"Would you be able to testify that you heard *Gombas*?"

"Well, now that you put it that way, no. I suppose not. I mean, there was a lot going on. Their voices were muffled."

Number Two looks like he's just been slapped with a month of unpaid overtime. And he's thinking about his dog shitting on the carpet. And his wife sitting there, watching it shit on the carpet. And him sitting here as a whole world of shitters just slips through his fingers.

"What did they do with the body?"

"The body? Well, I didn't... How would I know? Maybe they buried it?"

"They were above you, you say, on the cliff?"

"That's right."

"About how far above?"

"Hard to say. Maybe five metres. Maybe ten." Tibor is sweating through his shirt. "I can go?"

"If we have any more questions," says Sarkady, "where can we reach you?"

"The Gellert Hotel." The lie comes fluently.

"Nice place."

"Gorgeous." Tibor has one sleeve in his coat. He's standing up. He's so close to gone.

"So you like a downhill home stretch."

"Pardon?"

"You said you started your jog at the steps of Szent Gellert. So you ran all the way along the rakpart, to the other side of the hill to begin."

Right. "I always like to start on the flat. Build up a little steam." Tibor does a weird, fake little show of running. Why did he do that?

"Ah."

"Anything you need, just call. I'm really very glad to help." Tibor gives Sarkady a meaningful look, to let him know that Tibor is more than happy to mind his own goddamn business. Sarkady nods. Sarkady knows.

Tibor steps out of the station into the Budapest evening. The snow falls reasonless and unreasonable, and Tibor walks as quickly as he can without slipping. He is afraid. So afraid he can't even care that he's afraid.

The street throngs with fatigued workers. Tomorrow, first thing, he will go to the Canadian Consulate to file a report and, if necessary, ask for protection. That's where he should have started in the first place. He hadn't asked Ferenc if they'd found his camera. Fuck the camera. He scans the faces on the sidewalk. He glances back over his left shoulder, then over his right. As far as he can tell, he's not being followed, but to be safe he takes the well-lit sidewalk, on the side close to the rakpart and the river, to the hotel. He nearly laughs with relief when the ever-attentive Gabor raises his head from his computer with a calm, "Good evening, sir."

"Good evening, Gabor."

"Your mother is waiting in the restaurant, sir. Sir, are you all right?"

"Fine. Thank you. Just getting some exercise. Beautiful night."

"Yes. Budapest is beautiful in the snow."

Tibor turns toward the restaurant. He sees his mother at the far end. He raises his hand to wave hello. She looks at her watch. He's late. He leans forward to kiss her cheeks. The other side of the window, a car flashes by. When Tibor looks up, he sees under the halo of streetlight across the street, tipped against the slender trunk of a tree, a young man. He's watching them. He nods. He strolls away.

Ferenc.

Was it?

"Tibor? Tibor, what's wrong?"

It *was* Ferenc. The officer had followed him.

"Nothing. I thought I saw someone I recognized, that's all. No, not a friend. It's just been a really long day." Had he told Ferenc where he was staying? What had he told him? He couldn't remember. "At the police station? Oh, it was like your friend said—sorry, I've forgotten his name—Gyula, right? It was like Gyula said—no one cares about a mugging. Took a bit longer than I expected. Typical bureaucracy, that's all." He *hadn't* given him the name of this hotel. "No, really, I'm fine. Just tired. You're right, a bowl of soup." But the police would have ways of finding out. Was Ferenc here just to warn him? Or were they following him? *Stalking* him. "Do you mind if we eat in your room tonight? A quiet evening in front of the TV. How's that?"

3.

"Tibor. What happened to you yesterday?"

Peter. Finally. Thank hell. They squeeze together into the lecture hall. "You didn't get my message?"

"Sorry. Fucking pickpocket got my phone. Why?" Peter waves to someone at the front of the room. Imre. God, he's gained some weight. Tibor almost didn't recognize him.

"You heard about the head they found on Gellert?"

Peter shrugs. "Of course."

They settle into seats close to the aisle. Tibor leans in to Peter: "I was there."

"You what?"

"I witnessed the murder."

"Oh my God, Tibor."

"I went for a jog, early. I overheard the whole thing. The guys talking. The murder, the…Fuck. Everything."

"Christ, I saw it on the news last night. Organized crime, they think."

"Dr. Roland, are you feeling better?" The moderately attractive conference organizer. Ilona. Today, without the ponytail.

"Much, thanks."

She takes a seat in front of them and turns to keep talking. "That's a relief. Must have been a mild case. I had salmonella once, wiped me out for five days."

"Ilona, Tibor witnessed the murder on Gellert. He was just telling me."

"You're kidding. The head?" Ilona's hand flutters to her neck, as if worried for her own.

"Right. So obviously I went to the police and—"

"Why'd you go to the police?"

"To report it."

"Why?"

"What do you mean why? Because I witnessed a murder."

Peter gives him a look like, "And?"

"Well, that's the thing. The detective who interviewed me? He was one of the guys. One of the murderers."

Ilona's hand still hovers at her throat. Peter's shaking his head.

"I know. It sounds ridiculous. But the voice was identical. I'm sure it's him and I think he threatened me. I didn't even tell them where I was staying, and I get back and I look out the window, and there's Ferenc. That's the first guy, the first police officer. He must have followed me."

Lucia, another colleague, squeezes in beside Ilona, who says, "Dr. Roland witnessed the murder on Gellert, and it turns out the police are involved." Last time Tibor saw Lucia, she was starting her Ph.D. in law—something to do with the Roma or refugees. He used to be a little in love with her.

"Well, there's a surprise," says Lucia.

"I think I should go to the Canadian Consulate. Report this guy or...I don't know. Do something."

Imre has joined them now. He hovers in the aisle beside Tibor. "I don't know. That just sounds like more trouble."

"But it's the right thing to do." That's Ilona. "And they must offer some kind of protection."

Imre shakes his head. "No. You've done your good duty and now you can happily go on seeing the sights and minding your own business. I mean, look, these guys, they kill each other. It happens. Nothing to do with you."

"So what, exactly, did you hear?" Lucia asks.

"God. I heard the kid. I heard him die. And then after, they were arguing. The one guy didn't think they should've killed him. The other guy said he just does what Gombas says."

"Gombas?" Lucie interrupts. "Are you sure?"

The circle of listeners around Tibor grows, people linger in the aisle. Whispers carry the story out. At the front of the lecture hall, two of the three panellists chat while waiting for the third. The chair of the session looks pointedly toward Imre. "If we could get started, please. If we could get started."

Chairs scrape and notebooks flutter. Imre regains his place at the front, with some apologies. The session begins, but the focus is shot. Tibor feels it. People look to the front, they listen, but their attention is still with him, Tibor Roland, witness.

Agnes *feels* like she remembers Andrassy Ut when the houses were brightly painted and wealth moved at a strolling pace in sunlight filtered through high green leaves. But she would have been so young. Maybe she was remembering her mother's memories. Because all that was before the war, and after the war she was only nine, and houses were blasted shells that grew over with weeds and bush, full of broken treasures: pieces of teapots and palm-sized shards of crystal, and old thick glass bottles all mildew inside, rusting empty cans and stark white pieces of toilet bowl. She and Zsofi had raced along streets that had huge holes in the middle of them, past buildings without windows, black smoke stains up the walls like shocked hair.

Today, mottled limbs of plane trees scaffold the heavy sky. The air smells of diesel and cold, wet earth. Yesterday's snow mashes into grey grass in the pedestrian alley that bisects the avenue. She turns onto Csengery Utca. Narrow. Cobbled.

She's following the numbers: 75, 77, 79. There: 281. It looks exactly as Dorottya had described it: a corner building, with rounded corner windows on the second and third floors supported by a maenad with flowing hair. Dorottya said their instructions were to leave via the cemetery exit, but she and Zsofi had gotten turned around and had first emerged here, too close to the centre of the city, too risky. They'd immediately gone back down, taken the first left, and they'd got it right. Agnes peers through the locked gate into the building's front hall. Past it, the courtyard.

Two rows of buzzers. Twelve apartments. She's checking the names—Toth, Leeb, Kiraly—when a German shepherd fires out from somewhere, barking, teeth bared, and flings himself at the gate. She stumbles back. The thing growls, snapping its jaws between the metal bars.

"Bad dog," she reprimands. "Down."

"They trained him to do that." A young man stands behind her, bags of groceries gripped in hands nearly purple with cold. "He's a good dog. He thinks it's a game. Isn't that right, Cica?" At the man's voice, the dog named pussycat wags his tail.

The man is willowy, a weed. His shoulders slope with the

weight of the bags. He puts them down to find his key to the gate. "Who were you looking for?"

"No one. Just looking."

He's still searching for his keys.

"I lived here, once." The old skill returns so fluently; she lies as smoothly as a teenager.

"Ah." Still searching through his pockets. Clearly, he would prefer that she leave him be. He's too polite to push through and leave her standing there. This is the quandary she's put him in.

He's kind, but he's a busy man with things to do other than talk to her. He wants to go inside, read his newspaper, eat his bread and salami. She's holding him hostage. He finds his key.

"Which apartment are you in?"

He points up. "Second floor, back."

"Oh. We were in the back, fourth floor."

On Visegradi, they'd lived crammed all together in one room plus kitchen and bath. First the four of them, and then after her father's arrest, just the three.

He'd probably heard similar stories from his parents and grandparents. Probably hated them. Now, glossy shops lined Andrassy. Millionaire mile, it had become. Suits worth more than a Hungarian doctor's yearly salary. Gold necklaces for their millionaire wives. No shame in money, any longer.

"I never thought I'd be so nostalgic." She smiles senti-mentally, the attack dog now curled happily around his own tail. "I won't keep you. I just wanted to see if it was still here." She grips the gate and peers.

"Did you want to see inside?" Through his kind-to-old-ladies voice, she hears his reluctance.

"Really? I would love to." The gate opens. "This is my first trip home since fifty-six—you can't imagine how old I am. Isn't this amazing? An AVO secret policeman was killed at the foot of these very stairs. Did you know that?" She forges ahead, lie after breathtaking lie, defying gravity. The balustrade overlooking the courtyard has fallen away in parts, held together with bits of salvaged wood. "It used to be so well kept. Who lives up there now, in our old apartment?"

The man shrugs. He's trying to get away from her.

"Maybe I'll just go and see if anyone's home." She follows him up the stairs. "I would love to see what's left of the place. I wonder if my grandmother's kitchen table is still there?"

As soon as he gets to the second floor, he flees. "Hallo," he says. "Csokolom," as he pushes open his door.

Agnes waits until he's well inside, counts to thirty, then quietly, on kitten feet as her mother would once have said, creeps back down the stairs. Rugs hang over balcony rails on the third and second floors, awaiting their weekly thrashing. There's the sound of a vacuum from somewhere. Jangling keys, locking a door, then the gate in front of the door. *Clip-clop* of a housewife's brisk step. The door to the cellar is at the back of the courtyard, as it is in every old-style Pest apartment block. She edges around, under the balcony, just in case her young friend looks out his window. This door's unlocked. She slips in. Closes the door behind her. She's come equipped. She pulls a flashlight from her purse.

The steep stairs are exactly the same as the ones she remembers from the place on Visegradi. In that cellar, each family had their own storage space—for coal, extra or old pieces of furniture. The family next door had once been aristocrats, though they never talked about that. Their storage corner held heirlooms: oil paintings they had no room for in their apartment, a huge Herendi vase, a disassembled mahogany table. Her family's space was only for coal. They'd lost their house and everything in it after the war, when the Russians "liberated" Hungary. Most of this cellar is stacked to the hilt with old furniture. This might be a challenge. She puts the flashlight on a dusty record cabinet, reaches again into her purse. Tibor was always teasing her about her large bag. "An old woman's prerogative," she would answer. Now, she pulls from it the metal detector she purchased before leaving Toronto. Thank goodness she'd had the foresight to practise in her backyard before leaving. It wasn't complicated, but today there's no time to waste. She extends the collapsible rod, screws it tight, puts the earphones on her head, takes the flashlight in her other hand.

The thing is to be systematic. Start at one end, work progressively to the other. Any door to a tunnel would have to have some metal part, even if it was only the hinge. She begins at the corner closest to the stairwell. She doesn't know what she's going to do about the area covered in furniture, but maybe she won't have to figure it out. Already, the thing is beeping like crazy. She drops to her knees. Pulls the trowel from her bag and digs. A button. Start again. Two hours she works and the thing almost never stops beeping. Each time, she takes out her trowel and digs down. She retrieves: a button, several coins of different denominations, the handle to a cabinet, a chain link, many nails. She's working at the rate of approximately two square metres per hour. She's covered about a third of the space. She pauses for some water and the buttered roll she'd brought. If her husband, James, were here, he'd be laughing, but in a nice way, the way that reminded her she was loved.

He might even take a turn with the trowel, just to humour her. But James isn't here. He's been gone for nearly five years now. Nearly five years she has managed to go on living without him, and there's no point leaving a job only half done. She's sitting on the arm of a couch. As she pushes herself to standing, she looks down, between her feet. That's definitely a glint. She takes the trowel. She digs. Not a coin or a button, not a nail. Heavier. Sturdier. Circular. About the size of her hand. The floor is hard-packed earth. She needs a pickaxe for something this deep, not a trowel. Sweat beads and her breath comes heavier, clouding the freezing air.

Creak and rattle of the door. A heavy tread. Then faster. Someone coming down the stairs at a gallop. A snarling growl.

Cica.

The dog lands on her.

"Cica." The dog backs away. A flashlight shines in her face. "What the hell?"

She puts her hands up, to cover her eyes.

"What the hell are you doing down here?"

It's the kind young man. Is he really so kind, or was he pretending? There's no way to know, really. There's never any way to know for sure.

"My mother buried her jewellery box," Agnes stutters. Realizing she's holding her hands as though under arrest, she drops them into her lap. "From the communists."

He's trying to decide how to be, with her. Should he scare her away? Let her do her crazy, old-lady digging?

"You got the wrong building, lady. Mrs. Zena says her family's been in that apartment you said was yours since the end of the war."

"The wrong building? But that's impossible. I remember it so clearly. Maybe it was the third floor."

The man seizes her elbow, surprisingly strong for someone so skinny. Would anyone hear her if she screamed. If he killed her, how long would it be until her body was found? Would the dog eat her? "Lady, calm down. I'm just trying to help you up."

"I can get up by myself, if you will stop breaking my arm."

Once standing, she removes her gloves, dusts off her skirt. "Help me dig," she says. "If you help me for one hour I will pay you twenty Canadian dollars." He seems to be thinking about it.

"Forty."

He goes to the far end of the cellar. Scrabbles about there for a few minutes and emerges with a flat shovel.

"One hour," he says. "Show me the money."

He unearths the ring she'd thought was the handle to a trap door. It's a handle but to a large metal box, the size of a safe. She has to pretend that maybe her mother's jewellery is inside it, but when they get it open, it's full of paper — someone's banking receipts, envelopes, inventories, account books. When he lifts one out, it falls apart in his fingers. That was an hour. Forty is all the Canadian money she has.

He pockets it. "You gonna keep looking?"

The cellar now seems enormous, and her plan absurd, if not stark raving mad (as James might say). "Did you ever find a door down here? To a tunnel?"

"To one of those Soviet tunnels, you mean?"

Yes. The eagerness in her face.

"The ones that supposedly hid a thousand prisoners, a hospital, and a spa for the higher-ups, you mean?"

She feels foolish. She hates him for taking her money. Herself for giving it to him.

He leaves, chuckling, Cica at his heel.

Horrible, horrible country. She should never have come back. She's an old lady and it's not worth it. An old lady, driven by guilt (how original), pretending to be Indiana Ancient-Jones. She should go back to the hotel and sit in her room and not leave again until Tibor returns and then she should tell Tibor what she is really doing here. She should confess all the things she's kept locked in that black box in her brain all this time, not just this trip, but his whole life. Because what if she has a heart attack and dies? She doesn't want to die with that box of secrets unopened inside her. Even if you don't want to believe in a soul, as you get closer to dying, you find you do have one. And souls have to speak their secrets, release them into the world to be free of them. But she is not going to die today on Csengery Utca. She will turn back onto Andrassy Ut. Take the nearest subway back to the hotel room, blocking out the fact that for the minutes she's on the train she's *under* the Duna, under that wide, weighty flow that banks can hardly hold when it floods. Yes, she'll go back to the fancy hotel that makes Tibor hold his head like the world watches, and she'll order an overpriced lunch and charge it to her son. She's starving, suddenly. She's dizzy with hunger. She'll order the biggest dish on the menu, and she'll look out the massive window at the white parliament and will sort through the items in that unopened box and consider which ones to share with her son.

She turns onto Andrassy with these thoughts and this purpose clear in her mind, and as she does, looking neither right nor left, nor even seeing straight ahead of her, really, she steps into a living Duna of moving people. Flags snap. "Hungary for Hungarians." "Slaves no longer!" The last words are from a poem that she hasn't heard since 1956, the poem of the revolution. "Now or never," they'd shouted in those few heady days before tanks came in. "Slaves no longer!" But Hungarians have always been pushed around, pushovers, and that's why they shout it so stolidly. In orderly columns, the people push forward.

Marchers fill the street and she's pulled into its centre, borne forward, purse banging against her knees. Everyone but her wears the kokarda, that tricolour Hungarian rosette on their lapel, even though it's not a national holiday. When she looks behind, she sees the soldiers. Are they soldiers? Black boots stomp. A tall blonde girl locks arms with her. She can hardly see the sky for the shoulders and the banners. The marchers' pride is hard and shiny and happy. It snaps like flags. But an old lady like her, her bag so heavy, her heart so out of tune — she will trip. She will and they will walk over top of her because she is *not* a revolutionary. She never was. She left, you see. She left them all behind.

A group from the conference decides to get lunch at a little csarda up the street: good soup and huge plates of schnitzel. They file in, gather around two small tables, barely enough room for shoulders, but there aren't enough coat hooks. Tibor folds his and sits on it. He thinks of his camera. He had searched his hotel room, his suitcase, the pockets of all his clothes, even (irrationally) the ones he hadn't unpacked. What if the police were right now huddled around his camera, ogling, making lewd jokes about her breasts or his technique? What if they put it on YouTube? He shouldn't have shot the video in the first place, but it was almost an accident, really. Spur of one hot, unzipped moment. He'd been showing her photos from his trip to New York, so the camera was just there, on his side table within easy reach. It hadn't taken more than one arm slipping over her hip to push a button and he was in permanent possession of Rafaela's orgasm all the way from *ah* to *oh god*. It was mostly blurry. No picture of her face. Just her breasts, hips, the top of his head. Her moans. His moans. She might have guessed it was on, but she didn't say anything. Maybe she liked the thought of performing. He'd had the stupid camera with him on Gellert, right until that moment. Maybe he'd dropped it on the path, before he'd ducked under the overhang. Maybe he should go look for it.

Peter elbows him, points at the small TV above the bar. The news anchor is talking. It takes a moment or two for Tibor to focus. Then the photograph flashes on screen — a young man in a black peaked cap, raising a beer stein to the camera and grinning his face off, scarcely recognizable.

"The head found on Gellert Hegy has been identified as that of Janos Hagy, a Canadian citizen. Hagy's father arrived in Budapest today to identify the body. He has appealed to the Canadian government to work closely with the Hungarian police. He says he received no threats, and no request for ransom. He spoke to his son just hours before the murder is believed to have happened. His son was on his way to a party with a friend. He sounded happy and gave his father no indication that he was in any way in danger."

"A Canadian," someone says.

"Weird. I thought they said it was organized crime."

"Weird."

Everyone's looking at him.

"Tibor, you have to go to the consulate," Ilona presses.

"That guy, Gombas, he was up on major corruption last year—a scam that took millions out of the public purse—and he got away with it. On the news after the trial, he was calm, so ordinary-looking, forgiving everyone for judging him wrongly and all we could do was laugh at the farce. Not a single witness would testify against him."

The photograph is gone, replaced with the next news item. A reporter now stands in front of marchers wearing kokardas and waving red flags and shouting something about true Magyar.

Lucia looks as if she's waiting for something from him.

"No, you're right. Thugs like that, they can't get away with it." She nods. Exactly.

He knows he's on perilous footing here, taking such a definitive stance when really what he'd like most is to have a beer, talk about politics, and forget about young Janos Hagy and his gruesome end. But the way she's looking at him. And not just Lucia, everyone else too. They want him to step up. Their respect—no, their admiration—dangles like a fat, graspable peach just within reach. "And I'm the only witness."

He stares wretchedly into his beer.

Peter doesn't believe him for a second. He laughs. "Really? Look, if these guys are really with Gombas, you don't want to be anywhere near it, and if you're wrong about this detective, you'll only be making a fool of yourself. Possibly sinking some poor harmless guy's career."

"I'm not wrong about the detective."

"Fine, so you met a corrupt detective."

"A murderer," Imre corrects.

"But if you go to the National Police, or to your consulate, what's that going to solve? You think they'll ride in and arrest your guy? Just like that?"

Tibor feels the upswell of something, some feeling in his chest. Pride? Anger? It feels warm. It feels good. "I don't think I have a choice, Peter. It's the responsibility of the witness."

"Holy shit." Lucia's focused on the TV. A platoon of black uniforms stomp, but they're not police and they don't look like soldiers. It's the Magyar Garda, the quasi-militant front of Jobbik. They were supposed to have been disbanded last year.

"My sister's husband joined them," says Ilona. "It's unbelievable. Listening to him, you'd think it was 1938."

Everyone stares as the march pushes forward. The marchers look calm, unworried, definitive.

"Fucking fascists," says someone.

"It's frightening."

"They're as frightening as we let them become. They're a fringe element."

"It's true," says Imre. "Why are we taking them seriously? We should be laughing at them."

"Well, you're not Jewish, Imre."

The black-vested men and women look straight ahead, soldierly and undistractible, following orders they invented themselves.

Tibor feels the warmth dissipate as attention swirls away from him, consumed now with the upsurge in anti-Semitism. Will the ultra right-wing Jobbik win the next election? He tries not to feel deflated. Only Lucia says, one more time, pressing her hand into his arm, "If you need a lawyer."

. . .

After more conference and more beer, Tibor gets back to the hotel late and alone, despite what he thought was a pretty convincing effort with Lucia. He'd left a message at the front desk for his mother that he wouldn't be joining her for dinner. Easier that way. She was a grown-up after all, not a child. She could order her own dinner, entertain herself. When he gets to his hotel room, he turns on the TV. A pretty reporter is talking to the camera.

"Police have found evidence suggesting that the young man was being stalked. Warning that it's too early yet to say for certain, they suggest that it may be the work of a sexual predator. A friend of the murdered Canadian, Csaba Bekes, has come forward with information. The night of the murder, Bekes says, Hagy and Bekes attended a party together at this tear-down in Pest."

As Tibor watches, the camera slides to reveal the squat, the last party house he and Peter had visited on his first night here. It looks different through a news lens — more like the wreck it was, amateur, adolescent, not at all cool. The pretty reporter continues.

"By night, this place is a bar, its rooms filled with young partygoers. The beer is cheap and its guests, like Bekes and Hagy, are just here to have a good time. But one witness says Hagy left the party at 2:30 a.m. shortly after he spoke with a middle-aged man, likely a tourist as the two were speaking English. And Bekes reports seeing Hagy getting into a black Mercedes-Benz."

Tibor feels something sliding from underneath him: the facts, the ground.

He has the strongest urge to run downstairs right now, seek out the company of someone, anyone. To call Peter. "Peter, you ass. You skeptical, ironic fuck. I'm being framed."

Tibor lies awake, eyes open in the dark, trying to put things in order. This city is making him paranoid. It breeds anxiety. He has argued this in at least one academic paper. Why did people believe, in both 1956 and 1989, that the tunnels were under Communist Headquarters and not under 60 Andrassy Ut, where everyone knew political prisoners were held, tortured, and sometimes executed? Now 60 Andrassy is a museum that memorializes these horrors while, at the same time, refusing any responsibility for them. Appropriately, it's called the Terror House and you can tour its cellar prisons. There are no tunnels.

Similarly, he might now ask himself, Why would a Hungarian mob boss order the death of a Canadian boy? More pertinent: why would this Csaba Bekes concoct such a story about Tibor and how did the police know he'd been at the squat in the first place?

Answer: the camera.

4.

Tibor sleeps, or hovers just above sleep. There's an exam. He fails it. So they have to break him. First his foot. Then his hand. Then his knee. Then his elbow. He wakes when they get to the shoulder.

It's 5:17 a.m.

Agnes is also awake. She'd watched the moon rise over the right shoulder of the parliament. She'd packed her suitcase. She'd tried to sleep. At four, she'd risen, showered, dressed.

Now, she sits in the armchair, waiting for the sun. The parliament building is an Austrian girl's fantasy, she thinks, a fairy castle for a princess. It was never so white. In 1956, it was as grey-black as everything else, coated in coal dust and diesel gas, and it was better that way, more truthful anyway, more like the rest of the city.

At six, she calls Tibor's room.

"Tibor? Could you please take me to the Canadian Embassy this morning? My passport has been stolen."

She's pleased with the steadiness of her tone. Not a note of fear, not a tremor.

Tibor holds his hungover head in his palm, eyes closed. "Your passport? How?"

"I dropped my purse." She'd explain it later, the cellar, Cica, the marchers in uniform who'd pulled her in.

"You didn't put it in the safe?"

"I was *trying* to be safe."

"No, Mom. The safe in the room. That's what it's there for." Remember? What Gabor said?

"Tibor. Come here *now*, Tibor. I need your help."

Fuck.

Click. She hangs up.

Fuckfuckfuckfuckfuck.

Pants. Shirt. Shoes. Keycard.

Knock.

Unlock.

She looks like she's on her way to the mall, for her mall-walking club.

He looks like he drank too much.

"Don't look at me like that, Tibor. I know you have things

to do. That's why I thought we could go early. I did not lose it on purpose. It was stolen." She will not cry.

He sits. Out of frustration and fatigue, not to prompt a longer conversation.

"It was a mob. The fascists, the Arrow-Cross, they were marching."

"You were there? What were you doing there? "

"I was minding my own business, and one of those fascists stole my passport. There were so many people."

"Calm down, Mom. It's okay."

"I need to go to the Embassy. I need to go to the Canadian Embassy and then I need to go home."

"Our flight's not until the end of next week, Mom."

"I know that, Tibor." Why does he always assume she's losing her marbles? When she loses her marbles, she will tell him. "I will get a new flight. I don't want to stay. I want to go home. Today."

What on earth is she on about? He's the one in trouble, not her. "Fine. I need a shower first."

"Persze." But where had he been last night? Last night when she needed him?

Like a drill through the centre of his fucking forehead.

Tibor pictures how this will happen. They will go together to the Canadian Embassy: his addled, paranoid senior mother in her spotless Adidas shoes and pink velour track suit, and him, the addled, paranoid prof in his nostalgic Doc Martens and ski jacket. She will claim a fascist stole her passport while he insists that he is being framed by the Hungarian police for a murder that he *witnessed*. He can see it now: a disbelieving bureaucrat with perfectly aligned pens and eyes that barely flicker as he leans his polished head back to laugh—Hahahahaha—at the tourists. "You've been watching too much bad TV, my friend. Now go. Enjoy your holiday. Take your mother on a boat ride up the Danube. It's a beautiful city, even in this shit-grey month." And who could blame the guy? If it wasn't happening to him, Tibor wouldn't believe it either.

"I'm not losing my marbles," says his mother.

In the lobby, Gabor calls them a cab. "Ten minutes," he tells them. "However, as Hungarian taxis are quite prompt, it is best to wait near the door. Keep your hat on, as they say."

They stand by the revolving door. Tibor reads his newspaper. Agnes looks out for the cab, wishing to be home. When will it ever be the right time? she wonders. There is no right time. If she starts talking over lunch, it will seem rehearsed and it will take too long. It shouldn't be a conversation. She doesn't want him chewing while she unravels her past. He would no doubt take it personally, consider it *his* history as well. Strictly speaking, he'd be right, but is she willing to give him that?

"Tibor, I told you what happened in 1956."

He doesn't glance up from his newspaper. "Yes?" he says. Turns the page.

What could be so preoccupying him? Agnes slaps the underside of the paper. "I'm talking to you, Tibor." How familiar is that look on his face. It always makes her want to give him a little smack. "This is important."

Another look. He wants to smack her back.

"But I didn't tell you what happened to Zsofia."

"Zsofia?"

"My sister."

"Oh. Right."

The taxi pulls up. He gives the cab driver the address, then settles back into the seat. She can feel, without looking at him, that he's irritated.

"She fell in with the revolutionaries."

He is studiously not reading his paper.

"She killed an AVO officer, a member of the secret police. And then she disappeared."

"No. You didn't tell me that. Why didn't you tell me that?"

A good question. There is no answer, really. It just happened that way. Bad memories are not for sharing, especially with children. There's enough talktalktalk in this world already. She'd tried to write it once, but she burned her efforts. She never wanted to be like some she knew, holding on to those bad memories as if to let them go might cause disintegration. She wanted to live, to be happy in the most ordinary way. She does her best to explain this to Tibor, who fixes her with a vexed, irritable stare. She wants to tell him what she is doing here, searching for evidence of an escape. She thought it might feel good to finally confess what she had done. To explain why she had to be here. Why she had to search. But this is Tibor and he never listens.

The rest of the ride they don't speak. The car is loud. The seat vibrates. His mother sits, hands on her lap, weirdly slack without her purse. They get out of the cab in front of the Canadian Embassy and he says, "I'm sorry, Mom. That must have been awful."

She shrugs. The way only a Hungarian can shrug. They enter together.

The process for reporting a stolen passport is standardized, they find out from the receptionist. "It's happening more and more often these days," she says. "You can't be too careful." She doesn't say, The gypsies. She doesn't say, You stupid old lady, carrying your passport in your purse.

When she sees Agnes's maiden name on the form, she switches to Hungarian. Agnes answers in English. She wants none of this girl's presumptuous familiarity. In this embassy they are on Canadian soil. She will speak Canadian.

Tibor steers his mother to a chair in the waiting room and again approaches the receptionist. "I have a problem. I'm hoping you can help me." He whispers, leaning as close to the woman's ear as appropriateness allows.

His mother watches, questioningly. He gives her a reassuring, don't-worry kind of smile. To the woman, he whispers, "I'd rather my mother not be privy to this problem."

Her name is Manna. Manna stares, stolidly unresponsive. She's thinking underage hookers, venereal disease. Not *that* kind of problem. "I believe I am being framed for murder."

Manna doesn't bat an eye. Manna doesn't believe him. She says, "Oh?"

Tibor leans closer. "May I speak with someone in authority, please?"

"Do you have an appointment?"

I'm being framed for murder, and you think I'm putting it in my Daytimer? You have got to be kidding. Manna is not kidding. Manna has probably never joked in her life. Not in this office. Not in her job description.

"It's sort of urgent."

Manna clicks her mouse, surveys the computer screen.

"Tomorrow at two?" She scans. "Oh. Sorry. Make that four-thirty. Does that work for you?"

No, you fat, fascist bureaucrat, it does not.

"No, it doesn't. Listen." Tibor checks over his shoulder. His mother is perusing a newspaper. "I witnessed that murder on Gellert. Do you understand? One of the murderers is a police detective, Detective Tamas Sarkady. He intimidated me. He's had me followed. And now he's setting me up."

"I'm very sorry, Mr. Roland, but Mr. Sutherland is simply not available until tomorrow at 4:30."

"Do you think I'm making this up? I'm telling you my life is in danger. If Mr. Sutherland doesn't talk to me now, he'll be visiting me in prison." That was louder than it should have been. His mother has put the newspaper aside and is now approaching the desk with that firmness of intent he remembers from when he was a child and she was about to scold his teacher.

"I understand your concern, Mr. Roland. If you, and your mother"—she nods toward Agnes, who now stands beside Tibor—"would like to remain at the embassy for the day, or even a couple of days, you are welcome to do so. But Mr. Sutherland has a full schedule..."

"And who is Mr. Sutherland?" Agnes interrupts. She'd thought Tibor never stood up to anyone. Obviously, she has underestimated him. He has more of his father in him than she'd thought, and she feels a sharp, loving pain for this immature son of hers.

"The head of embassy security, Mrs. Roland."

"Why do we wait for a security guard? We will see the ambassador."

"I'm sorry, Mrs. Roland, but your son has expressed a security concern. Mr. Sutherland is the *head* of security."

Agnes remembers this kind of woman. The landlady of their building, who reported on the doctor. The pharmacist's wife, who took the bribe her father offered for her mother's medication and then reported him. The woman next door, Mrs. Nemeth.

"We won't be here tomorrow. That's too bad. Stephen will be sad that we weren't able to pass on his little gift for Ambassador..."

"Ambassador Nolan," Tibor supplies.

"And his dear wife. That's Stephen Harper. We promised him we'd stop by. Give the Nolans a sincere and off-the-record thank you for helping us keep those awful gypsies out of Canada. They went to school together, you know."

There's nothing more convincing than a woman in her seventies, Agnes thinks, as Manna ventures what might be called a smile and reaches for the phone.

In the hallway behind Manna, a door opens. Three men step out. One wears a sharply pressed blue uniform and police officer's cap. Even before he turns, Tibor knows it is Ferenc. Have they put out a warning against him? Reported him to his own government? "Thank you for your time," says Tibor. He grabs a pamphlet from the desk, takes his mother by the elbow, and hustles her toward the exit. "We'll come back later for your passport."

"Persze, Tibor. Persze. My arm."

Walk, walk, walk. Tibor lunges ahead impatiently, then stops to wait for her to catch up. Thank God she wears her Adidas shoes today. Could they not just wait for a bus? It's colder today, all yesterday's melt frozen fast, and the shade of tall walls hides patches of glare ice. She extends both arms like a kid on a balance beam. Chasing her son at break-hip speed. Ha. She wants to share the joke with him, but he's at least fifty paces ahead. What are they running from? Where is he headed?

For heaven's sake. "Tibor."

But the ice is faster and she's down as her son strides away. "Tibor." What is that look on his face? Apology? Alarm? He's jogging back toward her. She should tell him it's all right. I'm fine, Tibor. I was only a little frightened. And disappointed. And angry, mostly at myself. You see, I can stand on my own. It's too hard to speak. Whew. Dizzy. I'd rather sit. But there's no hurry. I know the march was only a march and I'm not a criminal. We can leave this country any time, like normal people. We can simply go to the airport and cross a border that is only a line taped on the floor. Isn't that remarkable? We can file onto an airplane, crunch our bottoms into narrow seats, and push off into a gunless sky. I'm too old to run, Tibor.

"I left without Zsofi. I left her in the revolution and she was only sixteen."

"It's okay, Mom," Tibor is saying.

Has she said this out loud? So it makes no difference, after all, to confess. She'd thought the black box inside her would shatter, but no. Still there. Might as well have kept it inside.

He's lifting her up. A good son, her Tibor. So protective. He's found a bench in the sun. He folds his scarf for her to sit on. That's nice. Solicitous and kind.

"Wait here. I'll find a phone and call us a cab."

. . .

She wakes in the dark. It's 10:30, according to the idiotic clock. Tibor beside her, clicking away at his computer. "It's too late to be working."

"Mom. How are you feeling?"

"Sore."

"You fell on the ice."

"I said sore, not senile."

"Do you want some soup?"

"I want to go home."

"I know. We'll pick up your passport tomorrow."

"Why did you have to run so fast?"

"Long story. I'll tell you tomorrow."

"I would like some water."

"Here you are."

"I would like to go home."

"Tomorrow, Mom. Like I said."

"I thought you were running away from me."

"I wasn't."

"I ran away."

"I know."

"I ran away from my family."

"You ran from an oppressive regime."

"I left Zsofi."

"It's okay, Mom. You told me, remember?"

"I did?"

"Gyula told me you were brave."

"Gyula?"

"I called him."

"Gyula was my lover."

"He told me that too."

"He talks too much."

"Call if you need me, Mom. You need to sleep."

"And tomorrow we'll go home?"

"Promise."

His hotel room is almost too quiet. Across the black Duna, the parliament pretends to float. Snow gusts.

Why haven't they arrested him already? They have the lying eyewitness, Csaba Bekes. They have the incriminating photographs on his camera. His footprints right next to where they found the head. And despite his lie, they know where he is staying.

They're not sure they can get away with it, was Gyula's assessment. Or maybe they just need a diversion. They need to look like they've *almost* got the guy, they're closing in on him, but somehow you slipped through their fingers.

The thought is not quite soothing.

He tried to call Lucia first, but when she didn't answer, he found Uncle Gyula's number. Whoever he was, judging by his clothes, he was obviously pretty well to do. And Tibor had to admit he was reassured, dealing with Gyula. Sometimes, a well-connected older man is just more solid, more credible, than a young, politically outraged woman.

Tomorrow, Gyula would meet him here around three. One more time, Tibor would walk through every event in detail, as best as he could remember. The party at the squat. The moonlit jog. The voices and the names he was positive he hadn't misheard. Gyula would put in a call to the National Police. Then they would go together to the consulate at four-thirty. And then what? He wouldn't speak unless someone could guarantee his protection. Gyula had agreed that was the right tactic, so that's what he'd do. But he could also just leave. As long as there was no warrant for his arrest, as long as he was only the useful diversion, he could simply book an earlier flight and, with his mother, fly away home.

"You might want to consider that," suggested Gyula. They talked with low voices so as not to disturb his mother as she dozed. She'd sprained her wrist but thankfully nothing worse.

Now, he clicks on the TV to catch the eleven o'clock news. Compulsive. He can't help himself. Strange sense that he's eavesdropping on his own life. Or the trap that'll close on it. Another witness has stepped forward, confirming that Hagy left the party in a black Mercedes. Detective Tamas Sarkady says they are getting closer to putting together those last few hours of Janos Hagy's tragically brief life. Police have not yet found the body. Anyone with information is urged to call.

Next, the boy's father. He's just some ordinary-looking businessman in a blue, button-down shirt but clearly shattered, straining for dignity then splitting apart. Please, if you have any information. Please come forward. Whoever did this. Has to be arrested. I just want justice. For Janos. For my son. Who could do such a thing? I loved my son.

I loved him.

Oh, my son.

My son.

My son.

The boy grins out at him from the TV. Cool hat. A pimple on his chin.

And Tibor stares back. And Tibor hates the boy. He resents

his smile and the pimple that reminds him that the boy couldn't have known what was coming. The boy looks like a posturing, suburban, self-entitled little fuck. He hates that their lives are now linked.

But there's no getting around it.

Because he was there, when he was there. Because he is the witness, and he is the murdered. A connection not of blood but of circumstance. Not of love but of debt. To what? To the dead. To the dead, Tibor. You owe it not to Janos who lived but to Janos who died. It's not his fault. Whether you tell or whether you run, you'll carry that snapshot of the boy in your head for the rest of your life, along with the fleshy *thunk* of an axe. No posturing now, no pretend. This is your soul speaking.

"Shut up," Tibor says.

Midnight. Gabor's not at the front desk, and Tibor feels strangely deserted. But wait, there he is. Out of uniform, chatting up the good-looking bartender. That seems wrong, out of character. Seriously precise Gabor shouldn't have a personal life. Most definitely, he shouldn't flirt.

Gabor leans one elbow on the bar. "Edward says I can indeed apply for positions elsewhere. If my English is strong enough and if my performance is virtually flawless."

She swipes her cloth over the ring Gabor's water glass has left on the counter. "I can't imagine leaving."

"You see, that's the problem with us. Lack of imagination."

She shakes her head. "The problem is the forint and the fucking taxes. Do you really think they'll be hiring foreigners in Germany? In England? Have you read the paper lately? We might be at the bottom of the shitter, but it's the same shitter."

"No, you will not dash my dreams with your determined pessimism, Eva. I will get out of this particular toilet, you watch."

"Right. Send me a postcard."

"I will find the meaning of life, you just wait. I'll go to India, to Tibet, but I'll find it."

So stiff-necked Gabor is a dreamer. Hilarious.

"Mind if I join you?"

The look on their faces—kids caught smoking dope behind the bleachers. Almost funny except that it makes him, Tibor, the party-busting grown-up.

Gabor stands. Nods to the girl. "Good evening, sir," to Tibor.

"Would you like something to drink, sir?"

Would he be there if he didn't? "Gin martini?"

"Persze."

Persze, it's a lousy martini. He should've known better. Cheap gin, lukewarm. Whatever. He sits at the window, the only customer. The girl swabs the counter again. She cleans glasses. She's busy, busy. A notably North American training they must get here. Never stand idle. Always *look* like you love your job. Fucking Soviet, really. Well, and how is he any different? Glad-handing his way through conferences, smarming up to editors and more important researchers. And what great "networking" he'd done on this trip. Nearly vomited on his own conference paper. Had clung to his old friends, failing to approach anyone of any importance whatsoever. Well, that's it. He'd tried. But here was the truth. Even if he did the right thing, testified, whatever, what would it gain him? He would still die alone, having achieved nothing. His mother would be the only one at his funeral.

Halfway through the martini, Tibor realizes that he's no longer scared, even though he should be. Out of sheer habit, his mind has veered back to its favourite topic: his own ridiculous incapacity. It's thoughts like these that drove him out on that ill-timed run in the first place.

"Slow night," he says, approaching the girl who has already put that bright smile on her face in readiness for his order. He eases onto a bar stool. "How do you like working here?" Dumb question, but he's not feeling flirty, just lonely.

"It's all right." She looks wary. Because she thinks he might come onto her, make things difficult? Her eyes slide toward the front desk.

"I promise I'm not coming onto you. I'm just so tired of my own company. You know?"

"Persze. I could call my friend. She is always up for a drink." A pause.

The girl says it so neatly. Like slipping a beer mat under his drink. Which she also does.

"Um." He's blushing.

She reaches into her pocket, pulls out her phone.

"No. I mean, no thank you. I'm fine."

I'm *fine*?

She shrugs, drops the phone back into her pocket. Picks up a glass. Polishes. Looks up, smiles a smile not of the customer-service variety and not at him, but someone behind him. Tibor turns, half expecting the connubial friend, a bright-faced teenager in teetering, hopeful heels, and he's about to say, "I really don't..."

It's Ferenc.

With the pressed uniform.

But Ferenc is not in uniform. He's wearing a soft grey sweater under a suit jacket. Soft-sweatered Ferenc nods at Tibor. Does the nod mean he's recognized him? That he is watching him? That Sarkady knows where to find him, that he can find him at any time and take him out at gunpoint or... "I'll wait outside," Ferenc says.

The bar girl smiles again, that not-for-sale smile, that flattered, smitten, girl-with-a-crush smile. The madam is dating a cop? *The* cop? *His* cop?

I need to be somewhere else.

"Mr. Roland?"

Knock-knock.

Is it night? *Knock-knock.* No, he can see a crack of white daylight between the curtains. Is he hungover? No, just foggy. It's 8:13. It's not sleeping in if you're on holiday.

KNOCK-KNOCK. "Tibor Roland?"

He sits.

"Detective Sarkady here. We've just got a few questions for you."

Fuck.

Tibor stumbles, fumbles, finds his pants. Where'd he put that card with Gyula's phone number.

"I'm calling my lawyer," he shouts, punching the numbers in. "I won't speak to you without my lawyer." What does it matter

Gyula's not a lawyer. He's Hungarian and he's rich. Through the door, he hears mumbling.

"Gyula?" Tibor whispers into the phone. "Gyula, they want me to answer some questions."

"We don't want to waste your time, Dr. Roland." *Doctor*. How do they know this? he thinks. "It'll just take a minute."

"No. No, they're here. At the door."

"You can ask your lawyer to meet us at the station."

He whispers into the phone, "No, of *my* fucking room. Detective Sarkady. I don't know who else."

"Your evidence is important to our case, Dr. Roland. We just want to go over some of the details."

"They want you to meet them . . . us . . . at the station. Okay. Right. No, I won't. Okay. You'll have your lawyer pick me up? Really? That's just . . . Thank you."

"I will meet you with my lawyer at the station," Tibor calls. Silence.

No mumbling. No knocking. Just breathing, which is his, and a pounding, which is his heart.

Gone?

Or waiting?

"I think they left."

He puts the phone down. He pads to the door. An innocuous white business card pushed underneath.

The peephole shows an empty, concave hallscape. He puts his ear to the door. Only the echoey hum of empty, ventilated architecture. Fourteen floors of empty halls, fourteen empty flights of concrete stairs, an elevator shaft, also empty. The brisk, purposeless airing of room after empty February room, and Tibor might just be the only man left alive up here. This is irrational but seems nonetheless real.

He picks up the business card. Detective Tamas Sarkady. Organized Crime Unit.

Fuck.

Tibor allows himself one full minute of hating Janos. Then he showers. Shaves. Brush the teeth, make the face nice. Take the elevator to your mother's floor and knock on her door, and make up some story. "Protect your mother from this," was Gyula's advice. And he would.

His mother opens the door before he's finished his knock. "I didn't know what to say, Tibor. He said, 'Are you Tibor Roland's mother?' I said yes."

Fuck. Persze.

"He said, 'Is this you?' He had your camera, Tibor. He showed me my picture, and he said, 'Is this you?' What am I going to say? No, it's not me? Obviously, it's me. He said, 'Is this your son's camera?' I said, 'I don't know.' He said, 'Does he own a camera like this?' I said, 'I don't know.' He said, 'Did he go to a party on Wednesday night?' I said, 'I don't know.' He said, 'Do you, or does anyone you know, own a black Mercedes-Benz?' I said, 'I wish.'"

She'd opened the door already talking. She led him into the room, talking. They had his camera? They showed his mother? Oh God, not Rafaela. "Tibor, is this about the mugging? I didn't know what to say. Are you in trouble? They wouldn't tell me. Interrogating me. That's what it felt like. They always come in pairs. Why? They wouldn't explain a thing." Her fingers grip her bandaged sore wrist, which Tibor had so tenderly wrapped for her. He takes her good hand. He leads her to the chair. He takes the bed.

"I'm sorry, Mom. I'm sorry I didn't tell you. It's nothing to worry about, I promise."

He should take better care of his mother. He keeps losing her, running away and spraining her, and now this. Why is his love so clenched?

Tibor tells her everything, the whole story from start to finish. He has to stop once, to get a glass of water. He pours them each one from the bathroom tap, noticing that she's used the hotel-provided shower cap. He always wondered who used the shower caps. He explains that he'd overheard a murder; he doesn't explain that they chopped the body into pieces. He tells her about the hole in the hill, and the dropped head. She only once interrupts him: "A hole? What kind of hole?"

"Deep, that's all he said. Deep enough that no one would ever find the body."

A hole in the surface of Gellert Hegy? A hole—or a tunnel with an entrance as steep and deep as a well.

"And Gyula's lawyer will be here in just a few minutes," he says. "We're going to the National Police first, to report Detective Sarkady. And then to the embassy—we'll pick up your passport, tell them what's happened. It'll be all over soon. Then, Gyula says, his lawyer will drive us to the airport."

"Gyula?"

"That's right."

"You told Gyula?"

"Yes. I thought he'd know what to do."

She puts down her glass. Her good hand is trembling. "Gyula lies."

"What are you talking about?"

"And Gyula drives a very nice car. A very expensive car. Not a Mercedes, but very expensive."

And?

"His son's a policeman. Did I tell you that? And Gyula's an engineer. I don't even know if he finished his degree. How does an engineer make that much money?"

Tibor hears the *snap, snap, snap* of his calm coming undone. "Mom."

"A policeman earns nothing in this country. Next to nothing. That's why they are all corrupt."

"Mom."

"Why wouldn't he accept a bribe? What keeps a man honest if he earns nothing and the politicians take his nothing and they give nothing in return?"

"Mom, Gyula's your friend."

"I haven't talked to the man in fifty years, Tibor."

"Right. But he's your friend. Mom, stop." She's pulling clothes out of drawers and tossing them onto the bed. She uses hotel drawers, Tibor thinks.

"Get my suitcase. You cannot go to the National Police. Why should you? Did you ask to be a witness?"

"Mom, stop."

"Did you know this boy? He's probably a drug dealer. An addict. A waste. And now he's dead, okay? Why do you have to risk your life? No, Tibor. It's time to go. And don't talk to anyone. Don't speak to *anyone*."

"Mom. It's not 1956."

"Yes, it is." She turns on him. "It is. It is *always* 1956. People do terrible things. You think they won't, but they do. They spy and they lie, and they will tie a man by his ankles and they will light him on fire and they will watch as he burns. They will *watch*. Why don't you listen to me, Tibor? You never listen to me."

Agnes halts on the word. Sees her adult son in front of her. Shocked. Worried. Frightened. Has she lost her marbles?

"I am being irrational."

Tentative relief. She hadn't asked him about the naked gasping woman or how his head ended up between her naked thighs. That wasn't very nice to see. But the policeman only showed it to humiliate her. The peasant. The peasant who is after her son. *Her son*. Why has she come back?

"But I still do not trust Gyula."

Relief, gone. Worry, back.

"He always lied, but now it's different. He's damaged. Damaged all the way through."

"I really don't think, Mom..."

"All right, fine. Maybe I am being irrational. However, I am your mother, and I want to leave this country right now because it *makes* me irrational. And I want you to come with me because I am old and I am afraid to go alone. Especially with my sprained wrist. So."

So what are you going to do now, Tibor Roland? her look says.

"We still have to get your passport."

"I found it."

"You found it?"

"I forgot. I put it in my zipper pocket. Ta-da."

He could strangle her. He might.

"What are you waiting for? Get packed. It's still early. We can be gone before they think to look."

The train to Vienna rattles and clanks. Graffiti obscures the view, which is nothing to write home about. Towers of panel apartments give way to squat little houses in smushed little yards. Dogs chained to fence posts. Dull factories. Duller, treeless landscape. Two hours and they'd be crossing the border. Another, and they'd be in Vienna.

I am not afraid, Tibor thinks, trying it on for size.

Aha? says his soul.

Don't give me aha. I'm not pretending.

So why are we escaping?

This is not escape.

Tell that to your mother.

In the seat opposite, in the compartment they share with two faceless American backpackers, Agnes lets the winter fields slide by her eyes. There's nothing underneath that earth but more earth. The bones are old. They're dust. But now she knows the tunnels exist. And if the tunnels exist, then it's possible that Zsofi escaped. And if Zsofi escaped, then she, Agnes, did not kill her.

Two hours to Austria.

How long can she hold this reprieve, whole as a stone, before she can't?

Now or Never

Tuesday, October 16, 1956

"I found someone who'll take us for 350 forints."

"I might love your navel more than your right knee."

"If we catch the train for Sopron, we can jump off before the station."

"I thought I loved your right knee best, that scar, but now I'm reconsidering. In light of this splendid, neglected navel."

"It's cold, Gyula, and you're not listening."

"But I am. I'm listening to your stomach. It's rumbling."

"I've been skipping lunch to save the money. You know that."

"Poor, hungry belly." He kisses it.

"Listen to me. If we're really going to do this, we have to be ready."

"What is there to get ready?"

"Our things. Our clothes. Do you have any shoes other than those ones?"

"What's wrong with them?"

"They're not very sturdy. I thought I'd leave these ones for Zsofi—look how thin the soles are—and I'd take her old school shoes. She hates them."

"We have only two hours together, Agi. Why are we talking about shoes?"

"Because we have to be ready."

"I know that." His palms cup her cheeks. "And I'm ready. I'm ready to follow you to Mars, if you want. But until then, we're here. Can we just be here?" His lips on her ear loose goosebumps all the way down to her hip.

Margit Island teems with lovers just like them. Half hidden in the treed autumn park nearly evening, they speak just above a whisper. If Agi added up all the minutes of conversations with Gyula, how many would be whispered? Their entire courtship murmured on an island in a river.

"Soon we won't have to lie," she whispers.

"Well then what on earth will we do for fun?"

"Whatever ordinary people do, in an ordinary place. Do you think I'll be able to take a teacher's diploma in Canada? Or maybe they'll take my Hungarian qualification?"

"I don't know. But I'm sure it'll work out."

"You'll find work. I'm sure you will. You'll have to learn English—well, we both will—but your cousin Balazs will help us, right? Did you write to him?"

"Agi, please stop talking." His voice at her ear drops straight through her. His hand slides over the rough wool of her skirt to the small of her back. In two hours she will walk back to her family's dark apartment on Visegradi in a dense part of Pest while he heads in the other direction, over the bridge to Buda, to the gardens and steep climb of Rozsadomb, where all the party officials live, including his father. He'll study for a couple of hours before sleep or hunch over the little shortwave radio that bears news, sometimes, from the outside. When they leave this stupid country, they'll have whole nights together. She'll wrap her legs around him and, finally, she'll take him inside her.

"Your neck," he says.

He names every part of her and she loves it, the words parting skin from touch. She bristles. He brushes.

"Under your collarbone."

Agi hadn't expected love to be so literal, didn't expect she'd need so bluntly, feel fat with kisses and greedy for more. This is a surprise. Also, how terrifying every evening to let him go. Because he's careless. This has always been true, but for the last two weeks he's been listening to that shortwave radio every night, meeting with friends from the university, and their talk is getting more daring. Maybe it's because he's still a student while she's been teaching high school for two years, but he sometimes seems unbearably naive. He and his friends, they say they want the right to learn English. They want to stand up against the suppression of free thought at the universities. They want all Stalinist professors fired. Just last week, Gyula visited the British Legation to watch Western films. He came to her elated, full of talk: capitalist modernity and cars and ease. Yet just the week before, one of his friends had been arrested for doing exactly the same thing. A few days ago, he deliberately missed a meeting of the Communist Youth Organization and was fined fifty forints. The money is one thing, but the next time could be much more serious, and then what? He has no right to be so careless, now that she loves him.

He presses her back against a smooth-skinned plane tree. The sky seems bluer through its pale, spreading arms.

"This hip."

He's the only thing that stops her brain from whirring and

worrying. Even as his finger reaches through layers of clothes and deep into her, he can make her laugh. Another surprise: that love can be hilarious. That it can be so easy and so pure. She's taken him into her mouth and tasted him and felt no shame. She's tasted herself on his tongue and marvelled. Joy could be both simple and possible. Now, dry leaves crackle under their feet. She's trembling. Sun's sinking. He buries his face in her hair and she holds him tight, so tight around his ribs, so tight the cold sky will have to crack from the sheer force of their love. One week and two days.

This city where Agi and Gyula whisper is full of holes. Gaping craters where bombs dropped. In pavement, deep fissures left by tanks. Vast gaps blown into the sides of buildings. Windows shattered and not yet replaced. It's all damage from the war, but the war's been over for more than ten years and some houses that are now only shells, holes of houses, have become gardens. Weeds and poplars sprout where people once dined, slept, or danced, sprout through the wreckage where children are warned not to play. Agi wanders home past several of these holes, which she no longer sees because she's forgotten what used to be there. As a result of the holes, there's not enough room for the population. This is a paradox for engineers and revolutionaries both: how can it be, with so many holes, that there is so little space to breathe?

At the beginning of the month, the government decreed to reopen a hole, an unmarked hole where bodies had been flung three years ago. Three years ago those same bodies were considered to be enemies of the state. The bodies were retrieved, names reattached, and political histories rewritten to reflect the valour these men had shown, and the true love they had harboured for the state that had executed them — wrongly, the state now admits. This is one of the reasons Gyula's talk is braver these days: the reburial of Laszlo Rajk — Rajk's redemption, you might almost say. On October 6, he and three of his unjustly executed comrades were given a state funeral. The newsreel played in every theatre in the city for a week. Rajk's wasn't the only rehabilitation. Since September, hundreds of political prisoners have been released, and Hungary's Communist Party swore that this was the end of Stalinism and of terror, its conclusion signalled by the digging of a new and proper grave. This may all be true and hopeful, but Agi still shares a single-windowed, dimly lit flat with her sister and their angry black knot of a mother.

Agi turns the key just as the door flings open. Zsofi grabs both her hands and pulls her into the kitchen, where their mother sits gripping the wooden spoon, pot of soup on the stove forgotten. The radio is on as low as possible, shutters closed tight.

"Szeged students have separated," Zsofi whispers at full volume.

Agi pulls her hands from her sister's grasp — what scents has she carried in from the cold and from Gyula? — and she crouches on the other side of the radio. The announcer's voice reaches them from somewhere beyond their borders. Students at Szeged University have separated from the Communist Youth Organization.

Agi meets Zsofi's eyes. "How?"

In June, they heard that students in Poznan, Poland, had held a demonstration and the entire city had joined them. The city called for freedom and yet no one had been shot or arrested. So now, months later, the restlessness has reached Hungary. But Szeged? A small, inconsequential university town to the south—what made them do it?

The soup is steaming the unheated room, filling it with the dense, digestive odour of cabbage. Gyula will be listening to the radio now too, and before long he'll be on his way back over the bridge to Pest and to his plotting friends.

Zsofi's fired with hope, exuberant with it. "Do you think the same will happen here?"

Abruptly, Margit clicks off the radio. "Jo etvagyat"—bon appétit—she tells her daughters, which is to say, "The walls have ears," and she places full bowls on the table in front of them. Silently, they share a quarter-loaf of bread. Shoulders straight, silver spoons precisely balanced on slim fingers, they eat the soup that no one likes but that they've all gotten used to. The three pairs of hands are almost identical: long and gracious, blue veins close to the surface. Margit insists on formal table manners and a leisurely pace, even if there is only bread and cabbage soup. Agi looks sideways at her sister. Zsofi's knees under the table joggle frenetically and she counts between spoonfuls to make it look right. When they finish eating, Agi clears the plates. Margit stands and picks up the radio to take it with her. She knows better than to leave it with Zsofi, who would turn it on and forget to keep it low and to listen for footsteps outside the window.

"Anyu," Zsofi pleads. *Mom.*

No answer.

Zsofi throws herself back in the kitchen chair theatrically, legs sprawling. As soon as her mother's out of earshot, she leans forward. "Did you see Gyula? What did he say?"

"He hadn't heard yet."

"Lorand will do the same. They have to — they can't let Szeged stand on their own — and then once Lorand separates, the rest will follow." Eotvos Lorand is the university where Gyula studies engineering. Leaving Hungary means that he won't finish his degree, but once they settle in Toronto, he can start again. He's young, smart, and brave. Nothing scares him. He'll learn English and he'll work and he'll go to school at night, and it won't take long before he will be building bridges and skyscrapers in a city without history.

Zsofi's still talking. "God, I wish she'd let us out at night. I bet there are meetings happening right now, all over the city, and we're stuck in here without even a radio. Doesn't it make you crazy? I bet Gyula's at a meeting."

"I'm sure we'll hear all about it tomorrow."

"But what about *now*?"

Agi runs the dishes under a trickle of cold water from the tap. "Now we're here and we can't do anything about it. Keep your voice down."

"How can you be so calm? How can you just pretend nothing is happening?"

It's hard to know these days if Zsofi is really angry or just putting it on — enjoying the colour of a new mood, a new spat, another new Zsofika, as Agi calls her when she feels soft.

"Nothing *is* happening, Zsofi. And I'm not calm, I'm just not hysterical."

"I'm hysterical? Hysterical for wanting to go out at night?

For wanting to see my friends and speak my mind? For *hoping*? Well, I'd rather be hysterical than be you. How long have you and Gyula been playing kissy-face on the island? You're old enough to get married, but you don't. You could leave tomorrow, but you don't."

"Zsofi, please." She waits for the drama to disappear from her sister's eyes. "We're leaving next Thursday. It's all arranged."

"Oh, Agi," Zsofi bursts, clasping her. And then, "When will you tell Mom?"

"Tonight, I guess."

Agnes takes a long time with the few dishes, carefully drying each bowl, spoon, knife, and pot before putting it in its place. Zsofi has already sought out the warmth of the other room, where their mother sits writing—as she does each evening—to her husband who's been gone three years. She writes in miniature script to save on paper and she keeps the letters in the small glass-fronted bookcase, one of the few items of furniture they'd managed to keep from their original home. She doesn't complain anymore about the things she's lost or sold—the elegant house in the Buda hills, the Herendi porcelain dinner set, the dresses, the mink stole, silk stockings, good leather shoes, fine cheeses and wines, the books (so many books) and the paintings, all *liberated* by the communists. She stopped complaining the day her husband was arrested. Agnes would prefer the complaints to the sound of that nib on paper.

She has to tell her. Somehow, she must find the voice to say, Anya, I am leaving. With Gyula.

But not tonight. Her mother snaps the lid on her pen, shuffles the paper straight, and abruptly stands. She stuffs today's illegible letter in her pocket. She takes her coat from the wardrobe and wraps a scarf around her head, checks that she has house keys in her pocket, and without a word to her daughters leaves, locking the door behind her.

This happens sometimes. They can't predict what day or time it will happen. They don't know where she goes or what she does. Sometimes, she's away for many hours, sometimes only one. Once, they tried to follow her, but she knew they were there and the look on her face as she spun to face them—lost, beseeching, needing mercy—filled them with such deep shame that neither had ever tried it again. She just goes and they know she'll be back and in an unspoken agreement they don't talk about where she goes because the room feels lighter with her gone and neither wants to admit such an ungrateful truth.

She has a name, Agi's mother—all mothers do, though never to their children. She is Margit, like the island that, leaf-shaped, splits the Duna in two. Her husband is Miklos, and tonight she goes to tell him the news about the students in Szeged: some change is coming, Miklos, again. But no change has ever held. It always turns back, turns bad. Better not to change at all because nothing ever comes of it but more terror, more blood, more loss. What will she lose this time? What straggly bit of hope should she stifle? Hope is the worst hurt of all. And yet, every time change seems possible, hope comes back. It sprouts tender green from what was black and shivers in the breeze as it reaches for light. And then something happens. Something always happens. The axe falls, the tanks thunder in, soldiers or police break down the doors and force their way in with their angry, fearful shouting voices, and everything is black again but worse because for a short time hope made her remember the feeling of love. She will not hope this time. She will not. That is what she plans to tell her husband.

It's a long walk. Sometimes she takes the streetcar, but tonight the weather is good, the air crisp. She's there in just over forty minutes: Koztarsasag Ter, Republic Square. The buildings that surround the wide square are massive and magnificent—pillared, stone or stucco, where gods and angels bear aloft the weight of balconies and the pomp of nineteenth-century empire, now long gone. The Communist Headquarters is located in one of these buildings, but Margit isn't interested in the buildings that form the periphery of the square but in the square itself. Or, more precisely, in one specific sewer grate at the far end of it.

She's a small woman. In a dress, on Miklos's arm, she was right. People might not have called her beautiful, but pretty and stylish, with a sparkling sense of humour. If her daughters heard her described this way, they might not believe it, and if she stops for a moment to recognize that truth, it would make her too unbearably sad and she has enough sadness to bear already, so she doesn't stop. She proceeds to the sewer grate, clenching the letter in her jacket pocket. When she gets to the grate, she ignores the armed guards at Communist Headquarters—they're used to her—and she lowers herself to her knees. Placing her hands on the cobbles, she sinks until her whole body presses flat to the ground, her face just to the grate.

"Miklos," she begins. "I don't want you to feel any hope whatsoever."

During the war, Margit had done what everyone else had done. She'd mended her dresses, used newsprint for toilet paper or stuffed it into worn boots for warmth. She'd cooked what was available, stretching out the spice and the fat, hoarding bits of paper, making balls of ends of thread and string. She'd stayed cheerful for the girls, sought the safety of cellars when the bombs fell, told them stories as the ground shook about heavy-footed giants, gods flinging fire, Athena springing fully formed from the forehead of Zeus. She'd prayed for her husband to come home safe from the front. And he did. Shrapnel scarred his left arm and chest purple, but his heart was still hers and it beat underneath hers so fiercely when she pressed herself onto him that first night that she felt the war end inside her and she cried—for peace, for ordinary happiness—long after the shudders had stopped. All would be right again, she'd believed, with her husband back in her arms.

And then, eight years later, he was arrested and put on trial—a drama, a farce—and found guilty of plotting to sabotage the building of the Szabadsag Hid. He was the engineer in charge, and he *loved* that bridge—the utile grandeur of it, its purposeful, elegant, weight-bearing bastions. Plus, he was a good communist. Why would a good engineer and a good communist make a bridge that would only fall down? Though she was never told where he was held, or the length of his sentence, she knows he is here in Koztarsasag Ter, underneath it, lodged beneath the city in the prison tunnels that keep spreading, spreading, spreading, honeycombing the earth until finally, surely, the thin crust of surface would give way and all these once-grand buildings would fall in. She has no evidence that he is here, or that he can hear her, but in the total absence of evidence, she is certain. Of course, they would stow an engineer underground. Where else? Perhaps he is overseeing the digging of more tunnels, ensuring the structural integrity of the enlarging warren. Perhaps he is breathing through a long straw, catching the air that finds its way down through the sewer and finally into the underground cell where he lies, waiting.

She heard him once. Only the once, but what more assurance does a desperate woman need? It was two years ago, eleven months after his arrest, a beautiful May evening. If he'd been there with her, they might have taken a long walk on Margit Island, a lover's walk, hand in hand, laughing at their troubles and their joys. And this is what she said to him through the sewer grate. She said, "If you were here, it might be a beautiful evening, Miklos, you bastard. You bastard, for leaving me alone on this beautiful night. I am ruining. I am withering without you. I'm getting old, alone, and drying out from lack of love. Where is your hand, Miklos? Where are your arms when I need them?"

She was sobbing into the ground, that night. That was unlike her. She hardly ever sobbed anymore. Why bother when it eases nothing? But that night, some combination of the warm evening, the prettiness of the budding trees — they just keep budding, the idiot trees — and the pain racked her right through. And that's when she heard him.

"Margit," a voice called from far, far below. "Margit, you are alive."

That was it, just that: *Margit, you are alive.* Was it her wish or his voice? His voice. He's there because he must be there, because it is the only possible answer.

And then, in September, thin hope dared to poke through. Hundreds of political prisoners were released. An end to Stalinism. Hundreds who'd been executed were "rehabilitated," some even dug up and reburied. A woman in her building, arrested for God knows what, came home. She was gone and then suddenly she was there, like Lazarus. She'd been held in some little prison near the Ukrainian border. Margit couldn't stand to look at her, at her family's happiness, the pain was so sharp. Why are you home? Why you and not Miklos? And the answer inside her was plain: because he's dead, you stupid, foolish woman. Your husband is dead.

So. Miklos might be dead, but, equally, he might be here. And so, in this space between what she knows and what is yet to come, she speaks through the stone, feels the warm, putrid updraft of the sewer against her cheek, and she pushes hope down with the pages and pages of letters she has written him these last few days through the sewer grate. In case he is under there and wondering whether there is still life up here.

Thursday, October 18

"It was incredible, Agi. You wouldn't believe it. Our first speaker was Karoly, you remember him? Big guy, big voice. I helped him write the speech, but it was good he spoke it and not me. You should have seen him up there. His voice filled the entire auditorium. And there were hundreds in the audience, must have been almost the entire university. He said that even though the lies and the violences of Stalin and Rakosi have been exposed professors still preach Stalinism. He said, 'Why are we still being examined on party politics, rather than architecture, law, economics? This must change. We must be at the forefront of change.' And the entire audience erupted in applause. It was like letting the top off. Suddenly, everyone had a voice. One student after the other got up and reported what these professors had done in the name of communism. I sat there, and I felt like I was somewhere else. Were these the same students I'd been in class with for the last two years? It went on until eleven o'clock."

This is why he didn't meet her on Margit yesterday. She sat there on her books in the park, arms around her knees by their tree, waiting and believing the worst. He'd been hauled in to the principal's office for questioning about some paper he'd written, too honestly. He'd been arrested on leaving the British Legation. He was right now sitting in some cramped room, refusing to answer questions. Or answering them. She waited the full two hours before giving up, the sun already set by the time she got home.

When they'd first met, just six months ago, what she loved was his daring. He was speaking quietly, but fervently, to a group who'd gathered round him at the entrance to the university. She had just started teaching at the high school nearby.

"We have been brought up amid lies," he said. "We continually have to lie. We cannot have a healthy idea because all ideas are choked by our habit of lies. If we want to be truly free, we need first to have freedom of thought." At that very moment, a professor passed and Gyula, without missing a beat, turned his talk to a recital of the latest Soviet accomplishments.

It wasn't just that he was an accomplished liar, but that he could turn it into such a lithe performance; he lied like a dancer. Her friend introduced them. He gave her a smile. She was smitten. That love could be so ready, that was another surprise.

Now, Gyula's arms about her waist, he's full of some new feeling. He vibrates with it. "We're meeting again tomorrow night, all the students. On Harmashatar Hegy. It's happening, my love. Something is happening. I don't know what, but even if what we accomplish is small, just a minor change at the beginning of many minor changes, that's something." He's got his arms around her waist, but his dark eyes shine bright with future, his lank black hair blowing. "This is the time."

He and his co-revolutionaries—not comrades, no, revolutionaries—they're planning manifestos, writing demands they want to put in front of government. This is no longer just talk; it's plotting. "Gyula, you will be arrested."

"No. This time the change is real. Can't you feel it? The press was at the meeting in the auditorium. The *Szabad Nep* and the *Magyar Nemzeti*. Did I tell you that?"

But that was about confronting professors, Agi thinks, not the Communist Party itself. But she doesn't have long to think because Gyula's mouth is at her ear. "Don't worry, Agi. I promise, I will be careful."

"One week," she says.

"And then we'll be married, and I will take you to an actual bed and will remove every last bit of your clothing and kiss every last bit of your body."

She smiles so easily, sees this future so clearly. "Promise?"

"I promise. And maybe by then even Hungary will be free. Can you imagine that, Agi? What a wedding present that would be."

Two hours later, Agi pushes fearless across Margit Hid into the wind, up Szent Istvan Korut, and dances left onto Visegradi Utca. In the bins of the vegetable store, the usual old potatoes, carrots, apples, the inevitable cabbage, turnip, kohlrabi. In Vienna, they will eat cake. In the window of a women's shop, flagrant and drab dresses hang side by side, listless and ugly, but in Toronto, she'll wear red. The butcher rolls down his shutters. Dog shit litters the asphalt sidewalk. She hops over it. Two men loiter, smoking and talking in front of her building. They're old and colourless and they know nothing of love. Her keys clang as she unlocks the front door. The elevator is still broken, so she takes the stairs that curve round it to the fourth floor. She walks along the courtyard balcony to their door, noticing that Mrs. Nemeth's kitchen light is on. She turns the key in the lock. Mrs. Nemeth would be peeking through her shutters now, to see who's there. As always, ready and willing to report suspicious activity. How suspicious is Agi, tonight? Very. Very suspicious indeed, with happiness glowing all over her face. So she tiptoes back to Mrs. Nemeth's shuttered window and says clearly, "Good evening, Mrs. Nemeth." There's no answer, but Agi senses a soft, plump woollen step to the side.

In the kitchen, Zsofi is cooking.

"Is Mother home?"

Zsofi nods toward the other room.

"How is she?"

What kind of question is that? Zsofi's look says.

Going into the next room where her mother sits, Agi clicks the radio on, tunes it to the National Radio, and turns it up loud so they can speak underneath it. "Anyu? I need to tell you something."

Pressing pen, pressing, pressing. Her mother doesn't look up.

"I'm leaving next Thursday. With Gyula."

Her mother doesn't lift her pen from paper. Agi tries to remember the mother from her early childhood, the one who'd known how to smile. This mother's lips have flattened and thinned to the width of the lines she writes relentlessly.

"We want to make a life together but not here. It's impossible here. Can you understand that?"

Scratch, scratch on the paper. "Persze, Agi. Of course, I understand."

Agi counts the moments, the scratches irregular and furious.

"Is that all you're going to say?"

Agi's mother doesn't put the pen down, but she holds it still. She looks at this daughter, this self-centred and stupid girl whom she loves so much she can hardly unclench her teeth enough to spit on her. "Is that all? I don't even know this Gyula. I've never met him. And now you tell me that you 'love' him, that with him you're going to run away and get yourself arrested or killed. What do you want me to say, Agi? Congratulations?"

"You could say good luck."

"Fine. Good luck. If you survive, send me a letter."

Her mother goes back to her writing, and Agi to the kitchen where her sister waits, eyebrows raised.

"I have to get out," Agi says.

They leave without dinner and without a word to their mother. They lock the door behind them. They walk bravely past Mrs. Nemeth's window, skip down the stairs and into the misting night. Side by side they amble. In this neighbourhood, there's hardly anyone out. A few people leave a warm csarda, closely huddled. One man up ahead walks his dog and smokes. On Szent Istvan, the streetcar trundles by. For lack of another destination, they follow it toward the Nyugati train station. Her mother nearly stole her happiness, but now, out in the autumn evening with her sister, she feels it returning. And tomorrow she will see Gyula, and together they'll make more happiness and they'll run away with their happiness, take it right across the border, far away from her mother, from this city with its holes that cramp and the fear that breeds mothers like Agi's.

"Can I trade you shoes?" Agi asks. "Not now, I mean, but Thursday?"

Zsofi stops. "You're really leaving, aren't you?"

"Yes." Now that she's told her mother, it feels more certain, more concrete than ever. "Yes, I really am."

Suddenly, like a child, Zsofi is crying. Fat tears roll down her cheeks. She hasn't thought this through, or maybe it never seemed real, as it didn't to Agi yet either. Leaving. It seems impossible, and yet Agi knows that people leave every day—are arrested, die, escape—while others are left behind. Everything here would remain the same, except Agi would be gone. The streets, the withered vegetables on Visegradi, Mrs. Nemeth hovering at her window, the men who stand smoking at corners, the crowded apartments and streets, and their mother. Their silent, angry mother would remain and Zsofi alone with her.

"Zsofi." Agi takes her little sister in her arms. "As soon as I find work, you'll join me. I promise."

The other side of Bajcsy-Zsilinszky, a group of students pours out of a side street. They're not talking. As they separate, they shake hands self-importantly. Another meeting, talk and dreaming in a city where dreaming out loud has been for years forbidden. The students disperse. The city's quiet. They can see right through the vast windowed wall of the train station where people hover, waiting, barely lit by the hanging lamps. The whole thing—the glass held together by black lines, the ordinary people getting ready to queue—at night looks strangely prettier than it is, and Agi thinks, I will miss this place.

Margit hears her daughters go out together, and in the space they leave behind she thinks, So this is it. One day, it will be only her here. Because of course once Agi goes, Zsofi will follow. Agi is more mother to that little one than she's ever been, not because she doesn't love but because her love is stopped up inside her, wizening, and if it comes out, it comes out as spite, anger, a slap, a rebuke. It was different when Miklos was around; he could always find a way to make things easy, make her laugh, to find the lightness inside. They had ten years together before the war, and eight years after it. Eighteen years, all together. Shouldn't that be enough? Shouldn't you be able store up enough love and laughter and happiness, enough that you could mete it out and make it last to the end of life?

Margit fills the pages, and minutes pass. She writes tighter and tighter, turning white to black. What can she possibly have to say to this husband likely dead? Everything, is the answer to that. Everything he's not here for—or how will he know it, how will he understand what his wife is becoming, has become? He should know every hardship that touches her, every minute she waits in line, every time she fails her girls, every damn stupidity of that menial job typing and sorting at the Unicum factory that is draining the last bit of intelligence she has, and the spying Mrs. Nemeth, and the house meetings and the things she has to say to be safe, and he's not here to be her one true place in all these lies. Margit knows her relentless writing is in some way pathological. She read Freud before the war when she was young and had the time and the brain to read, and so she labels it: compulsion, sublimation, control, her own version of the *fort-da* game. In Freud's story, a little boy, his grandson, replays the distress of his mother's departure and return by repeatedly throwing his toy away and calling it back. He throws it away; his mother is gone. He reels it back—a miracle—his mother returns. Pain and then joy. Pain and then joy. Over and over again. Just so, but without joy, Margit writes Miklos away; she calls him forth. She refuses to believe he's dead; she knows he's dead. She writes to suppress hope; she writes because to write is a form of hope.

> *Miklos, Do you know what your self-centred daughter*
> *did today? She's gone and fallen in love. She's in love, no*
> *matter how much I warned her never to be in love because*
> *look what it does to you. She's going to run away and*
> *get married. She's been lying to me, Miklos, because she's*
> *frightened of me. What kind of mother scares her girls into*
> *hiding? This kind of mother, Miklos, the one I've become,*
> *and I can't be any other way because this life is hard*
> *without you and I have lost my love. I am angry so they*
> *reject me, so I get angry. Don't you see? They used to love*
> *me, but now they don't. Who wouldn't be angry at that?*
> *And if you come home, you will be frightened of me too.*
> *That's what I fear.*

She writes for hours. She writes the same information five times over, ten times over. She writes him away; she calls him forth.

Monday, October 22

Gyula comes to Agi at a run. Late but at least he's come. She could cry with the relief of it. He's fine; he hasn't been arrested after his foolish meeting on the hill. He carries his coat in his hand in an afternoon suddenly warm as summer, loping across the bristled grass.

"Gyula, I told my mother."

"Told her what?"

"That we're leaving. And you know what she said? She said, 'Write me if you survive.' Can you believe that? Can you believe a mother would say that?"

"Who cares what she says. It doesn't matter. It doesn't matter like we do." He kisses her hard, but he can't stay long. The Student Federation has presented its petition to the government. Among the fourteen items they listed, they called for the withdrawal of Soviet troops. He grips her hands. "They have to listen to us, Agi. It's time. They've come so far already, why not take the next step? They *must* agree to our demands."

She stops him. "You put your name to a petition against the government?"

"Five members presented it on behalf of the federation."

Could he really be so foolish?

"The time for hiding is over, Agi. It's time to stand up for ourselves. As the poet says, 'It's now or never.'"

"But petitioning the government, Gyula? Signing your name."

"We've been afraid long enough. *Slaves* long enough." The poet's words again. Illicit words. They were revolutionary words when they were first written, a call to arms to rise up against Austria. Look how well that went. But the statue of Sandor

Petofi still stands in his park, his hair flying, the very picture of Hungarian yearning. Now Gyula.

"Only three more days, and we won't be."

He looks blankly at her. And then he understands. He sees her now, and she sees that he sees her, a focal centring. He's planning what to say next.

"Maybe we don't need to go."

"What?"

"If things change, Agi, we don't need to run. We can be here and still have exactly what we want—freedom and hope and possibilities and...everything. Everything we want but here."

"But we've been planning for months."

"I know, but that was before."

"Before what, Gyula? Before you signed a petition?"

"Agi."

"And now what do you think will happen? Really? That your petition will with one blow flatten the Soviet state?"

"Agi."

"Stop the AVO from spying and torturing? Make everything right?"

"*They*'re the ones who made the first move, releasing the political prisoners, talking about a new friendship with the Soviets. We're all on the same side, mostly. Just get rid of Rakosi and Gero and things will happen."

"Get rid of Rakosi? For God's sake, don't be such a child." Without realizing it, she is hitting his chest, pushing him off.

"I'm a child?"

"Yes."

"I'm the child? All you can do is talk about your precious exit plan, what shoes to wear."

"It's *my* plan now? Funny. Just yesterday, it was *ours*."

"Plans change. *History* is changing."

"I haven't changed."

"So maybe you should. This is our moment, Agi. Hungary's moment."

Wary even now, more than ever now, they fight in whispers.

"Our moment? What about *our* marriage?"

"For God's sake, I still love you."

"But you'll break your promise to me."

He's extricating his fingers from hers. She grips.

"I have to go, Agi. We're meeting in"—the bastard checks his watch—"in fifteen minutes, and I have to be there."

He kisses her cheek. Tells her not to cry, they'll work things out, everything will look better tomorrow, promise, promise, promise, I love you. And then he leaves, loping up the hill to the bridge and across the Duna to the spired grey parliament to learn the fate of his revolutionary hope.

Later that night, after a wordless supper, after the dishes, she spills everything into Zsofi's shoulder, trying to cry without a sound so her mother won't hear. Zsofi pats her back, uncomfortable with this role and unfamiliar with her sister's emotion. Finally, she says the only thing that occurs to her to say, and she hopes it sounds wise: "You have to let him be true to himself."

It's not wise at all. It's trite. An insult. But it's also all that Zsofi is capable of. So Agi straightens, wipes the tears from her eyes. "Maybe you're right," she says.

"Of course I'm right." Zsofi replies, pleased with her achievement and the conclusion of this small crisis. A moment later, she is watching herself in the darkened glass of the window, pulling her hair into new coquettish twists. "The thing is, he's very inspiring. His speeches, I mean. To the federation, he's invaluable."

To the *federation*? They're a bunch of idealistic, naive, careless, dangerous, big-talking children. And what does Zsofi know about it?

"People are quoting him, you know. He's a real leader. Everyone loves him."

Everyone? What everyone? What kind of love? Abruptly, Agi stands, furious with the superior look in her vain little sister's face, this dispensing of wisdom as she admires her own beauty in the glass.

"I'm going to bed."

Tuesday, October 23

Agi doesn't need a radio to know that something is happening. Her students are buzzing with it: the university students have gone out. Not just Lorand, but the Technical University too. They're marching. Thousands of them. Her classroom empties. One girl shoves a flyer at her. "Come, Miss Teglas."

In her vacant, windowed classroom, sun glaring in, Agi reads the leaflet the girl has given her. It lists eleven slogans, and she can read Gyula's overblown urgent rhetoric in each of them.

Poland sets the example; we want the Hungarian way!

New leadership, a new direction, requires new leaders!

Children of Father Bem and Father Kossuth, let us go hand in hand!

Children of workers and peasants, we go along with you!

We demand a new leadership; we trust Imre Nagy!

We shall not stop halfway; we shall destroy Stalinism!

Independence! Freedom!

Long live the Polish people!

Long live the Polish Workers' Party!

Worker-peasant power!

Long live the People's Army!

The day's too warm for a coat. She leaves her jacket on the hook, screws the leaflet into her cardigan pocket, and joins the stream of students and teachers.

On the grassy Petofi Ter, it's louder and more chaotic than any parade or festival. Messy placards — "Independence, Equality, Friendship!" "A New Policy, A New Direction Calls for New Leadership!" — picket around the statue of Sandor Petofi, whose banned words Gyula recited at her yesterday. Hungarian tricolour flags wave from open windows, their red, green, and white stripes torn at the centre where the Soviet red stars have been slashed out. The shouts and cheers are joyfully terrified, like children on swings, a hundred thousand children on a hundred thousand swings, urging heels to sky. She can't see Gyula in the throngs that pour into the small square from all directions, yet he's made this happen. How? Somehow he's done this, he and his fervent, political, and careless friends. As she scans the crowd for Gyula, a student climbs the statue. He shouts the illicit words of the poem. At first, it's just him. Just his one voice, swinging wide over the crowd: "On your feet, Magyar, the homeland calls!" But before he reaches the next line, the others have it: "The time is here, now or never! Shall we be slaves or free? This is the question, choose your answer!" Agi, too, joins in. "Slaves no longer!" they declaim, Agi declaims. "Now or never!"

They're moving. She goes with the mass, a stranger takes

one arm, another stranger the other. And now she's marching. Marching with elated strangers, marching up the broad, veering Kossuth Lajos Utca to Bajcsy-Zsilinszky. At every step, the crowd swells. From apartment windows flags wave, holes where the star used to be. People step out of little shops and businesses to cluster onto the sidewalk, shouting, "Eljen!" *Long may you live!* The shouting voices ricochet, brace, and bounce. In this whispering city, people yell, "Now or never." Agi yells. For the possibility of freedom, and the end of lies, but also at her mother and her mother's fury. At the things taken away and the things too ugly to save. At the broken plumbing and the unfinished subways, and the ones locked away, and the ones returned. At the men who took and the men who lied for those who took, and the women hollowed out with the pain of it. And then, at some point, someone, somewhere, from some window starts throwing paper. Paper flutters down on them. It takes a moment to understand and then she sees: they're Soviet pamphlets, Soviet books, Soviet words, and people are throwing them out their windows. Marchers cover their heads and laugh. They march over this ripped-up stuff, this meaningless, featherweight, ephemeral stuff—for it has no more heft and far less might than a thousand, a hundred thousand, Hungarian voices unleashed.

Across Margit Hid, the crowd heaves. When Agi looks back, the river of people behind her seems to have no end. They keep walking, and the swell carries her, and the bridge miraculously holds as the evening sun lights the Duna on fire.

At Bem Ter, on the other side of the river, they stop. It's a small square, smaller even than Petofi, not big enough for the crowds that keep coming. Shoulders push at her shoulders, and she breathes into another woman's neck. They shuffle to make room for more, but there's no more room to be had. Just off Bem Ter, the Radetzky Barracks holds soldiers. Have they come to challenge them? But she's barely thought it when she realizes what's happening. Guards and soldiers are spilling into the crowd, yanking reds stars from their sleeves. They're shouting with the crowd, "Down with Gero. Down with Rakosi. Out with the Russians!" One of them comes up behind her and lifts her up into the air, onto his shoulder, in sheer jubilation. With him, she punches the sky: "Now or never!"

Is that Gyula? Over there by the statue of the lion? Yes. And he sees her, waves two ecstatic hands. "Now!" she shouts just as the soldier lets her down.

Now! Full force and thick with love, the crowd pushes back, back over the Duna. To the parliament. The sun has sunk below the horizon by the time they get there, and Agi stands in Kossuth Ter next to an old woman, as old as her mother, whose hand grips hers. There's no such thing as a stranger tonight. They stand together as Magyars. They wait for something to happen. Kids have clambered onto the roofs of streetcars that have halted, electric current collectors lowered to the street. People chant their different demands. "Put out the star on the parliament. It wastes our electric current." "Russians, go home." Until all the shouting gathers into one: "We want Imre Nagy. We want Imre Nagy." And tonight, this seems possible. He was prime minister once, for a few months, until he was ousted by the hard Communist Rakosi and the terrors began again. But maybe it's possible. Maybe the sheer force of their voices will bring him back to power. Yes, and maybe her father will be returned to her unharmed, and maybe the borders will be opened, and she can just walk across it. Maybe there will be meat in the stores, and loud, raucous laughter in the streets, and she and Gyula will get married and be happy here, in Budapest. Right now, as thousands of Hungarians stand together in a square, shouting loudly for the return of Imre Nagy, all this is possible. But wherever this singularly honourable comrade is hiding, he doesn't appear. The chanting goes on and on, the crowd swells larger and larger, and still Imre Nagy doesn't step out onto the parliament balcony to hear what the people have to say.

Suddenly, they're swallowed in darkness. Someone has turned off all the lights—inside the parliament and all the streetlights surrounding Kossuth Ter. They stand blind. Agi feels the woman's hand tighten around hers and bends her head to the woman's ear. "We're fine. As long as we're all together here, we're fine." But she hardly believes her own words in a night so pressing, so purposeful.

A match flares, lights a single scrap of paper. Another match. Another scrap. To another scrap, another match. And another. And another. Scraps flare, pass, and vanish. Agi finds the screwed-up flyer in her pocket. She touches it to the flame offered by the hand in front of her. She lets it burn. She touches it to another's and so it goes. Tiny lights flicker and fall as wisps of paper burn. When she sees Gyula, she'll apologize. She'll stand by him, shoulder to shoulder, and try to see things his way.

At the parliament, suddenly two lamps. The crowd buzzes. "It's Nagy. Shh. It's Nagy."

"Comrades." The loudspeaker launches the word over their heads.

"Boo," the crowd responds.

And again: "Comrades—"

"No!"

"My esteemed Hungarian fellow citizens."

The cheers drowned out his next sentence. Agi hears hardly a word of what follows, but the crowd grows restless. People turn one to the other. "What's he saying?" Something about friendship. Soviet troops will stay. A new friendship? With the Soviets?

An entire city has left its post and wandered out into the streets to proclaim itself free, and this is Nagy's response? He was their only hope and he's offering friendship with Russia? No. No, this is not enough.

The crowd turns. Angry and right, it thrusts deeper into the clotted streets. It breaks apart. It finds itself. To Radio Budapest. It crashes against the wall, it storms: "In the name of the Student Revolutionary Council, let us in! We want our manifesto read on air! For all of Hungary to hear. For the world to hear."

Broken glass crackles and crunches under Agi feet. Somewhere, windows have shattered. She's in one of the side streets when she hears it: the unmistakable stutter of gunfire.

Wednesday, October 24

In the early morning, Agi sits with her mother, both fastened to their chairs and to each other by the same impossible unknowing. She watches her mother's hands, clenched together on her lap. She watches the movement of her mother's unforgiving mouth as she murmurs prayers or incantations into the air, and Agi closes her eyes because she hates this and she doesn't know where Gyula is and Zsofi hasn't come home so she waits with her mother. The same wait. The same room. The same hands.

Somehow, in the long, chaotic minutes after those first shots into the crowd, the revolutionaries procured weapons. They shot their way into the building. She still doesn't know if Gyula was in there, or if he was captured by the AVO, the Allamvedelmi Osztaly, the secret police. Or if he'd been shot. She fought her way through the crowd moving in the opposite direction and she saw bodies but not his. That wasn't proof he was alive, but at least it wasn't proof that he was dead. She stumbled into the square, desperate. She seized strangers by the arm, "Have you seen…?" Trying to find the words to describe him, receiving in return either compassion or a brutal "How should I know…?" She turned a corner and stumbled into a girl who fell into her arms. Agi helped the girl to the shelter of a doorway where they both collapsed, tucking back into the shallow alcove. How could the night have turned like this? The girl could be no more than fifteen years old, the same age as Agi's students, and she was bleeding from her stomach. Her blonde hair curled bright from underneath a beret. Agi held the girl as fighters and ordinary people clamoured by through air that stank of bitter smoke and filled with the dust of buildings blown apart.

"Hush," Agi whispered. "What's your name?"

"Eva." The blood seeped through Eva's shirt and coat, and though Agi pressed her hand to staunch it, the blood kept pumping.

"Eva, that's a pretty name. We're safe here, Eva. Don't worry."

Not that it mattered.

"I've got a little candy in my pocket," Eva said before she lost consciousness. "Would you like it?"

When Agi walked in to the apartment shortly before four that morning, her mother had been awake in the dark, sitting in the same stern wooden chair she always sat in to write her letters.

"Anyu?"

Hearing her daughter's voice, Margit said nothing. She did nothing. Not a hug or a "Thank God," and Agi felt deserted. She stripped off clothes stiff with the stranger's blood and went to bed, but she didn't sleep. Explosions and fear kept her awake, sporadic gunfire ricocheted. Her mother muttered prayers. And now they sit.

Margit twists a piece of string around a ball of string ten years in the making, thankful that one daughter is here, though that's not nearly enough. If she had opened her mouth last night, she would have said nothing kind. If she'd opened her hand, it would have slapped. Such nonchalance. Such easy, careless nonchalance with her love when anyone can see she can't afford to lose any more. No, if Margit could do it, she would put them, her precious daughters, in a box, wrap them up tight, incant prayers over that box to protect them, assign soldiers to guard them with guns and grenades and loyalty as fierce as her own. *Miklos, your daughters take their lives too lightly.*

From the street, a loudspeaker crackles and bellows: "Hungarians, Hungary needs you. Support our heroes of the revolution. We are all on strike. Do not work today." As if anyone could even think of working after last night. Whatever today might ordinarily have been, it is not and nothing is certain. Ordinary time is over. This is revolutionary time. This? This waiting inside a cold apartment for news? This is his revolution and she doesn't even know if he's still alive, or Zsofi. Agi flings yesterday's bloody cardigan over her dress, remembers that her jacket is still hanging on its hook at the school where she left it yesterday afternoon. She says not a word to her silent mother, and she slams the door on the way out.

Visegradi teems with people. They mill about, they pull toward Szent Istvan Korut. Some walk, some march arm in arm and sing. Many like her just stand in doorways, watching. A car trundles by. It's past ten and there's an air of holiday festivity but purposeful. Someone's singing the national anthem. Flags wave. She pushes through it all. This is impossible. How will she find them if she has no idea where to look? On Szent Istvan, she hears the sound of shooting from somewhere up near the Nyugati train station. Cars burn, a bus rocks, crashes onto its side. The air smells of burning gas and metal. Who will bury the dead? Old men clatter by with guns they must have kept from the war. Teenagers and young people clatter with weapons too. She stops one. "Where did you get the gun?"

"Technical University," he shouts. "It's the armoury now. Lots left if you want one."

The university an armoury? In one night, an entire city has turned itself inside out. Hungarians have become loud. Russian books have become flares. She, Agi, has become a revolutionary, and tanks have blown new holes in the city centre. She can't imagine Gyula with a gun, but then yesterday she wouldn't have imagined last night, and tomorrow, *tomorrow*, they are supposed to leave for the border. Skirting Szabadsag Ter, she hears someone shout that the Csepel munitions factory has gone out on strike and the workers are sending arms, truckloads of them. "Death to the AVO," shouts a woman in a faded housewife's dress. Her face shines with justice as she walks with purpose, locking arms with the woman next to her. "Now or never!" the women shout, and others join them. Agi hurries. The Technical University is on the other side of the river, at least ten kilometres from here, and streetcars stand, stalled and abandoned on their tracks. Still, it's good to have a destination. Her feet hurt already on the cobbles and she wishes for Zsofi's thick-soled, ugly shoes. Tomorrow's shoes. Approaching Jozsef Atilla Utca, a knot of people tangles round a lamppost. As she passes, they hoist a man from his ankles up the post. AVO. His car burns on the road. Calmly, an older woman in battered, once-stylish high heels walks to the burning car, dips a rolled paper into the fire, returns to the dangling, bloody man, and touches the flame to his left shoulder, his right, his hair. He screams as he ignites. Agi runs.

She runs until her chest hurts and stops, finally, on the corner of a street where a high wall hides a garden. She realizes she's sobbing: "I can't. I can't. I can't." I can't. What does this even mean? This can't be my life. I can't lose him. I can't run. She crouches like a small animal against the stone wall. She shudders and she rocks. "I can't."

Enough. The voice in her head is her own: as bossy and abrupt as she is with Zsofi sometimes. Get to your feet, hulye. Are you dead? No. Are you hurt? No. So stop your crying. Find Gyula. There is still time to escape. This is the best time to escape.

By the time she gets to the university it's three hours since she left home. A truck's parked out front. Students form a line, passing rifles from one hand to the next, loading the truck. Everyone is wearing an armband of red, white, and green to indicate their allegiance; they are fighting for Hungary. "Gyula Farkas?" she asks. "Zsofi Teglas?" She makes her way from one revolutionary to the next. No one knows. She follows the line back to the gymnasium, where hundreds and hundreds of crates are spread about the floor bearing Rakosi's stamp. So, Csepel's munitions have arrived already, arms stolen from the enemy. In the corner, a radio blasts. Martial law has been declared. No surprise, Hungary's most devoted Stalinist, Matyas Rakosi, is calling the revolutionaries *counter*-revolutionaries and fascists, traitors who threaten Hungary. He swears he will cut them off, like so many slices of salami. Soviet reinforcements are on their way. A boy jangling with bandoliers dashes into the gymnasium: "The soldiers have joined us," he shouts, and the old wooden auditorium resounds with cheers and stomps.

Agi wanders into the hall. An older man who looks like he'd be comfortable selling cabbages and turnips assumes she's here to enlist and directs her to Room Nine, on the second floor, where they're dispensing armbands.

"I'm looking for Zsofi Teglas and Gyula Farkas," she says.

"Farkas? I just saw him. Try that way." He nods toward a hallway lined with portraits of principals, some now slashed or dashed to the floor.

She passes three doorways, and as she approaches the last, she hears his voice. Gyula. "We must establish a radio transmitter somewhere in Buda. Who can do this?" At the open door, she pauses. He's sitting on the teacher's desk, surrounded by six fighters. Grenades hang from his waist. A gun is slung from his shoulder, sleeves rolled up. Three days ago, he was an ordinary student of engineering, awkward and gangly as he ran toward her on Margit.

"I could likely figure it out. If we can take a transmitter from the radio building, bring it up to the top of Harmashatar, maybe?" says one of the men.

"Good. We need to be in touch with Gyor, and with other student groups. There's no organization, no communication between our groups, an enormous weakness. We have to rectify it."

It hardly sounds like Gyula—so abrupt and decisive. He glances up, sees Agi by the open door.

"Agi." He bounds across the room and plants an exuberant kiss on her lips. Agi feels her cheeks light up. Is this part of the revolution too? Everything coming out of hiding, including love?

"Farkas, what did General Kovacs have to say?" This was a different young man, but they all looked the same to Agi—too young, too fired up.

"That's what I'm telling you, Marton. Next time, be quicker about it and you won't miss the information." Holding fast to her one hand, he speaks louder, tenser, faster than she's ever heard him. "Every minute matters. Feri's got his hands on an armoured vehicle. He can drive it. Can someone else manage the defence?"

The rattle of machine-gun fire is constant, if distant. Explosions blast, but everyone here ignores them. She tries to follow the conversation, but it's obvious she has nothing to add. The others have forgotten her. His hand lets go. She stands, purposeless and awkward, beside the revolutionary.

Finally the group breaks, and Gyula turns back to her. "Did you see how organized we are already? Did you see what's in the gymnasium?"

"Thank God you're safe, Gyula. Last night, I thought maybe you were at the Radio and—"

"From Csepel. Rakosi's own weapons, turned against him. And you know what General Kovacs said to me today? 'The most faithful allies of the army are the students and the workers in the city, and the peasants in the country. Together, we have risen against Soviet domination.' It's happening, Agi. You see? Just like I told you. Soon, we will be Hungarians on Hungarian soil again."

He's talking at her, face shining with fervour, his black eyes bright with it. All the apologies she'd wanted to make dry on her tongue.

"Gyula, they're burning men alive out there—"

"AVO men, Agi."

She can't even begin to answer this. "There's talk the border guards have left their posts. It would be so easy, Gyula. We'd just have to walk—"

He looks at her in confusion. "I'm fighting for my country."

He's lived through one war already, as she has. He knows what Russian tanks can do as well as she does. He knows the terror of hiding in a cellar for days, weeks on end. He had to clean Russian boots, bring them cigarettes and goose fat and beer. "But you will *lose*, Gyula."

His face goes smooth, mercenary. "Get out of my way."

"Gyula."

"I have things to do, Agi. Now let me go."

She'd grasped his sleeve without realizing. He strides away, shoulders set, grenades rattling loose around his waist.

When Agi leaves, the apartment walls close in. The fighting's not many streets away. Margit hears the ricochet of bullets, the shouts. What is Miklos thinking, where he dwells, down below? Can he hear the guns, the jubilation that fills the air? Is he tempted by that jubilation to hope? Don't you dare hope, Miklos, thinks Margit. Don't you dare. But before she even has a name for what she's doing, she's putting down the ball of string. She's standing, getting her coat on, wrapping a scarf about her head. With a key, she's opening the cabinet beside her bed and she's taking out the gift Miklos gave her after he came back last time and she told him what the Russians did and he couldn't have stopped them. It's only a pistol, but she has a full carton of bullets. She puts the box of bullets in one coat pocket and the gun in the other. If there has to be a revolution, then fine, let there be a revolution.

She walks with the long pistol in her pocket. She looks like any ordinary mother with a scarf tied round her head, with her little net shopping bag at her wrist. She moves not quickly, not nimbly, but steadfastly, one dogged foot in front of the other. People run from corner to corner. They duck and dodge. The noise and the fighting intensify as she nears Koztarsasag Ter. With every block, the screaming and the shouting get louder; bloodstained people run for their lives or are dragged out of the way or walk dazedly with their arms around friends. There's a pretty, ringletted girl holding a gun as if it were a dolly in the alcove doorway of a shop. She's dead. There's a man sprawled face down on the street, his back blown open. He's dead. There's an elderly woman, just like Margit, still holding her shopping bag in her left hand, splayed on her back. She's dead. Where will these dead be buried? Who will dig their graves and mark them? Who even knows who they are, these dead-in-the-street, these accidents and fighters, these corpses.

On the square itself, there's no fighting. A standoff. The Soviet tanks sit, with Russian soldiers inside them, guarding Communist Party Headquarters. The revolutionaries stand in front of them, jeering, daring, but not shooting. Margit walks bravely—she doesn't feel brave, but this is how she must seem to anyone watching—to her usual sewer grate close to the centre of the square, between the revolutionaries and the tanks. She takes the pistol out of her pocket and she lies face down on her belly.

"Miklos," she shouts into the sewer grate. "Miklos Teglas, this is your wife, Margit. Do you hear me?"

She hears nothing. Nothing and nothing and nothing. Every twenty minutes, she calls. And waits. And calls, and waits. While the battles rage around her, she calls and she waits and she calls and she waits and finally, finally, she hears something. Not as clear as the last time—maybe he's farther down—but there's something. A clink. A murmur of a voice, more than one.

"Miklos, sooner or later, the revolutionaries will attempt to seize Communist Headquarters. I know it. I'm not hopeful they will win, but they will try, and when they do, you have to be ready." And with that, Margit drops the pistol down. She counts to ten before she hears a watery plunk far, far, far below ground, and then she drops the bullets. "Shoot that door down if you have to, Miklos. But don't get killed."

"Na." Margit pushes herself onto her knees, and from her

knees, one leg at a time, she stands. She looks toward the tanks. She brushes the dust from her coat front and her knees. She has done all she can do for her Miklos. Now, let the revolution do the rest.

Thursday, October 25

It's *Thursday*. And Agi is still here. All over the city, fires burn and guns shoot, but they need to eat so Agi goes out for bread. Along Szent Istvan, she walks past the corpses of three more AVO men hanging from their ankles from the lampposts. People are extinguishing cigarettes in their carcasses. She finds a bakery open. Waits in a line two blocks long as Soviet tanks crank closer and she tries not to give in to the fear that grows like a shriek inside her.

Agi was eleven when the Russians invaded Budapest twelve years ago. Their tanks screeched, metal on metal, grinding asphalt and pounding artillery that levelled whole blocks of buildings. Russian soldiers smashed through front doors, kicked over cupboards, and took what they wanted. Five hungry soldiers found Agi and her mother in the cellar. They hauled them both upstairs and four took her mother into a room while one of them, the fat one, touched her hair and talked to her as if she was his pet and made her suck. When the men came out of that room, they made fun of the one who'd stayed so quiet with the little girl. But he just shrugged, took out his still-wet dick, and pissed in the kitchen sink. The soldiers took their last potatoes. They took clothes, her father's watch, an alarm clock, a mechanical toy. They camped out in the house for days, four sharing her mother, while the fat one kept Agi all to himself. Somehow, the soldiers missed little Zsofi, curled up invisible under an old blanket in the cellar and during that whole time Agi kept Zsofi hidden, fed, safe. But now the tanks are back and Zsofi is missing.

Agi waits in line and tries to calm herself by reading the newspapers glued to windows and walls. Every surface on the street is papered with news — the usual newspapers but also other publications, without names, without titles, printed in haste. All these words, all of a sudden. It's a riot of print, hectic and urgent and loud. A man pushes a broadsheet into her hand. Janos Kadar has been appointed First Secretary of the Central Committee, replacing the feared and hated Soviet stooge, Rakosi. While the tanks are still grinding past, the loudspeakers announce: "Hungarians, put out the national flag. Raise the tricolour. Peaceful demonstration, this afternoon in Szabadsag Ter. Let's show them we want an end to the fighting. An independent Hungary." Finally, Agi gets the bread and races home.

When she takes bread in to her mother with a couple of the newspapers, her mother stiffly unpurses her thin lips: "Thank you." So unexpected, that thanks, it feels to Agi almost like love.

The first paper, *Szabad Nep*, announces: "We side with the insurgents!" The second, *Magyar Nemzeti*, the national newspaper, bears a message from the Revolutionary Council of University Students calling on the government to end the fighting, send the Soviet troops home. The third isn't a publication Margit recognizes, just some ordinary person's words, printed by the hundreds as if words were free. "Liberate political prisoners!" it reads. Followed by a list that includes her husband's name. *Miklos Teglas*. It stops the breath in her chest.

She reads it again. Miklos Teglas. And again: Miklos Teglas.

Someone, somewhere, knows that he is still missing, that her husband is gone but that still he has a name. He is absent, but his absence is here noted. Miklos. She puts her finger on the name. She takes it away. She puts her finger on the name, she takes it away. Here you are, she thinks. A blade of hope, a thin nothing of a green of hope wavers inside her. She puts her finger on the name again, and takes it away. Nothing vanishes.

Two hours later, maybe three, the sound of a key fumbling in the lock and Zsofi bangs into the kitchen, a bandolier strung across her chest, a tommy gun in her fist. She looks scared. Filthy. She drops the gun and throws open the cupboard door. She gulps the milk, tears hunks of bread in her teeth as Agi watches. She's crying and eating at the same time. Tears course down her cheeks.

"It was supposed to be a peaceful demonstration," she says, mouth full. "To celebrate the government's change of heart. To persuade them to let us be. There were old people there. Children. Little children."

Agi looks to where she knows her mother sits, on the other side of the closed door, not moving though surely she can hear her daughter's distress.

"The Russians were waving at us, being friendly. They don't want to fight, they were saying. 'We don't want this fight any more than you do.' Some girls climbed up on the tanks. Pretty girls. So pretty, and they were flirting. And then. And then. And then they fired. I don't know who fired first, Agi, the AVO on the rooftops or the Russians. But the tanks were firing and the guns. There must be a hundred dead on that square, Agi. Hundreds, maybe."

Hundreds. But not Zsofi. Not Zsofi. Agi takes her little sister in her arms and rocks her as Margit sits silent in the next room with the newspaper on her lap, finger on her husband's name.

Saturday, October 27

"Radio Free Europe supports the revolution. Britain, America, France — we are with you." All that day, the cars with the loudspeakers cruise the streets. People emerge for food, which they carry back in their net bags, dodging corner to corner, from one safe wall to the next. Implausibly, postmen appear. But everyone knows they're informants, and no one opens their doors to them, not even Mrs. Nemeth.

Zsofi and Agi keep to the kitchen, Margit to the main room. They don't bother keeping the radio on low, but turn it up, to listen to the revolutionary station, the Free Students' Radio, now somehow broadcasting, which calls on everyone to continue the general strike until Soviet troops withdraw.

"Agi. Have you seen Gyula?" Zsofi asks at some point — surprised, as if the question only now occurs to her.

Agi nods, terse. "Yesterday."

Zsofi fidgets. She stands, looks out the window across the courtyard where nothing's happening and the air is grey. "He's staying at the student housing by the Vermezo," she says. "All the revolutionaries are there."

"Oh?"

Zsofi looks everywhere but at her sister. At the clock. At the stove. At the calendar on the wall. "I can't stand it, this waiting around for something to happen."

She's assembling the gear she'd brought with her — gun,

bandolier. She's tying her hair on top of her head in a rough knot. "I can't just stay here, hiding. Not while others are risking their lives."

That is directed at Agi, pointed and harshly adolescent. Where is it coming from? Zsofi gets mean when she feels guilty. She's halfway out the door, this younger sister with her weapons and her blue eyes and her young, untouched skin when Agi thinks it. Just thinks it.

"Where are you going?"

No answer. Zsofi in her sturdy shoes tromps away. Agi follows. Grabs her by the shoulder. "Look at me."

"Don't blame me. You're the one who gave up on him."

They're face to face on the balcony overlooking the courtyard. Everyone in the world can hear. Their mother. Mrs. Nemeth. The postmen informants.

"Says who?"

"Says Gyula. He told me it's over between you."

"What are you talking about?"

"You heard me. It's over because he loves me. Because unlike you I'm not going to desert him."

He what? He *what*?

"How dare you!" Agi shouts.

Zsofi's already turned her back, so Agi lunges for her hair, yanks her back, but the knot comes undone in her hand and Zsofi twists away, races down the stairs ahead of her, hair flying, her ungainly shoes and the gear all clattering. She pulls the gun from her back for speed, reaches the ground floor four steps ahead of Agi. A man is walking through the door from the street toward them. He wears the revolutionary armband: red, white, green. "Now or never," Zsofi greets him. Exuberant.

Alive. He slings his rifle to the front. Aims. A moment of uncertainty—befuddled by Zsofi's beauty, maybe her love-bright happiness—and Agi screams, "AVO."

The burst of gunfire.

A terrible stillness.

Seconds pass before Agi can see what's in front of her.

The man's on the floor, bleeding. The heavy door bangs shut behind the fleeing Zsofi, and Agi sinks to her knees.

Sunday, October 28

The day before, when Agi went back upstairs to tell her mother what happened, Margit collapsed in tears. Agi couldn't remember seeing her mother cry since her father's arrest. She reached a hand out, thinking to comfort her, but Margit pulled away. "Why Zsofi? Why my little girl?"

That night, the entire building gathered as three men dragged the body onto the street. They ripped the tricolour armband from him, and with his own blood they painted on his back: *AVO*. They left the body there for others to hang. All the while, Mrs. Nemeth stayed inside her apartment. She'd been there for days now. How she ate, no one knew. But she wasn't coming out. On her window and across her door, someone had written in large black letters: *Informant*.

Sunday, Agi retreats in humiliation. She can't move her head without thinking of them, the two of them, together. Can't put a hand out in front of her without seeing her sister's on his skin. She only has room in her chest for one feeling, and that is the wrenching degradation of her own replaceability. She has only one desire, and that is to know what happened.

Precisely. In the minutest detail, with nothing left out. Zsofi never lied, but she may have misunderstood. What did Gyula do to make her believe it was love? Did they kiss? Make love? Did he predict Zsofi's body the way he'd predicted hers? Was the substitution so easy?

Then, that afternoon, the unbelievable announcement: "Soviet troops will withdraw from Budapest."

Monday, October 29

There's word that there's chicken at the market, and meat. All exports have been cancelled; the food is needed for Hungary. Margit goes out with a neighbour, big-boned Mrs. Lomax, with whom Margit had hardly spoken before now. She's one of the peasants transferred from the countryside to Budapest at the beginning of the 1950s, and she has never gotten over the shock of it. This morning she knocked firmly at the door to tell Margit and her family about the food. It was a kind of gift — "We know your girl is one of ours." *Ours.* One of our fighters, she means. Margit accepts it, bitter and grateful.

Since the announcement of Soviet withdrawal, the rattle of machine-gun fire has calmed. The corpses of AVO still hang from the lampposts, but as Margit and Mrs. Lomax pass, a group of men starts cutting them down, throwing the stinking bodies into a cart. Garbage litters streets and piles up in empty corners: tins, cinders, paper, broken glass. The women pause together as the tanks roll past back over Margit Hid to Buda. The radio hadn't lied. They really are retreating.

The meat is unlike anything they've seen in Budapest for years. Thick cuts of red meat and plump, young chickens. It takes them nearly three hours to get to the front of the line, and they try not to think it might be gone by the time they get there. It's not. Each hands over the forints, accepts a chicken from the butcher, who grins. A hesitant happiness hovers over everything.

"Maybe it's over," Mrs. Lomax volunteers.

Margit doesn't want to burst her bubble. "Maybe," she says.

Tuesday, October 30

The revolutionaries storm Budapest Communist Party Head-quarters in Koztarsasag Ter. The soldiers in the tanks guarding the headquarters switch sides. They fire at the building. They blast holes in it. The men who hid inside the building emerge. They're shot. More men emerge, one bearing a white flag. They're also shot. Shooting isn't enough. One man has his heart torn out before he's hung upside down from a lamppost. Margit has come, as she has come for years, to drop letters down the grate. She watches from a corner and feels her own heart wrench. It doesn't make the pain better, but it does something, maybe, to even the balance.

"Where are you, Miklos? Where are you?"

The revolutionaries are in the building. Someone shouts that they're battering down into the cellars, into the prisons. *Soon, soon, Miklos. Soon.* But then word from the revolutionaries emerges: "We can't find them."

What?

"There's breakfast for hundreds down there, but no prisoners. We can't find them," one man shouts. "We heard a voice though. The voice said, 'There are one hundred and forty of us down here.' We have to get them out. We have to dig."

Margit pushes past the man who's just dispensed this information, angling toward the turned-round tanks, toward the blasted building, striding over the dead and the nearly dead. And she forces her way through the revolutionaries too. "My husband's down there," she cries. "My husband is imprisoned down there."

A boy and a girl take her, one at each arm, and carry her out. They say, as if they were the grown-ups here: "Don't worry. We'll get him out. We're calling in the engineers."

"But he *is* an engineer."

"Don't worry," they repeat, the pompous children. "We will get him out. But you need to stay out of the way or you'll be hurt."

The fighting is over, really. The building is mostly destroyed and the revolutionaries have taken it, and the communists are dead and the AVO too and many fighters and some innocent of violence entirely, and so Margit fights her way through the shocked and jubilant and fear-drenched crowd and back to the sewer grate and falls to her knees on it, calling down into its deep, deep hole: "Miklos, don't you dare die on me. Don't you dare."

That night, the Soviet tanks withdraw. Columns of them make their way down the broad streets. The ammunition trucks too, long strings of them, puffing gaily as a parade. It's foggy on the Duna, and the tanks are leaving.

Have we won? Margit wonders, Agi wonders, the entire city wonders. Have we *won*?

Wednesday, October 31

Margit's body shut down when they took him from her and she was glad of it. Glad to feel herself drying out, getting lighter, thinner. It was the only way to deal with the blunt, drab wait. Everything was a wait. For food, for pay, for the streetcar. To start work in the morning, to get out at night. A wait at the post office, a wait for the meeting to begin, a wait until it finally ended, a wait until your daughters came home, safe. And underneath the various waitings with others or alone, the waiting for him. The worst waiting of all. Meantime, she didn't look at herself in the mirror, blindly twisted her hair back in the morning for the office work she did well enough. She didn't look down when she peed. She didn't watch the cloth as she bathed.

And yet now, her husband's hand washes her. A miracle. It trembles, but it remembers the round of her belly, the dip of her spine, the crook of her neck.

"It's different now," she says.

"That's okay."

"You can't leave me again."

"I won't."

"How can you promise that?"

"How can I not?"

The problem is he is a good man, mostly, and kind. She is the sharp one, perpetually dissatisfied, mad at life, and the last decade has only whittled her down. Down to this. She is only just past forty, but her knees sticking up in the tub are those of an old woman and the flame that used to lick her belly she'd doused. How can I not? he asked. He doesn't know how scared she's become. Years ago, when they married, she'd wanted dinner parties. She wasn't a frivolous woman and she didn't need riches — she'd shared his politics, after all. She'd *loved* his politics, their honesty and honour. But she also wanted laughs with friends under warm lights, a wedding anniversary every single year. He rubs her right foot, tucks thumb under arch, smoothes her toes straight.

"Do you want to tell me?"

He shakes his head.

Good. She can't bear to know.

Miklos had not been held under Koztarsasag Ter after all, but at Gyujtofoghaz prison. Yesterday, while Margit shouted into a hole, its doors had been flung open and hundreds of political prisoners poured out. A couple of strong young revolutionaries had brought Miklos home. She found him there, when she returned, in front of her door like a parcel.

She had bathed him first. Run the cloth over the burn marks on his arms, the smashed and twisted bones of his engineer's hands. He'd lain back in the tub as she raised one leg to wash, then the other. Legs so thin, they weighed almost nothing. Pulling the cloth between his legs, moving his slack penis from one side to the next, she'd bit the tears back. What right had she to cry? She helped him out of the deep tub and into a clean, warm set of clothes, too big. He lay in bed as she scrubbed the grey scum off the tub. He slept for six hours. When he wakes in the dark, he finds Margit in the bathtub crying silently in inches of water, and he takes the cloth from her hand.

Now the man who sits at the kitchen table fills the small room. Quietly, he thanks his wife for the bowl she puts in front of him. He barely meets his daughter's eyes, abashed before her sudden adulthood. He's skinny. He's lost teeth. The spoon trembles in his hand.

"Jo etvagyat," her mother says, her voice like the spoon.

That morning, when Agi woke up, both her parents were still asleep, arms around each other. She had to find her clothes in the near dark of the shuttered room and dress in the bathroom, jumping on the freezing cold tile, trying not to look at the stinking heap of rags he'd dropped there last night.

Now he turns to her. "Agi, your mother tells me you're a teacher?"

"Yes. Mathematics."

"Good. That's very good."

They hear gunfire and shouting, boots pounding on cracked stone. How can he ask such questions when the world is falling apart?

"Mathematics." He nods. He's run out of things to say, looks to his wife with a helplessness she's never seen before. At the sharp sadness in her eyes, he pulls it in. "Margit, how on earth did you make such a responsible, intelligent woman out of the hooligan I used to know?"

"I had nothing to do with it," says her mother. Her tone ends the conversation. They finish their bread in silence. If anyone's still hungry, no one says so.

Agi dries and stacks the plates. From the other room, the low mumble of her parents' voices. Her mother seems no happier now than when he was gone. There was no rejoicing last night at his return, no signs of joy on her mother's face this morning, only the same tight knot of a forehead. And Agi thinks, Why am I still here? Who am I waiting for?

Thursday, November 1

At 10:00 a.m., Gyula appears at her door. Gyula! For a moment she forgets. And then she remembers. He pulls her out of the apartment, away from her mother, but there's nowhere else to go so he shuts the door behind them and they stand there under the shadow of the balcony above. He holds her hands. Into her ear, he says, "The word from Vecses is that the tanks have turned around. They're pointed back toward Budapest. They've been playing with us, Agi. They're preparing to invade. Almost certainly, and probably very soon."

He's afraid but trying not to show it, acting strong, for her. "The Revolutionary Council is meeting tonight. Everyone needs to make his own decision, whether to stay or get out. You need to go, Agi. Just like you planned. If you go now, you can likely make it through. The borders are still open, you can get to Austria."

She looks at him, her Gyula. He's still *her* Gyula, isn't he? For one instant, she imagines Zsofi has never said what she said. Imagines stepping into his arms, the relief of that letting go because he would hold her just as he used to and everything would be fine. "Did you tell Zsofi that you love her?"

The question takes him by surprise. "What are you talking about?"

"She believes that you love her."

"But that's crazy. She's crazy. Are you listening to me, Agi? There's no time for this. You need to get your things together and go. Today."

"You didn't kiss her? Make love to her?"

"For God's sake, Agi." His hair needs a wash. At least six

grenades hang from his belt. His hands are black from shooting the gun that hangs from his shoulder.

"Zsofi's dramatic, but she doesn't lie. It's one of her weaknesses."

But Gyula lies. He lies all the time. He lied to his father about her; he lied to the school about his ideology; he lied to the police who stopped him coming out of the British Legation; he loves to lie. Did he lie to her? All that time, promising to come with her, pretending that escape was his dream too—was it just another lie? No, looking at him now, here in front of her, she knows that much, at least. He is a sincere man, a true man who feels deeply. Maybe he hadn't lied to her but hadn't chosen her either. When it came down to it, he chose this revolution. That didn't stop her from wanting him. It only made it impossible, and the one thing she will never do is love like that, love grievingly, love for what is not. She knows what that love looks like: it leaves holes inside a person deeper than life, so deep if you fell in you'd never crawl out.

"I love you, Agi. You."

"It doesn't matter anymore," she says, taking a step back.

"Come on, Agi, it was one kiss. In the heat of battle. A moment. That's all. "

One kiss, that's all. Of course it didn't matter, not to him. And it should never have mattered to Zsofi.

"Where's Zsofi now?"

"What did I just say?"

"No, that's not what I meant. I mean, I can't leave without her, Gyula. I have to find her."

"Oh. I don't know for sure. Likely the student housing near the Vermezo."

"Thank you," she says.

He leans in, touches his lips to hers. "My love," he says, and his voice drops right through her. As if nothing has changed. She bristles, he brushes. How can love possibly end? How can it? She wants to hold him so tight. Wants to hold him and never let him go. Wants his arms around her, and his heart, wants his soul, his touch, his breath.

"Agi, I'll come find you. I promise. When all this is over, I'll find you."

Moments later, from behind the closed door, she hears him go.

She makes it across the city in good time, without having to run to avoid shooters or explosions or armed or fleeing crowds. If it's true the tanks have turned, that this is, in fact, the eve of a new invasion, there's no sign of it. Budapest is calm, the air strangely quiet in the aftershock. People rest, bury bodies in parks and empty lots, line up patiently for food, walk at an ordinary pace, greet with an ordinary voice. In the housing by the meadow named Field of Blood for a different battle, she finds students massed, lounging, crowded in, dozing five or six to a room. She walks the hallways, takes it all in. The feeling of it. The youth and the camaraderie. They share cigarettes, food, clothes, ammo, and hope. They huddle for warmth. They dream of a future that will thank them. Of course they shared love. How could they not? They are joined together in this making of new epic stories where love runs ready and hot as blood. But Zsofi is her sister and that is love too.

"Zsofi Teglas?" Agi asks the first group she sees.

Shrugs.

"Zsofi Teglas?" she asks a woman in men's pants, coming out the door of a crowded room.

"Sorry."

Down one hall and up the next, Agi wanders. She has all her forints. She carries food and water in a bag. She wears the only shoes she owns; they'll have to do. On her head, a hat, and under the jacket she's borrowed from her mother a shirt, two sweaters, two skirts. She'd made all her preparations as her parents watched. Her mother's anger was ebbing, finally, running out and drifting around her ankles with the pages and pages of ink-etched paper that she kept letting go. Her father held one hand in the other, listening to the voices of his daughter and his wife and hardly hearing them. "Are you leaving for good, then?" he finally asked, after she had twice explained to her mother the plan, the route, how she would evade the guards at the border, how she would write as soon as she was safe. In Vienna.

"For good," she answered. And she kissed her father's cheek, the cheek of the man who'd once towered over her, but who had never been able to protect either his daughters or his wife.

"Zsofi," she calls.

Her sister lies curled into the arm of another girl the same age. They're dozing fully dressed on a bed, with their shoes still on their feet. She calls again, "Zsofi. Wake up."

Zsofi pulls herself out of sleep, blinking to make sense of the world. "It's me. Come on. Get up."

"What are you doing here?"

"It's time to go."

"Says who?"

"I don't want to fight with you, Zsofi. Please. Just come."

The other girl has woken now too, and three others in the room watch them.

"I'm not going anywhere." Agi knows that tone: stubborn Zsofi, digging her heels in, especially in front of an audience.

"Gyula came to warn me. The tanks have turned around. He thinks the Russians will invade."

Around them, a scuffle, a flurry of questions—"What? Turned around where? Where are they? When?" Zsofi, though, has heard only the first part of what she's said.

"Gyula came to you?"

"To warn me, Zsofi. If we can leave today, now, we can be to the border by tomorrow. It's still open, he says."

"But *he's* not leaving."

"No, Zsofi, he's not. But we can."

"If he's not going, I'm not going."

Zsofi flings her arms in front of her chest. Proud, fearless lover is what she means to project, but what she does project is stupid, foolish, lovesick girl with gritty crumbs of sleep in her eye. Agi steadies her voice, makes it warmer than she feels right now, tries to draw the better, smarter, realistic Zsofi out from behind this face. Like tsking for a kitten, offering plates of warm milk.

"He can join us, Zsofi. He said he'd join us. After. But he wants us to be safe."

"Grow up, Agi. He wants you to be safe; he wants me by his side."

Grow up? Since when…? She buttons the anger. "He doesn't love you, Zsofi. Not the way you think."

"Really? Then why did he make love to me?"

"He *kissed* you, Zsofi."

"Yes, and since then, we've been lovers."

The word sounds obscene, engorged in her sister's mouth.

Zsofi turns to her bedmate: "Isn't that right, Anna?"

"Gyula *adores* her," says the witless child.

Okay, enough. Agi grabs Zsofi's wrist. "You're coming with me."

"Am not." She kicks.

"Yes, you are." Agi drags her half off the bed, but Anna holds tight to Zsofi's other arm.

"She said she's staying!" Anna shouts.

"Zsofi, listen to me. This revolution is over. You have to stop pretending."

"*I'm* pretending, Agi? You wanted him to run away with you, to be your husband. I just wanted him between my legs. Which do you think he chose?"

Her sister gloats, so in love with her posturing, sure of herself, and her murderous beauty, sure that she'll win because she's always been the lucky one, the untouched and protected one, the brave one. So Agi lets go.

The Safe Room

He hears it first, the crack of his own skull against the brick wall, the pain a moment late. Two uniformed men stand in front of him. Just two weeks ago, they would have been the ones in hiding or running for their lives and this shows in their faces—their satisfaction, happy to be on the winning side again. Revolution over, Gyula, too, is once again exactly what he'd always been: a skinny, bookish man with the hands of a pianist, not a fighter. One punch to the gut knocks the air out of him before he can straighten. He crumples forward. Don't go down. The next one smashes into his cheek, and his shoulder lands on frozen ground. The toe of a boot meets his kidneys. The grunt of pain comes from outside him. Who else is being beaten in this stone-cold yard? Christ. He prays. No one to save him. There was never any other ending, and they all know it's only what he deserves. Another kick, this time to the hand protecting his skull. Fingers splinter. He screams. A boot readies itself above his knee. *Zsofi.*

They caught him on Aldas Utca. He heard the rumbling truck behind him, heard it slowing down. His left hand tightened on the satchel he held, meaningless. An older man walking toward him looked decisively innocent, and Gyula restrained his pace, reminding himself that from the back he looked like any comrade on his way to the office. Before leaving the house, he'd shrugged into one of his father's good coats — about three sizes too big, but it was warm and innocuous. At the last minute, he picked up the soft leather briefcase, its handle polished to a dark shine by years of his father's grip. If he'd seen himself in the mirror, he'd have recognized how inept a disguise it was. His unshaven face hovered pale and hollow-eyed above the clownishly large coat. The briefcase dangled, obviously empty of papers, from an ungloved hand. But Gyula hadn't checked the mirror, and now he just kept going because once the choice is made, it's made. No turning back. Maybe they were slowing for someone else — those hurrying, slender women up ahead perhaps, who were also refusing to look over their shoulders. He kept his gaze straight ahead and put one flimsy-soled foot in front of the other. He'd found these shoes a week ago on a dead man, and they were better than the ones he'd worn right out, but not by much. If he had to run, he'd slip. So he wouldn't run. In less than ten metres, he would take a left and let the truck continue on its way down the hill to the city. He counted every step. Perspiration streamed between his shoulder blades. He just had to get to a pharmacy. Or a hospital. Either would do. Zsofi wouldn't even know he'd left. He'd bandage her up. In a few days, they'd be sharing a can of ham by candlelight, and he'd tell her how, seized by fear, he couldn't turn around and all he could think about was his lousy shoes. She'd giggle like she used to.

"You. Halt."

Don't look back. Never look back.

"You." A shot. Gyula dropped his satchel.

He comes to in the back of a rattling canvas-covered army truck crammed full of men like him. His head is on another man's legs. He's not dead. The straining engine, the grind and clatter over broken roads fills his ears. His gaze finds its focus on the face of a boy opposite, no more than twelve years old. Blue eyes stare straight ahead, unseeing, from an unbruised face. He's not dead either. As the truck swerves, bodies shift, a man's elbow lands on Gyula's knee. Again, he loses consciousness.

It didn't occur to him to love her, at first. That seems impossible now, that he might have missed her.

The first time he kissed her, he hadn't meant it like that. It really was a misunderstanding. He climbed out of the tank, his mind swarming with the unimaginable: men with their heads beaten in, men upside down with their hair on fire, men's guts on the sidewalk in front of the store where he used to buy cigarettes, dead men and women and children too. A mind clustered with death. But he was a soldier, a champion. And he pushed himself up out of the tank's belly not victorious but petrified and guilty, and wishing for grace. And there she was, waving both arms in the air like a kid, her hair unbrushed and her smile all joy. *Victory.* She shouted, like he was some hero. And she threw her arms around him and when he kissed her she tasted like onions.

He noticed her in the cafeteria, waiting in line for the boiled potatoes and cabbage.

"Zsofi."

He meant to greet her casually, soldier to soldier, but when she turned, he felt a flutter in his belly and blushed.

"Thank God. Nobody's seen you all day, Gyula."

His tongue twisted. He had no answer. His heart hammering. Could she tell?

Yes. Yes, she could. She grinned now, sure of her power. "You look hungry. I'll let you butt in line if you want."

She came to him that night. The room was freezing cold, and under the covers he was fully dressed. Around them, the slumber, snores, sleep-mumbles of the other revolutionaries. She said nothing as she wrested him first from sleep and then from his clothes. No speaking, no naming, no imagining. No permission. No hesitation. Only a hurry of hands, the scrape of held breath, the fall of smooth hair in his face and her skin was cold, but her mouth so hot.

November 8, when it was clear the revolution was crashing, they hid in a burnt-out building along with six others. They had two nights together there. They found a shell of a room and called it their own. No roof to shelter them from the snow that had only just started falling so they burrowed under old rugs, made a cocoon, heated it with just body and breath. There was nothing more they needed. He fell asleep between her legs; he woke with his cock in her mouth. He licked her, bit her, screwed her. They fucked so hard they bruised. It was happiness so furious and so real it made everything else go away. Then someone warned them and they scrambled out of their perfect home and they ran, hand in hand, back ways that Gyula knew. To the safe room. They should have gone there first. Why hadn't they?

She was hit. He couldn't blame himself for that; it was so random. They were running, there was gunfire. It could have been anyone.

The truck stops. Outside the truck, men call out.

"Good haul?"

"Not bad for a day's work."

Tires screech and the truck's back door clanks open. Cold rushes in. Those who can walk are hustled off. Those who can't are dragged. He forces himself to sit up and, pushing against shoulders and grasping the cold metal of the truck's ribs, cantilevers himself to standing. A hand yanks him from truck to ground. The pain in his knee nearly overtakes him—a dark, dizzying, nauseating wave. *Don't fall.* And he's following the man in front of him across a courtyard, through an ordinary open door that could be anywhere but isn't. His bad leg is a stubborn old dog on a leash. Step, drag. Step, drag. Another door and a stairwell. He steadies himself against the wall to get down the stairs. He's slowing down the line. The man behind him—who?—comes around front and puts Gyula's two arms over his shoulders. One flight and another he descends, half carried on the back of this strong, two-legged soul. *Thank you.* At the turn of each flight, a grey-painted metal door bears a white number: -1, -2, -3. The paint is flaking. Some numbers are partial. But he's not going to die today. He can't die. -5. How deep is this prison? With every level they descend, panic mounts: panic -7, -8.

Agi's mother had always claimed there was a city down here, an insane negative of the world above, where her husband (against all odds) survived. Gyula pitied the woman for her irrational fantasies, pitied Agi for having such a mother. "She just can't bear the truth," he soothed, stroking Agi's cheek.

And yet here he is, dragged and hobbled, being carried deeper and deeper as if captive in someone else's nightmare. They reach an open door, finally, and still draped over this stranger, he proceeds through it: -11. The hallway extends the length of a city block, at least. Door after door after door. Four at a time, men file off. It's a dance, a measured courtly counting without music. A flat-nosed guard is in charge of doors. His keys rattle; locks unlock; locks lock. *Rattle-rattle.* He loves his keys. He hates these men. Cell 1108. You, you. Gyula's new friend dumps him on a thin, uncovered mattress. Two men follow.

"Welcome home, boys."

Keys rattle. Lock locks. "NO."

Gyula tries to push himself off the cot, but his knee buckles. "NO," he screams again, as if he's the only one condemned. As if anyone's listening. "NONONONONO."

"Look at me." The voice is stern, commanding, and in his face. It's the man who carried him. "I am Molnar Dezso, but people call me Gombas. What's your name?"

Gyula swerves, veers, focuses on the face: ugly, deeply cratered, eyes black as a gypsy's.

"*Look.* You're in prison, but you're alive. You hear me? They haven't finished you. Your name," the man repeats, firmly this time.

His name? What does it matter? He dropped it in the sewer, for Chrissake. They were eleven fucking storeys below ground and he'd never get out and if *he* never got out, *Zsofi* would never get out. A scream of terror gathers at the base of his skull, but the ugly face stays put.

"Your name." The man's voice is a rope. It smacks him.

"Gyula." For one, two, three seconds, it's true. "Gyula Farkas." He is in a small, cold concrete cell, with this man and two others. The others stand; they, too, watch him. I am Gyula Farkas, and the world holds steady. I am Gyula Farkas, and the pain in his jaw when he says the words pins body and soul together.

"Good to meet you, Gyula," says Gombas. "We will look after each other in here."

Gyula nods, but he can't breathe. The bare bulb in the ceiling pulses, erratic and accusing: *You took the key, you idiot. You took the goddamn key.*

The first time his father pushed the wine rack aside and unlocked the hidden door was a few months before the revolution. He explained nothing at first, only motioned for Gyula to go first. Gyula still remembers the scurrying underground fear as he dropped to his knees and crawled into the dark. He felt the earth closing in and imagined he could hear the soft sift of dirt falling. And then his father was there beside him with his flashlight. A moment later, his father found the switch and the room lit up. The safe room was square, about eight feet by eight, the ceiling just high enough for Gyula to stand, its four walls lined with rows of wooden shelves stacked upon bricks. The shelves held all kinds of necessities, many of which hadn't been seen in Budapest stores since before the war: canned goods—beans, ham, pickles, peas, peaches, sauerkraut; boxes of candles; stacks of fine white writing paper; rolls of rough grey toilet paper. At the centre of the room, directly below the lightbulb, was a small, cheap table—Gyula recognized it as the one that used to sit on their front porch—and a single chair. At the time, Gyula suspected his father must have his own reasons—smuggling, the most likely one—to create this safe, well-stocked room. He didn't ask. Though his father didn't explain why he'd suddenly decided to share his secret room with Gyula, the reason was pretty clear; Gyula's politics were going to get him in trouble eventually. And Gyula felt a deep, uncomfortable gratitude for this man whose hypocrisy he despised.

His father placed the key in the lock—a habit, obviously.

At the other end of the room was another door. "I was about eight years old when I found the tunnel," his father said, motioning to this second door. "No, not this one. I was on Gellert, running away from bullies. I squeezed myself into a crevice to hide and found myself in what I thought was a cave. I had no idea at the time how extensive, but I came back later with matches and candles." His fingers tapped a can of condensed milk on the shelf, and he looked at that rather than meet his son's gaze. "I spent hours underground, and not once did I see signs of anyone else. No one knows about it, Gyula. It's why I had the house built here. I'm sure there are kilometres upon kilometres of tunnel under these hills. So far, I've found only the one entrance, but there must be more. There must be, or they would have been of no use to them."

"Them?"

"Our ancestors, Gyula. The first Hungarians. The real, true Magyars." He looked to his son now, daring him to contradict or scorn his version of history as he opened the other door, the door to the tunnel. "Where did they go when the Turks invaded? Did you never wonder? They came here. Underground. I think they lived inside these hills, maybe for decades, maybe longer. They preserved our language, our culture, our Christianity."

Gyula expected that the second door from the safe room would open onto a beautiful and vast underground cathedral or a well-scaffolded hall that stretched beyond what he could see. But the door opened onto a narrow passage no more than three feet wide, five feet high where he stood, which dwindled to probably just two feet high.

"Through there, Gyula, right through that hole, a whole network of ancient tunnels. We just have to find the way in."

What was clear to Gyula was that his father was mad, delusional. Kilometres of tunnels? A thousand years old? But, at the same time, perhaps tunnelling in search of tunnels was no more or less insane than what his father did every day, which was to send men to Siberia and then come home to dinner with his family, make love to his wife, help his son with his math homework as if with a clear conscience and whole mind.

His father turned the key in the first door, from safe room to the cellar, and again motioned for Gyula to go first. Once they were back in the cellar that had once seemed so normal, his father placed the key in his hand. It was preposterous: ornate, too big to carry comfortably in a pocket.

"Door locks automatically," his father said. "I keep the key here." And he went to a corner of the cellar, lifted a stone from the wall. At his father's nod, Gyula snugged the key in.

They were on their way to the safe room when she was hit. He couldn't blame himself for that; it was so random. They were running, there was gunfire. But they made it. Yes. They made it to his parents' home, and he found the key in its hiding spot, and he opened the door with it. He lay her down on the floor. He covered her with his jacket. She was shivering. And then he lit a candle and he put a note beside Zsofi's head. *My dearest love, gone to find antiseptic and clean bandages. Don't worry, you're safe here. Try not to move too much. I'll be right back. I promise. xxx.*

Did he put the key in his pocket or had he left it? He checks. It's not in his pocket now, but it could have fallen out. To exit the safe room, he must have used the key to unlock the door. And then? He'd put it in his pocket. Had he? Or did he instead leave it in the inside lock, trusting that by the time he got back, she'd be conscious and open the door for him? He knows he didn't put it back in its hiding spot. He has no memory of that. So he must have left it. He must have. But what if he hadn't?

"Let me out."

Gombas knows who Gyula is, one of the student leaders. Gombas was from the Workers' Revolutionary Council. Before all this, he'd been a mechanic at the Csepel factory; he fixed the machines when they broke. At fifty, he'd never been married likely because of his face. It's how he got the name Gombas—looked like he had mushrooms sprouting on it. No surprise, girls didn't like to kiss it. What a painful time youth had been. But you'd think—at least, Gombas thought—that when he got older, it would be different. Everybody's faces wrinkled and bumped, women included, so he kept hoping maybe even just one woman would look on him and not find him ugly. But for reasons he never entirely understood, it just hadn't worked out that way. Or maybe he just didn't meet enough women. But he wouldn't change places with Gyula right now, not for anything. His girl locked in a cellar on Rozsadomb bleeding to death, that was a hell of a thing for the mind to bear.

He'd had to smack the kid, once, twice—on the cheek that wasn't purple—just to beat back the panic. And then he got the story. He could tell the other two didn't want to know. Both of them looking off into space, like the people sitting next to you on the bus pretending not to hear your wife scolding you. And fair enough. Why take on another man's terror when they each had their own?

"He can't keep shrieking like that," whispers one of them, the handsome one with the full head of shiny hair, Andras. Gyula's asleep, thank God. Some respite.

"If I was him, I'd be shrieking too," murmurs the other one, Pavel.

"Yeah, well, if he keeps it up, he'll get us all in trouble."

"He'll be better tomorrow," Gombas asserts. He might be wrong, but why should he have to listen to a handsome man's worries? And sometimes when you've got no choice but to keep living, you have to just say things like that. You muscle down your irritation, and you do what you can not to make things worse. The bulb in the ceiling goes dark. They could call it night, and it might be.

"I have to talk to the guard."

The lightbulb has only just gone on, and the clanking in the corridor suggests breakfast. Andras shakes his head, looks at Gombas. *What'd I tell you?*

"What do you want to say to the guard?" asks Gombas.

"I was thinking he could get a message out for me."

"Right." Gombas nods, pretending to consider it. "But, Gyula, right now the guard doesn't know who you are, yeah? You call attention to yourself, and he realizes he's got a member of the Revolutionary Council in his range, you'll end up in interrogation. You understand?"

That's a whole other level of terror. Had the kid not even thought about it before now? By the look on his face, apparently not.

Keys rattle. The door opens. A guard—not the flat-nosed one from yesterday but another, this one black-haired but equally plain, young, and blunt (do they all look like they just stepped off the farm?)—shoves two plates at Pavel, who'd stood up to take them, and then two more at Gombas. He closes the door and locks it.

Gyula's shaking, chest heaving, eyes fixed on the door. Gombas watches him.

"Here. This looks like shit, but you need to eat."

Gyula doesn't reply, doesn't move, so Gombas plants himself in front of him, bends down so his face is on a level. "You're okay, Gyula. You're okay. You just need to eat. That's all."

"GUARD."

Jesus Christ.

"Shut. Up," Andras shouts.

Gyula's trying to manoeuvre himself off the bed. The plate lands on the floor. What the hell?

"GUARD."

In one step, Pavel's reaching past Gombas to put a hand over Gyula's mouth. Together, they hold him down on the bed.

"If your girlfriend's still alive, shouting at a guard isn't going to help her."

Gyula bites into Pavel's thumb.

"Christ." Pavel pulls back.

"GUARD."

"For God's sake. Your girlfriend's *dead*, man."

In all the commotion, Andras hasn't moved. He sits on his corner of the cot and tosses his comment over top of Gombas and Pavel. He ignores the looks from Pavel and Gombas, focuses only on Gyula, who stares, uncomprehending.

"I'm sorry, but if she was bleeding, there's no way."

"She's not. She has food, water. I bound her wound."

The thing is, Andras thinks, the others are here because they were deluded into believing they could change the world, or change the Russians, which is all the same thing. He, on the other hand, is here for a totally different but equally stupid reason. He'd been at the border, almost across, and then at the very last minute he'd stopped. It was night. He crouched in a line at the edge of the woods with five others, waiting for a cloud to cover the moon. Across that field was Austria and freedom and a new life. Behind him was his world, everything he knew, his professional reputation, his nice-enough apartment, his local csarda, his language — every nuance of which he felt in the very creases of his soul. Across that field, he'd be nobody. Or he'd be shot. So that was it. When the others dove forward, blind and hopeful, racing over clotted frozen ground for their uncertain prize, he'd stayed put. And when the field lit up bright and sudden in the white glare of headlights, five dark figures dropped one after the other mid-flight, but not him. For him, instead, this ending: a single shit-bucket between four men. These three were willing to be deluded. He wasn't. He never had been. It takes courage to tell the truth sometimes. Even if it wasn't true, it was better this way. Better to think she was dead than to think of her dying.

The kid's still staring at him, half out of his mind. "She's not dead. She's not dead."

"I'm sure she's fine," Gombas soothes. "Food, water, and air, all a human needs to live, right? She's alive and for now, there's nothing you can do except keep your strength up. You can't let her down, right? So just sit, have a little bite of bread, that's right. Just a little."

He doesn't eat, but eventually he stops shaking. He turns so he's facing the wall, wraps arms around his head, and tries not to see the pictures that swarm when he closes his eyes.

There are too many hours in a day under a bare lightbulb in a room not big enough. They take turns walking the *T* formed by the two beds, hitting the wall and turning back. Gombas and Pavel talk about their ordinary, pre-revolutionary lives. They don't discuss Gyula. Pavel was a gym teacher, it turns out. So that explains why he's so fit, still, at forty-three. They don't invite Andras to take part in their conversation, and he doesn't try to join.

Andras takes his turn walking, then tries jumping jacks at the foot of the beds—just enough room. When he's done, Pavel stretches his body between the beds and does one hundred and seventy-five pushups, huffing his count. Gombas follows suit but only makes it to sixty.

They try not to listen to Gyula, who mutters, incants, rocks. Which version of the safe room was he in—Zsofi dead or Zsofi alive? As long as he doesn't know for sure which version is real, each is equally possible.

. . .

The flat-nosed guard opens the door. "Good day, boys. It's bucket time. Who wants shit duty?"

Gombas volunteers. A chance to stretch his legs.

He gets back. The bulb goes off. Night. Only one meal per day in here, apparently. What if they are forgotten? What if the Americans come and bomb the shit out of the Russians, and no one knows they're here? Stop thinking, Gombas tells himself.

Andras imagines food. Warm, crusty bread. Red, spicy goulash so rich the oil pools on the surface. Tiny, luscious pieces of beef. The meal he should have had the day he was arrested—Tanya always had a handle on black-market meat. That woman was worth everything he gave her. Don't think about her. Don't think about tits, ass, cleaving her. Don't think.

Pavel pictures the place on the ceiling where the lightbulb was. Eventually, it will come on again. Until then, he'll fill that invisibility with some other gaze—God's maybe. God. Really? Well, if you're going to find religion, this would be the place to do it.

Bulb goes on. Day Three. A black-haired guard comes. Gyula doesn't stir. The guard leaves. The three men look at each other. Pavel shrugs. They eat what they've got. Gombas tries to get Gyula to eat his. When he refuses, they divvy up what's on his plate.

Hours pass. Maybe. No one has a watch. The arresting officers took them. They take turns on the floor—pushups, walking, jumping jacks. Pavel does situps on the cot. The shit bucket stinks, but no guard comes.

Gyula finally stops knocking his head against the wall and

rolls over onto his back. He pushes himself to sitting, then tries to lever himself off the bed. His leg is huge, ballooned. He stiffens against the pain. "Gombas? Bring me the bucket."

Andras pretends not to see as Gombas puts the bucket in place, then helps Gyula to stand. It takes both Pavel and Gombas to suspend him over the bucket from the armpits. When he's done, they help him with his pants and ease him back onto the bed.

"Can I take a look?" asks Pavel, gesturing to the leg.

In his years as a gym teacher, Pavel had knocked displaced shoulders back into place, bound sprained ankles and wrists, splinted bones, and in the last few weeks, he'd helped out at the hospital. He learned a few things there: how to drain a wound, how to pincer a bullet out of muscle, how to hold a man to the table when there was no anesthetic to do the job. He took Gyula's lack of response as a yes.

Pavel puts a hand on the ankle first, then feels his way gently up, eyes on Gyula's face. When his fingers reach the knee, Gyula arches away.

"Good thing you don't have to go anywhere on that. Your kneecap's popped right out. I can't tell if anything's shattered in there, but I can at least push the patella back in for you. You can't heal with it like this."

Pavel has seen this look often over the last three weeks, this transfiguring fear as the whole person tries to retract from the body, from sensation, scuttling backward, inward, nowhere to go. The injured hated him in that moment, even if he was trying to do them good. They hate you, and then they feel better and they love you and their gratitude is deep.

"No," said Gyula. "Leave it. I'm fine."

Pavel's right hand rests just below the knee and he nods, affable, teacherly, understanding.

"Well, all right then. Whatever you say." He leans over, as though to push himself up. He doesn't look away from Gyula's eyes, not once. Left hand chops down as the right yanks the leg straight.

A Scream.

Zsofi wakes, takes the key from the table where he'd left it, unlocks the door, and walks out into bright day. She hobbles a bit, favouring her injured leg, but she'll go home to her mother, who will bandage her, feed her, hide her.

Zsofi finds the key where it's fallen from the table and unlocks the door and crawls through it and up the stairs, and she leaves the house, and in the garden she stops for a rest. A passerby sees her, takes pity on her, washes her, clothes her, bandages her wound, feeds her, and then calls the police. Zsofi, you can't assume everyone's on your side. For two weeks, all of Hungary was with you, felt your fervour, marched, and fought beside you shoulder to shoulder. But that's over now and everybody has to pick a side eventually.

Zsofi wakes and there is no key. Her leg is festering. She's feverish, and those blue eyes flash with terror. Gyula? Why did you bury me, Gyula?

Morning and the flat-nosed guard comes with breakfast. He has no name that anyone knows. He's square-faced, straw-haired, dull-eyed.

"How you doing today, boys? Holding up okay?"

Gombas and Pavel play along. "What's on the menu? No, don't tell me. Surprise soup?"

"How did you guess? Chef's special."

"Excuse me, guard. My girlfriend is locked in the cellar of my parents' house, 34 Verhalom, Rozsadomb. If you get her out, I promise, the house is yours."

Three prisoners bow heads to plates, pretending to have no interest in the answer. They swallow the watery soup, the rotting vegetables. The guard pauses. The dense, spicy sausage smell of his breath fills the cell. His uniform is rumpled and his hair greasy, but in the guard's dull eyes, Gyula sees the bright feather-flash of a bluebird in a tussled green tree. He *wants* what Gyula promises. Who wouldn't? He likely lives in a shared apartment in a dirty, narrow part of Pest, likely shares a bathroom with five others, likely hates this life.

"You think I'm stupid?" says the guard finally.

The door clangs shut. Keys rattle. Lock locks.

As soon as the guard's gone, Gombas dashes for the bucket. Explosive, spattering release. Hot and rich, the stench rises moistly, smothering. If he could have held it in, he would have, but when nature calls…It's the food they give them. Rancid fat, onions starting to turn. God, they'd suffocate in here. Another explosion. Spatter.

"Sorry about this," he mutters. How could he *not* apologize? Even if apologizing forced him to own this stinking failure of the body. Better to apologize than to feel only how utterly, unredeemably disgusting he is. Apology at least is manly. Is the social part of man. Another cramp. Please, God, let it be the last. Let this pass. Let him stand, put a lid on it, and move away from the mess he's made.

Andras and Pavel put sleeves to nose, breathing through mouths.

"Are you an idiot?" says Andras through his sleeve. "You're a prisoner and an enemy of the state. Even if you ever owned that house, you don't anymore. You think a guard wouldn't figure that out?"

Fuckyou.

"What's more, he could report you for trying to bribe him. And if he even believes you, he could take your information to the AVO, get Zsofi arrested."

Fuckyou. Fuckyou. Fuckyou.

Next morning, flat-nosed guard is back. "How you doing today, boys? Holding up okay?"

Gombas and Pavel play along. "What's on the menu? No, don't tell me. Surprise soup?"

"How did you guess? Chef's special."

"I have information on a very valuable enemy of the state," Gyula breaks in.

This was a good plan. A much better plan. Thank you, Andras.

The happy guard swivels his bland, imperturbable face toward Gyula. Good cheer hovers, stranded.

"She murdered an AVO, and I can tell you where she's hiding."

"Okay." Affable. Not insulting. Not anything.

"What do you mean 'okay'? Do you want it or no?"

"Sure. Sure, I want the information."

"Her name is Zsofi Teglas. She's at 34 Verhalom, Rozsa-domb. There's a safe room off the cellar."

"Thanks for the tip," says happy guard and turns to go.

"So are you going to arrest her?"

"I'm a guard, not police."

"But you're not listening. You could *use* this information."

"No. *You* listen to *me*. I'm just doing my job here, and trying not to be an asshole."

"But you *are* an asshole. By definition you are an asshole: you're a fucking prison guard." Gyula's shouting.

Good cheer is gone. Vanished. Never existed.

One step, two. The guard grabs the bucket, in one move overturns it on Gyula's head. Yesterday's shit runs down Gyula's face. It catches in his eyelashes and ears, on his unshaven cheek.

"By definition," says the guard. He's not laughing.

Gombas strips Gyula's shirt off and uses it to mop the boy dry as best he can. Shit smears, stinks. He gets him to drop his head over the side of the bed and pours what's left of the day's drinking water over his hair. With his fingers, he combs out the clots. Throughout, Gyula shakes, teeth chattering. It's cold in here, but it's not the cold that's doing this. No one speaks. Even Andras keeps his mouth shut.

When he's as clean as he's going to get, Gombas helps Gyula's legs up onto the bed and Gyula curls as best he can around himself, pulls Gombas's coat over his head. The coat is months of woolly sweat, a hole in the earth, an armpit. If he bites his lip hard enough, he can taste his own blood: salt and safety, a hurt that can't hurt him.

. . .

He wrote the note. Pen scratched over paper. He put it by her head, at first, where she'd see it when she opened her eyes. But no, that's not good enough. He folded the paper. He put it in her hand so she would feel it even before opening her eyes. And he turned the key in the lock to open the door. Yes, he can get this far, to the turn of the preposterously heavy key, the tumble of the lock, the pressure of hurry, in his chest, the fear. She looked so pale. The hurry, the hurry. Have to get something for that wound, maybe find a doctor, maybe find someone, someone to help him. Go upstairs. It still smells. Don't look into the living room where the bodies of his parents remain where they'd fallen, killed by the revolution. Don't look. Get a coat from the closet. Disguise. Hurry.

Don't forget the key, Gyula. Don't forget the key.

Where did he leave it? Why had he not put it, with the letter, heavy and reassuring, in his lover's hand? Why could he not remember?

He must have dozed off. He wakes coughing. Gombas is at his side, offering him water. He props himself up on his elbow to take it. It must be night because the light is off. The water is good. He slurps, loses some down his cheek. He stops coughing, but sleep is gone. How many minutes until the sun gets turned on?

Now. Sun is on. Gyula doesn't eat his breakfast. He doesn't sit up. He lies, facing the wall, shaking.

"If he doesn't want it, we should share it," says Andras.

It's all Gombas can do not to get up and stomp his heel right into that shiny, arrogant face. "He'll eat it."

The prisoners have lost their appetite for conversation. They take turns doing their jumping jacks, pushups, situps. The cell reeks of their sweat, but then as soon as they sit down, they're cold again. Gyula coughs.

He better not be getting sick, is what they're all thinking. One man gets sick, we all go down.

He coughs again.

It doesn't sound too bad. Could be just a cold.

Pavel does some marching on the spot, knees lifting, feet stamping. Andras does more pushups so he doesn't have to look at their faces.

The cough hurts Gyula's lungs and the convulsion makes everything else hurt. When he tries not to cough, he only coughs harder.

The day turns off. Gyula hacks and hacks. The bed shakes. Gyula's body is so hot in the middle of the night that Gombas dreams of firesides.

The bulb sizzles. Morning.

Flat-nosed guard delivers breakfast. Casts one look at Gyula, huddled under Gombas's coat. Says nothing.

The man's obviously ashamed, as he should be. False cheer is gone. Can't meet anyone's eyes. That's not good. An ashamed man is dangerous, mean, cornered. You have to be nice, nudge him back into humanity. And so Gombas says, amicably, "Got a bit of an attitude, this kid."

"You're telling me."

From under the coat, Gyula hacks and hacks. His skinny form shakes the bed.

"It's okay. He'll learn."

Gombas doesn't even try to get Gyula to eat. The three men share the boy's food without saying a word about it. Have they given up on him? Given up carrying him? They listen to his coughs and they spoon the foul stuff into their mouths, and they go on.

He takes the key from the lock in the door. He feels its weight in his palm, which is stiff with her drying blood. He had managed to staunch the flow with the tourniquet. Thank God he'd learned that trick. Well, thank you, Russians, for youth camp. He has the key in his hand. He looks down. He's wearing the same coat he's worn for the three weeks of revolution and it shows: one arm shredded from when he squeezed through a hole in the wall, the buttons gone, bloodstain on the front where a dying man had landed on him. He covers her with this coat because she's shivering. Find a new coat. Borrow your father's coat. Go upstairs. Go upstairs, though you know what you'll find because the revolutionaries who shot your parents were so proud of themselves when they returned to the dorm that night. They'd killed a true Stalinist. How could he be responsible for that?

He put his coat over Zsofi. He knows this. But was the key in the pocket of that coat? He has no memory of putting it back in its hiding place. No memory of walking up the stairs. He saw his mother's stockinged legs, at odd angles as if she'd fallen from a run. The soles of her crocheted slippers looked tatty. He remembers his mother's slippers but *not* where he put the key?

He coughs.

He's so deep inside his memory, he almost misses it: a

responding cough. And not from inside the cell, not a manly cough. No. Definitely a woman's cough.

He holds his breath. Has he lost his mind? Is he delusional? Is he still here? Still real? His body still reeks, still hurts. So yes, he's here. A moment later, he coughs again. And this time there's no question: the other cough is in answer to his. So he coughs twice. In reply: two coughs. The same timing. Cough-pause-cough from the other side of that door.

He tries it again: cough-cough-pause-cough.

In response: cough-cough-pause-cough.

He sits up. Gombas's jacket falls from his shoulders. Clumsily, he levers himself off the bed, using Pavel's shoulder as balance. He presses himself against the door.

Zsofi.

When he sees the flat-nosed guard the next morning, Gyula says nothing. Maybe Zsofi was here because the guard did file a report. Maybe it is coincidence. He isn't willing to bet either way just yet and he has no inclination to be grateful.

Time is now divided, split into two halves: pre- and post-cough. Day of first cough is Day One. Every night after that, he goes to sleep with a feeling of anticipation he hasn't felt since the days when he used to run to Agi on Margit Island. Eventually, another cough will come. Isn't it marvellous that day comes after a night, even in here? And the door, when you look at it, is only a door. And this room provides enough space, after all, for four men to live. The lightbulb glares down. The slops arrive. It's all evidence, of a sort, that there is a world out there. If there were no outside, there would be no electricity, no food. On the other side of that door are more prisoners.

Food is made and carried and cigarettes are smoked and Zsofi carries her shit bucket to the latrine to empty. And if there's an outside—which, without direct sensory evidence you just have to believe in—then why couldn't Zsofi be part of that outside?

So when he wakes, he does his best to tidy himself. He combs his hair with his fingers. He spits into his shirttail and rubs at his face. As if she's going to notice. This is not a date, but it feels like it. He almost laughs at himself. He brushes his teeth with his index finger. He pisses and he's ready. He would put all his love into this cough, all his longing, his devotion, the memory of their sex.

Gyula stands by the door like a suitor: hands behind his back, eyes facing the door as if he can see through it. Of course, there's no knowing if it's Zsofi. It could be someone else, but somehow he's certain. He just knows, the way a lover knows. When he hears the guard's keys, and Zsofi's approaching step, as he concentrates on the metal door, it's as if he can see her. There she is, beautiful despite everything. Should he cough first or wait for her? He is the suitor. Of course he should go first. He breathes in. Holds it. When she's right in front of him—yes, he *can* see her—he coughs. And in quick return, two short coughs. Two.

He grips his palms before him as though in prayer. She's understood. And she still loves him.

But wait. It's not over. After she empties her bucket, she'll come back. He counts the seconds to the return of her step, the guard's jangling. This time she should be the first. Will she know this?

Aha. She does. He nearly slaps the door in sheer glee. But no, Gyula, contain yourself. Don't give her away. Cough sweetly, so that only she can hear. Zsofi was never one for self-restraint, but now they will both be careful because this is too thin a thread to yank.

Under the pads of his fingers, unbudging cold metal. He is a man. It is a door. The other side of it, the woman he loves moves away.

Stay, stay, fragile happiness. Don't leave me. Not just yet.

How will he bear a whole day, or two, or three, or four without her? Or, how can he do anything other than bear it? How could they live like this, so close and yet unable to talk or touch, or look? A love expressed in phlegm: is this it? Is this to be their lot? But better than what he feared. Oh yes, better by a trillion times than what he feared.

Gyula tries to hold on to joy, tries with his clumsy broken fingers not to crush it, to palpate it gently, to keep it for himself.

Gombas watches this spidery young man clinging to the door, coughing tenderly as a poem.

None of them interferes.

If he wants to believe that his lover is here, just the other side of that door, and that she has chosen to contact him in a Morse code of coughs, let him. Why couldn't it be true? It is about as plausible as anything else these days — plausible as revolution, as public burnings on Andrassy Ut, as being locked in here. Sure. Why not? And true or not, it keeps him quiet. The racking cough is gone. He is sleeping through the night. He's stopped making trouble with the guard. Yes, this is fine.

Three days, and then a cough. Fifteen minutes, another cough. Then a day, a day, a day, Zsofi day. No other days have names.

. . .

A cough. Return cough. A cough. Return sneeze.

It makes him laugh. Variety: the spice of love.

Another day. He humbly waits. He prays, even. What's the point of atheism when you're locked in a room? It becomes as ludicrous as belief.

From the other side, a cough. Pause. Two coughs.

My love. He presses palms and forehead to the door. She's there. Inches away.

"What makes you so sure it's her?" asks Andras.

Gombas and Pavel glare, but really, aren't they wondering the same thing? How is it possible that a man can be persuaded by a cough? More than that, how can he be *happy*?

Gyula goes back to his spot on the bed. It's getting easier to move. Bit by bit, the pain in his knee is receding. That's love's effect. One day, scientists will prove that men in love fare better in battle because their love protects them. It makes them stronger and fills them with hope.

"I just know."

Andras scratches his beard. He hates facial hair, itchy and animal.

"Why don't you ask the guard?"

Ask the *guard*? Open his mouth, his heart, to the guard?

Clearly, Andras is just trying to get a rise out of him. For what? Entertainment? Well, it won't work.

"I mean, honestly, for all you know you're coughing at an old, axe-faced peasant. You must want to know. I mean, *really* know."

"Leave him alone, Andras," Pavel cautions.

"You should get him to open up the door when she coughs.

And then you could lay eyes on her again. Don't you want to *see* her?"

Gyula lies down, turns his back on Andras. He knows it's her. She's alive, and for now that's enough.

Days without a cough. More days than usual. Is she sick? Has there been an accident? Gyula tries to pace, but the others stop him. "There's no room," says Pavel. "Do some situps or something." But he's so worried and his worry chases him like slavering dog and yet there's nowhere to go.

And then, finally, after ten days, he hears the guard's clomping boots and, beside them, the girlish steps. And then, three loud hard coughs, one after the other: COUGHCOUGH-COUGH.

Gyula starts up, hugely grinning, but before he can reply, Andras starts banging.

"Guard. Guard, open up. We have an emergency in here."

"What's going on in there?" A hurried jangle of keys.

"No." Gyula leaps. He lands on Andras, smacks his head *slam* into the edge of the door as it is thrust in. His body goes slack so suddenly.

Zsofi, it wasn't you. Another girl, your age, blue-eyed, like you, staring at me the way I stared at her. Each of us the death of the other's hope. I wanted to die. It is too hard, this pain. I didn't mean to leave you. Please don't be scared, Zsofi. I'll make it right.

I might be a prisoner, but I'm an engineer and if I can't build up, I'll build down. You remember how buildings reflect in the Duna? If you look at it from the bridge, it's like there's a whole world down there, upside down. When I was little, I imagined living in the Duna. Shimmering windows open into watery rooms. Stairs spiral deeper and deeper, but nothing goes wrong and no one ever falls.

I'll make a city like that.

No. That's a child's dream and we're not children anymore, are we? Why gild when there is no sun? They don't turn the light on for me anymore. Murderers don't get light, they say. I tell them I don't need it. My name is Gombas now. Like a mushroom, a fungus, I thrive in the dark and some days the difference between dead and buried is inconsequential. I've got nothing to draw with so I'll do the calculations in my head. I'll make our tunnels safe. I'll calculate the weight the walls have to bear; I'll support the ceilings with steel beams. I'll dig to you, Zsofika, and under Budapest, we'll be free.

Brothers

Let's be clear about this. Csaba doesn't have a lot of great ideas.
Doesn't have many ideas, period, but he's good at weaselling
out of things. Something you learn as the younger child of
two, I think, as the younger, less intelligent, and less attractive
brother. He can talk his way out of pretty much anything,
and I guess that takes some smarts. Ever since we were kids,
whatever trouble we got into, it's always been my fault, not
Csaba's, because he's too little and too dumb. Too much of a
follower. And sure, most of the time this was true. Whatever
we did, it was always my idea. That's what I'm saying. I'm the
idea guy. He's the "not my fault" guy. But I'm not worried. Not
yet. I'm still smarter. I think faster, wider, longer. The difference
is ambition. You have to know what you want in life and then
go out and get it. Me, I always wanted a big car, big house, a
beautiful wife, and maybe a fling or two on the side. So that's
what I got. Wasn't all that hard. You'd expect it would have
been harder, the way everyone walks around, not getting any
luck for themselves. Decide what you want, then take it. That's
my advice. For free.

Which is exactly what I was doing walking along Andrassy at 4:30 a.m.: going after what I wanted. And what I wanted at that exact moment was to be a long way away from Csaba's friend Janos and the dudes who were about to seriously mess him up. And sure, I was smoking a fat spliff that Janos kindly left in his coat, but given I left all my fucking cash in the coat *he*'s wearing, fair's fair, right? So that's what I was doing—that's all I was doing—when the fucking cop car pulled up beside me and asked me if I knew Csaba Bekes. Do I know him? He's my brother. And what do you care?

But Csaba's like an idiot savant when it comes to getting out of shit. Like I said, guy can talk his way out of pretty much anything because he doesn't *look* smart enough to lie well. People underestimate him. Maybe I underestimated him. Because suddenly, Csaba has his one great idea. First idea he's ever had in his life. To give him credit, it's a pretty good one. This is what I'm thinking as I sit here, in this interrogation room, getting interrogated by a cop who doesn't look tough at all. Looks like a math teacher. Maybe he's a smart cop, but don't worry, I'm smarter. So let's go:

INTERROGATION, *Scene One.*

"Well, my brother's lying." (That's me: bored, belligerent.)

"Is he? Why would he do that?"

"Sibling rivalry? How the hell should I know? For God's sake, he's the fuck-up, not me. I'm a businessman, I run my own company—what the fuck would I be doing beating on a gypsy in the middle of the night?"

"The thing is, though, Mr. Bekes, we have two witnesses

who saw you and your brother running from the scene of the crime, and your running shoes show blood on the soles and we think if we test it, we'll find the blood is from Mr. Zoltan Kolompar, who died of internal bleeding—but you may know this already—at approximately 1:00 a.m. this morning."

"Well, the shoes aren't mine."

"Ah."

"They belong to a friend of my brother's."

"And I suppose he killed Kolompar, then persuaded you to wear his bloody sneakers because, what, you needed an image makeover?"

"Where's my lawyer?"

That's a short one because of course I have to talk to my lawyer. I know how this works. I tell my lawyer how it's going to go. He takes lots of notes. He corrects my story where he has to, where it's going to get me into too much trouble. He says things like, "Will your wife corroborate that?" and "Did you speak to anyone at the club? Anyone who can vouch that you were there?" and then he says, "We can work with that. You ready?"

You bet I am.

INTERROGATION, *Scene Two.*

In the room, me, my lawyer, Detective Rev, and Detective Roth.

"I'm telling you, it wasn't me. It was Csaba and his best friend Janos. All this"—I waft my hands top to bottom, from the poser hat to the really-not-my-style Maple Leafs bomber—"and the shoes. They're his. Do I look like a hockey fan to you?"

Detective Roth interrupts too fast. "So you're saying Janos

and Csaba committed a murder, then Janos, what, calls you up? Calls you up and says, 'Laci, can I give you my clothes,' and you say, 'Hurray. Tradesies.' Is that what you're telling me?"

"No. That's not what I'm saying, but if you'll listen to me for a moment, I'll explain. It's rather complicated." (I know I'm being pedantic and arrogant. It's on purpose. Makes people mad. I also know the word *pedantic*, which is more than you can say for most dudes in construction.)

"We'll try to keep up," says Detective Rev.

He's the smart one. I can see that he knows how to be wry and unperturbed. That's fine, let him. Because he's going to have to listen to me for as long as I want to talk—and believe me, I'm in no rush—and my story will exculpate me from this bullshit pile of evidence. Which I have to agree looks bad. Never mind the shoes don't fit. If it can help them frame Laci Bekes, they'll make them fit. In addition to the aforementioned witness report, they also have my brother and his idiot friend (in hockey bomber and shoes) at the bank machine near Margit Hid. They have a drug dealer willing to testify he sold me dope. They've got Csaba's phone in the dead gyp's pocket, and then they've got Csaba himself swearing up and down that I did it. Me. His brother. Murder a fucking Rom? Like I've got time for that. But that's all right. I know the truth of it and I've got my story.

I give my lawyer a look. He nods. That's for show. We've been working together a lot of years, Mr. Teleki and me. And he has just given me the one piece of information that will exculpate me, veritably. And when I'm finished here, I'll start on feeling bad about the events I put in motion, as they say, but for now I'm thinking if you got 'em, smoke 'em.

Rev clicks the tape recorder. Get your head straight, Laci. Get your face on. This is one deep pile of shit to get through.

"It started yesterday. Well, no, before that. A few weeks ago I bought this beautiful piece of property up on Rozsadomb. Gorgeous. View of the Duna, Margit Island, Kispest. Floors are fine, inlaid parquet, French doors open out onto curved balconies—I love those—and it's got this wide entrance, sweeping staircase. Elegant, you know, real old Magyar elegance. Trees in the back look five hundred years old. It was a deal."

Detective Rev gives the other detective a look. Yeah, they're thinking. A Laci Bekes kind of deal. Let them think what they want; no charge has ever stuck. They want to say, Get to the point, but they won't. One, because they figure they've got me. Two, because they figure they've got me. They're wrong both times, but they don't know that, and I've got Gombas after me, so, believe me, I'm in no rush.

"So I was in my new house, and I decided the one thing it was missing was a wine cellar. I mean, what kind of self-respecting Magyar doesn't want a cellar full of wine? There was a cellar, of course, but old style. Mud floor. Stone walls. You can't store wine down there, not the valuable stuff, not the stuff you want to keep. Last owners used it for preserves. Shelves and shelves of peaches in syrup, sauerkraut, pickles. Like you can't just go to the market and buy that stuff now? Peasants. Whatever.

"I hired a guy who specializes in wine cellars. There's an art to it, turns out. You have to know all this stuff about temperature and humidity regulation, and condensation and insulation, and it's more complicated than you'd think. You don't want anyone but an expert designing for your wines, trust me. So we go down to the cellar together to take a look around and he figures out what we'd have to do to support the structure, and by this time I can see my bill is mounting, but I love wine and I got a veritable collection of the stuff so I give him carte blanche. Go ahead. Do what you have to do. Just make it elegant.

"First day into it, they're pulling all the old shelves off the walls. Foundation's brick, right. Have to waterproof the shit out of it. So they're on the last wall and what do you know? Behind all that shelving, there's a door. A metal fucking door straight into the earth. They stop work. They call me up. I'm at a job site, just outside the city. What do I want them to do? What do you think I want them to do? Blow it.

"Metaphorically, I meant. I mean you can't blow up a door in the foundation, you risk jeopardizing the future stability of the entire edifice. No, I mean torch it. Do what you have to do. Get it open. Because you never know, do you, what those old communists hid in their basements. House used to belong to Farkas."

Aha. That got their attention.

"Not Gyula, his father. That old boy's picture's in the hall of shame at that new museum, the Terror House. You probably knew that, though. So I'm thinking maybe the old boy hid some Russian guns down there or something. Maybe he's got some 'liberated' art. I mean, a secret door to a secret room? I was dreaming all kinds of shit. Shit that'd make me rich. Fuck the job site, I took the fast way home. Got there about an hour later, and the boys had the door off already. The room behind it was about ten by ten. Brick walls. Shelves on every wall but most were empty. Obviously someone had lived down there for a time. In one corner, empty cans of all kinds of German shit from before the war: sauerkraut and pickles and ham and fruit. You get the picture. But the weirdest thing, another door. But this one wasn't metal. It was wood, and it was open, off its hinges, earth spilling out of it. Looked like a cave-in. The rubble had half knocked over a table, pushed it into the corner. Creepy. I got shivers. Backed right out of there, the other guy too. Except something caught my eye. Under the cobwebs and dust, on the ground by the overturned table, something that looked like a scroll.

"Now, I've read the fairy tales same as you have, Mr. Rev— sorry, *Detective* Rev—and you know there's always warnings about what you find in a place you shouldn't be. But I took the scroll. I mean, who wouldn't?"

Rev is getting edgy. He thinks I'm spinning this out too long. He's got dinner waiting at home, maybe a hot wife. No. Not likely. Maybe an ordinary wife, then. Or a dog that needs walking. Well, that's your problem, detective. You're the one who took me in. You might as well just sit back and enjoy.

"Keep going, Mr. Bekes."

I was taking a long drink of water. But, okay, I put the cup back on the table.

"Okay, it wasn't a scroll. It was a five-page letter, rolled up, tied with a ribbon. I untied that ribbon. I unscrolled that letter on the table in that creepy room. First thing I see: dated November 10, 1956. Next thing I see, 'Dear Gyula.'"

The detectives are thinking I'm full of shit. Rev gives me a pretty decent sardonic, I'm-humouring-you kind of look. Do they teach these things at cop college? Amazing.

"And I suppose you have that letter, Mr. Bekes? You can produce that letter?"

"I wish I could. Yes. I wish I could. It would certainly make my story more persuasive, but you have gone directly to the root of the matter. The letter is the veritable issue at stake.

"I read the letter. It was sentimental crap, teenaged love — When you first kissed me, I knew it was real — that kind of thing. Some predictable complaints about living in someone's cellar, on and on about someone named Agi, and do you love her, Gyula, or do you love me? Did you go to her and leave me here? When will you come back, and kiss me again... Love, your Zsofika. You get the picture. Well, you and I both know Gyula Farkas was one of our heroes of the revolution, and this was his father's house, so obviously it was his letter and just as obviously, I figured, it would be only right to let the man know what I found."

"And this letter written more than fifty years ago magically clears you of murder?" This is from Detective Roth, and Rev visibly stiffens, irritated with his less subtle colleague who thinks he's funny when he's bullying. My lawyer's just staying out of it. Nothing ever shows on that guy's face. Same face, no matter what. Useful for his profession, but I wonder if it changes when his wife is blowing him. Probably not. A little "umph" and that's it, is what I think. Umph and then ah. And then, thank you, my dear.

I see no reason to give them the whole background — I'm a modest guy, why flash my tits, right? — so I tell them, "Gyula 'Gombas' Farkas. Can you believe it? I'd been trying to get a meeting with him for months, but no way am I in his league and no way is he doing me any favours. So I sent him an email. I told him about the cellar, and the five-page letter I'd found there—to him from Zsofika. Within the hour—within the fucking hour, boys—I get a call. It's Farkas. He wants the letter and not only that, he's coming over to my house to get it. Tonight. Nine p.m. It's now two p.m. So I say, 'Of course, Mr. Farkas.'

"And I figure Farkas knows I'm angling for his favour. He knows it, but he wants the letter. I figured he'd want it, but he *really* wants it. Wants it so bad he's willing to come to my house, so bad it won't wait until morning. I will be honest with you now. I will tell you what I was thinking. I was thinking Gyula Farkas is going to be grateful to Laci Bekes. He's going to be grateful and munificent and all I had to do was the decent thing."

If Rev is smart, he might have a question or two about all this. Isn't it coincidental that I buy Gyula Farkas's family home, and isn't it handy that I find that room. Honest to God, I bought the house from my buddy—private sale—and he gave me a good deal on it. The room and the letter, well, that was just God giving me a break for once. Doesn't everyone deserve a lucky break?

"So I'm feeling pretty pleased with myself. It's afternoon, a few hours to kill before my goose lays the egg, so to speak. I could go back to work or I could do other things. My wife hates dust, noise, and construction workers, so she's up in the bedroom with a designer friend planning paint colours, no idea what's going on underneath her. 'I thought you weren't going to be home 'til after dinner.' 'Guys downstairs had some questions for me.' 'I don't know what I've even got in the fridge.' 'No, no I'm going out again. But I've got a guy coming over after dinner. At nine.'

"I didn't tell her who it was. She gets all worried when she has to meet important-type people. I love my wife. She's great. But she's not used to having money, and sometimes she says she wishes she was back in that shitty panel in the Eleventh District where we started. I don't really believe her, but she likes to say it and I let her. So I'm on my way out the door, and my phone rings, and I answer it. Nothing important, just business. And then I think kifli and salami would be good right now and maybe a beer, so I'm on the phone and I'm making myself a snack, and then I remember I left something on my desk, so I'm back in my office. I know. Details. Whatever. They matter. I finally leave the house, I go to Maria's, we fuck like teenagers, I go to my favourite csarda for a bowl of goulash. Belly's full, balls empty. It's about seven and I figure I might as well head home, get prepared for this meeting. Not that I had much to prepare. Hand the guy a letter rolled in an old ribbon, show him some hospitality, give him a tour of the old house if he wants it, listen while he tells his old man stories. How hard can it be?"

Rev is looking bored. A practised bored, spinning his pen, doodling. Roth is getting interested. Can't help himself. There's a man who should never commit a crime. Gives it all away and doesn't even know he's doing it.

"I'd left the letter on my desk before going out. Positively, I had. No doubt in my mind, I had left that ancient goddamn letter rolled up in that dusty old ribbon, right there next to the computer keyboard. And there was the ribbon to prove it. 'Kato? Kato, cica?' I'm calling her, and I'm scrambling through piles of paperwork, opening every drawer in my desk. 'Did you do something with that letter on my desk?'

"I'm getting more than a little worried, right. I mean, I had Gyula fucking Farkas to face. This was my chance. This was my fucking shot at the big game, or at least a *ticket* to the game. Finally, Kato hears me. She appears at the door to my office, looking worried, wearing red. Woman dyes her hair cherry and then she wears bloody scarlet. This is what I mean. What kind of woman makes that mistake? And that look on her face. Not helping, not doing anything, just standing there. Dumb as a cunt. I mean, drive me up the fucking wall. 'What did you do with it, Kato? That letter. It was right here.' 'I don't know what you're talking about.' And then she looks scared. Why does she look scared? I treat her good. I don't beat on her. What have I ever done, to make her give me that face? Makes me fucking lose it every time. 'I left it here. Right here. Here is the ribbon.' I wave it at her. 'Which means that somebody took the paper out of the ribbon and moved it. And I don't see anyone else here, do you? So where did you put it?' 'I swear, Laci. Laci, I swear I didn't touch it. I didn't even come in here. I never come —.' 'Well, it didn't get up and walk away. Don't just stand there, you stupid cunt. Help me find it.' We looked for that letter for an hour. I swear to God I thought I was going to lose my mind. I retraced my steps through the entire house. I even checked the fridge, the drawer where the salami goes. I mean, what the fuck? It was supernatural the way that letter disappeared into thin air."

Detective Roth snorts. Rev just keeps his eyes on me. I don't know about this one. He's thinking. And I don't know what he's thinking. And that's unusual, I have to say.

"By eight-fifteen, I said fuckit. Fuckit, I don't have it. But I told Gombas I have it. And I need this break. And what the hell, I read it. I remember what it said, basically, which is not very much. And so I said to my wife, who was on her knees pulling files out of the filing cabinet and crying, I said, 'Get me your diary.' 'What?' 'JUST GET IT.' She started keeping a diary when she was sixteen. It was a gift from her grandmother. Kato wrote in it a little, but she never filled it. Women and their diaries, right. They always think they have secrets to spill into it, and then it turns out they don't. It was old paper. Not that old, but old. That rough, cheap paper and brittle. It would do. I sat her down in my chair at my desk, and I gave her a pencil and I told her to write. 'November 8, 1956. Dear Gyula.' And I told her to keep the writing really small and tight together, like you know you're going to run out of paper. 'When you put your arms around my waist that day you jumped from the tank, I knew it was love. I knew it was you that I loved, my sweet rebel.'

"I talked and my wife wrote until her wrist hurt. We had to cover five pages, one page for each day, which brought us to November 15, and to be honest I couldn't say I read it so carefully to know what each page said exactly. Not exactly. But this Zsofi woman, she complained about the cold, and she complained about her leg, and she said she didn't feel so good, and she missed him, and whatever. Love. Love, love. And do you really love me, or did you leave me here to die? I embellished to fill in the gaps with some 'I want you, Gyula. I want you to hold me like you used to, to fill me, to call me your Zsofika.' I mean, it's a love letter. They're all the same. We rolled it up, tied that ribbon around it.

"I will be honest with you now. I was nervous. I mean, this

is Gyula Farkas we're talking about here. But I got debts to pay, and if I could do Farkas a favour—well, money flows a lot easier when you're connected, right? He shows up at nine on the dot. I offer him a drink. No, thank you. A glass of water? Coffee? No and no. Anything? Just the letter. We're standing in the living room. Kato offers him a chair, but he doesn't sit. So she has to stand up again. The whole time standing there, he doesn't look around the room, doesn't look anywhere, just straight ahead to the patio doors, but at this time of night, they're just mirrors so really, he's only seeing himself and the room. Kato's getting uncomfortable, the way she does. I go to my office to get the letter. I hear her trying to make small talk about the house, and how he must have loved growing up here, so pretty, such a pretty neighbourhood, the house is pretty too, and the garden is pretty, and that tree outside is big and pretty. I get back with the letter. He hasn't even taken his overcoat off. Well, and Kato didn't ask to take it. Damn that woman. I give him the letter, all rolled up and tied exactly like the first one. He notices the ribbon. I notice him noticing, but he says nothing. He slides the letter into the breast pocket of his overcoat like it's a cigar. He touches a handkerchief to his lip.

"'And you said you found it in the cellar,' he says. He's so courteous. I don't know why I didn't expect that—tall, skinny, and courteous. When you see his photos in the paper, they don't show how tall he is. And soft-spoken, that was the other surprising thing. 'If it's all right with you, I'd like to take a look.'

"He knows the way downstairs, obviously, but he lets me lead the way. My guys had taken down the door, so from the foot of the stairs, he can see right through to the rock fall, the pushed-aside table, the pile of old cans.

"'It was in there,' I point and respectfully stand aside. 'By the table.'

"Gyula Farkas picks his way past me over construction rubble and, gripping what was left of the door frame, steps inside. I watch from where I'm standing at the foot of the stairs and then, as I'm watching, Gyula Farkas drops to his knees. Just drops. At first I think maybe he's having a heart attack or something, and I go to help him, but then I realize he's not. In his fine suit and overcoat, he's on the dirt floor and he's bending forward, putting his hands to the rock fall almost like he's a Muslim, praying into it.

"I think to myself, I shouldn't be here. My house, why shouldn't I, right? But that's what I think, and before I know it, I'm turning away so I'm surprised when he says, 'Was this rubble here? When you opened the door, I mean. Was it already here?'"

"'Sure. Yes. That door there led to a tunnel, right? Well, the tunnel must've caved in. Could've happened any time, but I think it happened a long time ago. Look there.' And I pointed to the table. 'See how it was pushed by the rock. See how dusty it all is. If it was new, the dust would look disturbed. The letter too. It hasn't moved in ... well, years.'

"As I'm talking, he's nodding. We're like two construction professionals down here, just talking business.

"'And this door, was it locked from the outside?'

"'If it was open, my men wouldn't have had to drill it out.'

"He's still facing the spill of earth and rock while he's talking to me. It takes him a while to stand, and when he does, he comes back through the door and right past me to a cellar wall we already cleared. He runs his hands over the brick, looking for something I guess, but seems he doesn't find it because then he's heading up the stairs, leaning pretty heavy on the banister.

"He says thank you as he leaves. He says this has meant a lot, seeing this place again, and the letter. He says, 'I may have misjudged you, Mr. Bekes.' He says, 'I know you'll keep this private matter between us.' He says, 'I'll be in touch.'

"And really, that's all I wanted, was a 'be in touch' with Gyula 'Gombas' Farkas. That's all I wanted, and I got it. I fucking got it. The car's pulling out of the driveway, headlights swoop white over the entrance hall, and I'm just about busting. 'Did you hear that?' I say to Kato. 'Did you *hear* that?'

"Kato doesn't really understand about these things, or why her husband is suddenly doing some kind of crazy dance around the house, but she's happy, you know. For me. Time to celebrate. So I tell her, don't wait up, and I call a buddy of mine, and I say, 'Drinks are on me,' and I'm out the door."

Rev says, "Could you excuse us for a minute, please?" And they leave me with my lawyer. Is he trying to make me nervous? Trying to throw me somehow? Hard to say, but I haven't even got to the best part, the part that clears me, so they better come back.

INTERROGATION, *Scene Three.*

Everyone takes his position as before.

"Do I keep talking?"

"Sure. Keep talking."

They switch the machine on again.

"So did I party? Yes, I did. From one club to the next. And I smoked a little dope and I drank a lot of beer. I was at it hard for must've been four hours and then I'm sitting with these gorgeous blondes from Sweden when my phone buzzes in my pants. It's my buddy, on his way home. Poor asshole doesn't have my stamina and he's got a wife who'll hang him by the balls from a Christmas tree. And he says to me 'Laci, I don't know what you did, but Gombas is looking for you. Two dudes. At least one is packing. They're on their way to Akacfa.'

"Jesus fuck.

"Jesus fucking Christ, fucking Kato, why did I trust her to write it, Jesus fuck, probably spelled it all wrong.

"So I'm standing up now, getting ready to sprint, and then I thought, No. No, then what? Then they keep coming after me. Better to just tell the truth. I lost the fucking letter. I remember what was in it, but I lost it. I'll find it, but you have to give me a day or two. And I was thinking, There goes my favour from Gombas. If I could just delay them. And then it hits me. I must have taken the letter to Maria's. Did I do that? Sure. Sure I must have. Which means it likely fell out of my coat pocket when we were fucking. Sure, I fuck with my coat on. Don't you when you're in a hurry? So if I call Maria, tell her to find the letter... No, no time. All this, I'm thinking to myself at lightning speed, detectives. Because if those boys are on the hunt, then I'm the fucking duck and there's no time to lose. And then I thought, I need a decoy. And *then* I had my idea: Janos. That's my brother's Canadian friend, Janos Hagy. That's right, the guy who owns this incriminating Toronto Maple Leafs jacket. Can you see where this is going now? Okay, so the thing about Janos is that he's a *little* smarter than Csaba, and he thinks I walk on water. He is ambitious, though, I give him that. Wants to be my right-hand man, so he'd do anything for me. People always say we look alike. Like twins, almost. So

I call him up. I say, 'How fast can you be here?' Like I figured, he was just happy to be asked."

I reward myself with a very long drink of water to give them time to put it together. Yes, they're putting it together.

"Mystery solved, detectives. *This* is why you found me at four a.m. in a murderer's jacket and a murderer's shoes. Janos was happy to help. Pretend to be Laci Bekes for an hour? Shit, the kid nearly wet himself. Now, I recognize this wasn't the finest moment of my life, setting up an innocent to take my beating, but honest to God I just wanted to buy myself some time. Time to find the fucking original letter and work out some major butt-licking apology. Who'd have thought a guy like Gombas would give a shit. I mean, it's a *love* letter. From fifty years ago. Which means that twat has got to be seventy years old by now. As I say, I'm not proud. I'm not at all proud of what I did."

I look at my feet, give them a good penitent and troubled stare.

"I told Janos what he had to say to pretend he was me, and I left. Found my loser brother waiting for me halfway down the street, mad as anything because I always choose Janos over him or some shit like that, because I never take him seriously, never let him in on the business. I shook him off. Told him to go home and cry to his mother. Should have been a bit nicer, I suppose, or I wouldn't be sitting here right now, taking his fall."

You see how it all comes together.

There needs to be a pause, don't you think, after a realization like that? Do you taste it? Move on.

"You want to catch yourself a gypsy-murderer, you look for a Canadian kid named Janos Hagy, staying with his grandma in the Thirteenth District. I can give you the address. And when you find him, you'll find he's wearing a good quality brown leather coat, and in that coat pocket, you'll find both my wallet and my goddamn car keys."

These detectives will have questions. Sure. I don't think we're done here. They might want to check out my cellar. See if the creepy room is real. Let them. I've got nothing to hide. And if Gombas is after my ass, this as good a place to be as any. And besides, my lawyer tells me an unidentified head was found on Gellert early this morning. Who the hell drops a head on Gellert? Gombas, that's who. So do these boys want to take me seriously? You bet. They *want* to believe Laci Bekes now. Yes, oh yes, they do.

After Budapest

Two weeks ago, he looked her up on Facebook and there she was: smiling radiant, Daniel's face next to hers, his arm out-reaching, holding the camera, retarded kid nowhere in sight. How did some people manage to look so happy? He thought he was over her, but when he saw her there, Daniel's face mostly overwhelmed by her hair, he felt a blip of something and, in nearly the same moment, irritation. You idiot, Tibor. All those little fantasies about bumping into her, and how happy she'd be to see him. How they'd go for a walk, or sit side by side on some ordinary city bench somewhere, and he'd tell her everything that had happened in Budapest—the murder he'd witnessed, the cops who'd tried to frame him, his mother's sudden irrational fear of her old boyfriend. To Rafaela, he could confess, finally, how terrified he'd been. And her forehead would wrinkle in concern, and her eyes would look on him with forgiveness. Yes, forgiveness. Not because he deserves it, necessarily, but because he suffered, *is* suffering. Because he needs it.

The phone rings. He answers.

"Tibor. What are you doing?" Never *how* with his mother, always *what*.

Reflexively, he closes Facebook. "Working. I'm working, Mom."

Outside his window, a fat grey squirrel travels an improbably thin branch. Tibor toggles up and down his lecture, a couple of pages, all crap. And not nearly enough crap to fill the two bloody hours alone behind that podium.

"Good. When you finish, you can come for dinner. I want to show you my pictures from Budapest. I made a slide show. With music."

"That sounds great, but I'm at a rather crucial point in this lecture. I thought I might push through."

"I don't know how you can work at night. I always think the best ideas come when the mind is relaxed, awake. You'd be better to work in the morning, after a good night's sleep."

That's a laugh; he hasn't slept since Budapest. "I like working at night. No distractions."

"I don't want to distract you, Tibor."

And now it's raining. The squirrel huddles under its tail. Last thing he wants to do is make the trek to North York to see a slide show of Budapest. He was *there*, for fucksake. "How about tomorrow? I'll come for lunch. I'll bring you korozot from the deli."

She pauses before replying. Just so he'll hear how selfish he's being.

"Persze. And don't worry about the korozot, we'll just have the chicken paprikas I made for tonight. I can reheat it in the microwave."

Tibor looks at the huddled squirrel. He looks at his un-written lecture. Persze, he shuts down his computer. "Chicken paprikas? Why didn't you say so?"

. . .

The house smells like paprikas cooking. Like lemon furniture polish and old cushions. Like his mother and like rain because once every day, sometimes twice if there was company, and no matter what the weather she'd open the front windows wide to air out the house.

"Hallo," he calls out. He drips on the hallway rug with his bag of korozot.

"I'm in here."

He follows the voice down the short parquet hallway to the kitchen, where his mother sits at the kitchen table, already set with green oval plastic placemats, white paper napkins in the blue plastic holder, green cut-glass tumblers, watching the news on TV. She looks up with a smile and holds out her hands for his face to kiss.

"It's pouring out there. Your hair looks nice."

He puts the korozot in the fridge. There is no need to present it to her. She knows he's brought it as he always does, and she will find it there tomorrow morning and it will be nice. It will be nice for her to sit in her yellow kitchen and eat the Hungarian korozot that she hasn't requested and that her good son has brought without expecting thanks. She waves her hand at the compliment, her eyes now focused again on the television news.

Two teenagers were shot last night. The suspect is described as black, average height, wearing a black head scarf. They show the parking lot where it happened, the TV lights glaring on the slick asphalt, a tarp that you know covers a body, a club at the end of a strip mall. Now, the day after, the story is focused on the police and the family. The family believes the police don't do enough. The police are increasingly worried about gangs in Scarborough. The mayor looks worried too.

Tibor spoons the rich, creamy stew out of the pot onto two plates placed ready beside the stove. In the oven is his favourite potato casserole. The bread is sliced and in a basket on the table. Beside the bread, a small bowl of minced peppers.

There's a comfort in the habits, he has to admit, in the not needing to be asked to serve the stew or to check the oven for the potatoes.

"Jo etvagyat," she says.

As usual, there's little conversation while they eat. The TV news continues. He comments that paprikas is the perfect meal for a cold day, and his favourite potatoes are even more delicious than usual. They eat and they mop the last of the creamy sauce with their bread and they watch the news together. And then, a Hungarian accent. A middle-aged man, wide forehead crimped in two deep horizontal lines: "I am asking the Canadian government for help to solve my son's murder."

The father pleads, heart broken, as the camera fixes on his face, which now fills the screen.

The reporter takes over. "Hagy's son's head was found in a park in Budapest, more than a month ago. The body has still not been recovered. Hungarian police believe the murder to be linked to the city's organized crime, but they will not say how. Here in Ottawa, a spokesperson from the Prime Minister's Office says Canadian officials are watching the case but will not intercede in the investigation." Flash to the father, standing empty-handed in what must be his son's bedroom, before a poster of red Formula 1 Ferraris. "No news is sad news for a father who should be celebrating his son's twenty-first birthday today."

At the table, the silence thickens. Reporters keep reporting. Iran. Afghanistan. People interviewed express anger, outrage, grief—the usual. And it's horrid that it's usual, but the world is not small, as people insist. It's huge. It has too many people and too many wars, too many disasters, and compassion only stretches so far. The bad news continues for approximately four minutes before the local weather.

"Rain! Expected to turn to *freezing* rain tomorrow!" There really is no Schadenfreude like a weather forecaster's. "Wet snow later in the week, turning to flurries by weekend. Don't pack away those boots just yet, folks."

Tibor's mother clicks off the TV and turns her face toward her son, clearly expecting he should have something to say. Tibor stands, takes the dishes off the table. He runs the dishes under hot water before putting them in the dishwasher.

"I think we should contact him, Tibor."

We? He presses start and is rewarded with the soft roar of pressured water. Tibor dries his hands on the faded floral towel. He feels more tired than he has ever felt, more tired than he thought it was possible for a human to feel. He hasn't slept since Budapest. Days just keep blurring into dusk, then into dawn. Last night, after finally drifting off at one, he woke at two, finally gave up at four, turned on his computer, and tried to work.

"He deserves to know."

Really? The man wants to know what happened to his boy on that pitched, rocky, and heretical slope at the ass end of a Budapest night? In what way is this Tibor's responsibility? He's just so fucking tired he can hardly get through his day, never mind take care of this.

"It won't help," he says finally, tersely.

The rain pelts against the windows. They stare at each other across the kitchen in the warm, ordinary house that has been Agnes's own, alone, for nearly five years now. Here is her son, her only child. He stands with the dishtowel in his hands, waiting for her to concede. She usually does concede, not because she believes him, but because he needs it so badly. Sometimes, in moments like these, she wonders, does she love this son of hers? And the answer is in her bones and in the emptiness at her centre that he once filled, as she and Zsofi had once filled the emptiness at Margit's centre. She doesn't believe in unconditional love, but she does believe in this, this love that happens without her permission, that slides beneath her better judgment. When Agnes's father had disappeared, her mother crumpled up whatever love she had left, pressed it into something that allowed nothing in, a sharp bitterness that she nurtured. That substitution too likely happens without permission. While Agnes created a kind of moderate happiness here, found a man to love, made this son with him, her mother had filled the holes in her life with lists of losses. Agnes was not her mother. This was a relief. But neither was she her son.

"Come, Anyu," — the diminutive, he hardly ever uses it — "let's look at those photos." And he leans over, puts his hand gently on hers. His father used to do exactly this when it was time to change the subject.

Everything is all ready to go in the basement office: two desk chairs positioned in front of the computer. They sit, side by side, stiffly upright. She clicks play.

Disconcertingly, the first photo is of Tibor on the airplane, fast asleep, book open on his lap, mouth slightly ajar. "Ha," he says. And he has a visceral, somehow embarrassing sense of how much she loves him. And then, Budapest. Lights spangle the Danube at night and midday the parliament shines sugar white. The chain bridge spans, the castle imposes. Trees in the cemetery weep. It's a beautiful city and there is Gellert Hegy, but from a safe distance. There is an old building. Another old building. A new building.

In Vienna, as they visited museums and pastry shops, it was as if Budapest had never happened. As if by tacit agreement, she didn't speak of Gyula or her missing sister, and he didn't speak of the boy's head or Detective Sarkady. It was easier that way. It was bearable. They spent a fairly pleasant week touristing in Austria. He changed their flights, and they flew home from Vienna without a hitch. The Budapest police, it appeared, weren't looking for him. Apparently, they didn't need his testimony. Apparently, he was not being framed. He was both relieved and chastened by this realization.

Now, as the image shifts, strangely, to what seems like the entrance to a cellar, he says, "Who was Gyula, in 1956?"

"Gyula?" She shrugs. "He was any boy, a good liar. Sweet. He believed in his revolution."

"But you didn't?"

On the screen their hotel, modern and innocent, pots of blooming pink at the entrance.

"For a day, maybe. For a day or two, I did."

She juts a chin at the screen: Margit Hid, yellow streetcars jaunting across it. "The first day of the revolution, we marched across that bridge. I was there."

The next photo: the fountain in Szabadsag Ter that comes up out of the pavement in four walls of water, then suddenly sinks. "Zsofi was joking with the men in the tanks. Flirting, more likely. No one thought they'd fire."

The wide boulevard of the Korut, bisected by the tram tracks, lined with imposing, nineteenth-century buildings in grey and yellow and green. On one, the pilasters lifting the corner balcony are Zeus, or some other strong, bearded God who holds things together. "I saw a man hung from his ankles at that corner. AVO. A woman set his hair on fire."

Rows of cakes under glass. "That café was always busy, even when there was no coffee and no eggs for cake."

The photos slide. Agnes narrates. And it helps with that feeling that she'd been living with since Budapest, the feeling that she was two people: one, Agi, the lover of Gyula and sister of Zsofi, and two, Mrs. Agnes Roland, inside this tidy bungalow enclosed in a green lawn, encircled by wide asphalt road. How impossible. How utterly impossible, to live a life so decisively divided.

She'd believed that in Budapest she would bridge it. She thought she would find the tunnels, and in this act, this foolish act of belief, she would somehow across the span of years and politics recover the girls they used to be. Such beautiful, such difficult, such *girls* they'd been. Every year, looking at long-limbed, glossy-haired, smooth teenaged Canadians, she'd thought, I was that young once. And every year, it became more remarkable. *That* young? That young, they had been each other's safety. The feel of those skinny, childish arms around each other, Zsofi's shoulder blades just under the surface, the strength of that wrap.

Decisively divided only because — *all* because — faced with her sister's conceited, immature, unfounded, and smug claim to a love that should have been her own — that *had been* her own — she'd thought, Fine. You think love will save you? Learn the hard way.

When she knew, she *knew*, that if she'd kept talking, Zsofi would have come round. She always did. Eventually, the posturing would have dropped, reality would have penetrated, the utter and terrifying futility of a teenaged girl standing up to Soviet tanks. Agi could have — *should* have — forced the issue, argued longer, made her understand, but she didn't because she was mad. Mad-jealous, mad the way only a sister can make you mad. Making that dash across the road, through the forest with so many other frightened souls she'd been fuelled not by desire for freedom but by fury. Furious with Gyula, with Zsofi, with her mother. They had put her in this position. *They* had left *her* to do this alone. That injury, that resentment had propelled her, had filled her lungs and pushed at her back like a mob. The colour of resentment is not red but violet as bruises, and it smells of others' sweat.

Thanks to two angers — Zsofi's hot, hormonal, and jealous, and Agi's foul, spiteful, and dark — one sister had been swallowed by war as the other stumbled to freedom. And Agnes had lived with that while raising this child. She'd felt, in the gestures that were her mother's, in her lovemaking with a husband who was not Gyula, in laughter she did not share with Zsofi, the incommensurability of their fates, and the irredeemably locked door of the past. She had left. She was no longer that girl. No one here called her Agi. And while she sometimes tried to reason with her past — it would not have been better for anyone had she stayed; Zsofi would still have disappeared, imprisoned or killed; Gyula would still have been arrested—how could it have turned out any differently for a murderer and a revolutionary?—she remembers her anger and she despises her stupid young self.

Perhaps Zsofi had escaped with Dorottya to Vienna, only to suffer a more ordinary violent death—hit by a car, caught in a house fire, drowned in a boating accident, strangled by a boyfriend that she, Agnes, had never met. Or maybe Dorottya had the wrong Zsofi. Maybe Agnes's Zsofi had been shot by the Russians along with dozens of others, her body tipped anonymous into the Duna, the floor of which must surely be thick with bones. Maybe she died of a gunshot wound on the street, was buried in a park, the grave unmarked. There were as many ways to die as to live, no doubt, and some secrets are never known, but what Agnes knew, what she had always known, was that Zsofi was dead. How it happened, when it happened, who did it—all these questions were inconsequential, in the end. Zsofi had been gone for more than fifty years. She had only lived sixteen. At some point, the vacant mass of unlived life outweighs the lived. She was a child, she'd died a child, and Agi had gone on.

"There is the building where we lived," she says. "That day that Zsofi killed the man, we were fighting. About Gyula, if you can believe it."

This is more than his mother has ever shared with him. She did all this, went to these places, revisited old terrors, all the while taking pictures like any tourist in walking shoes. He wouldn't have expected this of her, somehow, this directed and purposeful retracing of steps.

The field by the university. "Rebel stronghold," she says, and it sounds medieval.

As Tibor leaves, he says thank you. "Thank you, Anyu. Csokolom." And she knows he is, truly, thankful and that he would like to say more but doesn't know how because after all he is her son, and she is his mother, and this is the best they can do.

At 4:00 a.m., as usual, he's awake. He hauls himself from bed to desk, flicks on his desk lamp, jabs the computer on. He opens his unfinished lecture. And he writes:

> *My mother lost her sister during the revolution. She doesn't know what happened to her. The sister simply disappeared. As happens in any war, some victims are never accounted for. My mother also believes, along with many other Hungarians who lived through first the war and then the revolution, that the Germans, and then the Soviets after them, constructed a network of tunnels deep under Budapest. In the period of Soviet occupation, Hungarians thought that the party bosses had stores of luxury foods down there, that people were imprisoned deep underground, that the building of the subway, which halted before the revolution, was only a pretence, a grand entranceway to a parallel, underground, secret city.*

He has never, in a lecture or at a conference, or in a published paper, spoken of his mother's experiences of Budapest. Only now does this strike him as odd.

He remembers when he first realized that she must have emigrated in 1956. "You stood up to Stalinism," he enthused. He must have just taken his first class in Eastern European history.

"What do you study? Stalin was dead by 1956."

The revolutionary taking of Communist Headquarters had been documented in *Life Magazine*, which he pored over at the university library. Black-and-white photographs of the violence, a blond uniformed man, maybe AVO, his head launched back with the force of a revolutionary bullet. Faced with these photos, Tibor realized he had to reconsider everything he thought he knew about his mother—and he'd made his decision, then, that he would figure out what happened during those brief weeks of freedom. This was how he thought of it at the time. He, Tibor Roland, was connected in the first person to these brave young men and women who'd fought and lost. He now understood that these events shaped not only his mother—and that bowl of silence she carried imperturbably through all the rooms of her life—but his own past, his self. He was a child of these circumscribed facts, of all she'd left behind. And he felt, well, he felt that it added something to him. Not mystery, not quite, but something.

"But Stalin-*ism*, Mom."

"*Ism* did not drive the tanks."

"So you fled when the tanks came in."

"I *left*," she corrected as she sliced an apple or folded a tea towel. He can't remember a conversation with his mother when she wasn't also doing something else. She pours cream into the chicken paprikas, or polishes the table with lemon oil, or takes a sharp knife to the crusty accumulation between kitchen sink and counter as if there was not enough time in her day to simply talk.

"I walked across the Austrian border with dozens of others. There were Red Cross trucks waiting for us on the other side. And that was that. So"—brushing crumbs from the table—"I have no revolution stories."

"But what about before you left?"

On her gleaming table, he opened the folder he'd brought with him: photocopies of images from the November 1956 *Life Magazine*.

She folded the damp cloth in her gloved hands. She wiped the seat of the vinyl chair. She hardly glanced at the photo of that blond man hauled out, blood streaming.

"I wasn't there," she said. "I had nothing to do with that." Removing yellow gloves, placing them neatly over the side of the sink, parallel with the blue J Cloth — as if such precision mattered.

He asked her so many questions, that time and others, and rather than answer she just busied herself around them not because she wasn't there, he now realized, but because she *was*, if not at Koztarsasag, then other places. She'd seen a man hung by his ankles and burned. He'd somehow failed to imagine this.

It's hard when reading the past to remember that in the middle of war, the survivors don't know they will survive and no one knows which side will win. From the distance of now, it seems the winners and survivors are protected from the start, tethered already to a future safely assured. As a historian, he should know better. He writes:

Here are two witness accounts of the events in Koztarsasag Ter the day that Life Magazine *so famously photo-documented. The first is from a revolutionary leader:*

I was with a group of revolutionaries who captured an AVO secret policeman. The others wanted to kill the man, but I only wanted to interrogate him. I'd learned that underneath the Communist Headquarters, which

*bordered Koztarsasag Ter, was a secret prison. Arrested
students were being held there. As we stood there debating
the fate of this secret policeman, I felt pounding coming
from underground. The prisoners were right there. Right
under our feet. Before I could take the AVO away for
interrogation, another revolutionary struck the man
with his rifle barrel so hard that the man's skull burst,
smattering us all with his brains.*

    *The second account comes from an architect involved in
the building of the Communist Headquarters who insists
the crowd of revolutionaries in Koztarsasag were all seized
by some kind of mass hallucination.*

    *These people said they could hear sounds from buried
prisoners. When even bulldozers couldn't unearth the secret
prison, the revolutionaries sent a message over the radio,
asking for anyone who knew anything about the prison
to call the radio station. One of my colleagues called in to
report that our firm designed the building, so a soldier
came to my office requesting information. I reviewed all
the building plans of the Headquarters. There was no
prison. I called the original architect and engineer, and
they agreed with me: there was no secret underground
prison. There never had been.*

    *No resonance imaging has ever shown any evidence of
the tunnels' existence. And so the tunnels remain a mystery,
riddling the modern post-Soviet city. It's tempting to call
them an urban myth, born of wartime terrors. And yet…*

Tibor looks up. The sun is still hours from rising, but the city
radiates its own bruised yellow glow. And yet?

And yet he knows because he was there, that there are tunnels under Budapest, deep holes in the surface where the murdered go.

The woman who pours his double-double looks Ethiopian. Tibor invests his "thank you" with extra special warmth. *I see you.* That's what his thank you says: *I recognize that you're worth more than this.* Half his brain is making these reflexive, habitual social moves. The other half hates himself, so he stops.

He chooses a table at the window facing onto Davenport, as far from other customers as possible. Hagy was the one who suggested this Tim Hortons on the side of a busy main artery into town. At three, cars sit bumper to bumper waiting for the light to change and dirty March snow wetly falls.

Tibor doesn't want to be here. He wants to be anywhere but here. But here's the thing: sometimes, at night or during the day, some random, sharp-cornered memory of Budapest forces its way up — of Gellert's night slope, of Detective Sarkady, of that panicked dash from the embassy over ice, his mother's fall, the obscene head — and he has to stand or do pushups or walk to the store or drink till he finally sleeps. But there is no way to dodge the sharp soreness that has insinuated itself like a splinter in a softly willing region of his brain because he is the witness and if he walks away, he will still be the witness, and the murdered may or may not stay buried, but he will still be the witness and the murderer may or may not go free, but he will still be the witness because the witness remains and this is his shame.

He knows this now.

The man who enters is similar to the one on the news

but shorter. On the TV cameras, his shoulders and grief had seemed to fill the screen. In person, he no longer fully inhabits himself. His black leather bomber inflates a less stocky build. His jeans bag. At the door, he pauses and looks around. He strains with the effort of normalcy, hands shoved in pockets, shoulders thrown back with habitual confidence, but as his scanning eyes finally land on Tibor, he looks like a man willing his knees not to give.

Somehow he walks. Calmly, he takes his seat in front of Tibor. He folds his broad hands on the table. He looks straight into Tibor's face. And he waits.

Under

Gyula's spade hits rock. Get under, thrust it out. Soil crumbles. Should be flooded down here, but it's not. It's dry. It's dry because it has a roof and walls and they're waterproof. So the tunnel is waterproof. He's sweating. Take the coat off. That woman upstairs is finally quiet, her yapping and pounding done. It takes time for people to accept their fates, and then they do and there's just silence. His throat is dry from the dust and he wants water, but why should he be so kind to himself? His muscles will give him hell for days and his conscience maybe too for the woman upstairs who so kindly let him in, but this is nothing. Hell is nothing. He's been there once before and he survived. Fucking Laci Bekes. His spade goes deep. He hefts it out. To forge Zsofi's handwriting? To show him the cellar and this goddamn room, to treat Gyula Farkas like he's some doddery, sentimental old man, all the time pretending to be respectful, pretending to have some fucking message from the dead. To *forge* it? No, Laci Bekes does not get to walk away from this. Not from this. Laci Bekes has seen him on his knees, on his goddamn knees at this pile of earth. Well, very soon that piece of shit will be on *his* knees, begging for mercy at the top of Gellert Hegy. Each time Gyula rams his shovel into earth, he feels the shock of contact travel up his arm and into his shoulder. He used to think of Zsofi Teglas every day. In prison, he thought of nothing else. Locked underground without another human voice for months, he had only his guilt and his love. One had to win out. On his release, he didn't come back to this house, didn't come knocking on the door, demanding entrance to the cellar. He didn't look for her because it no longer mattered. He was not the same Gyula. Underground, he lived without light. He ate whatever crawled on him. He thought he was dead, but when he felt his own urine hot against his thigh knew he was alive, and forgotten. It is not possible to emerge from that darkness intact. In the end, here's all he knows: people hate and people die. Some are set on fire. Some have their beating hearts dug out. Some are tortured until there is nothing left of the human inside. Some are buried alive. The end doesn't matter. Gyula Farkas survived because he is a survivor. He survived because surviving is all that remains. And that doesn't bear thinking about either.

It's quiet down here. All he wants is the sound of his spade against rock.

I promised you, Zsofi. Didn't I promise? I will tunnel under this city to find you. I will burrow to get you out.

I would like to thank Julia Creet for taking me to Hungary; Ilona Roth for lessons, friendship, and Budapest nights; and Gabor Leeb, my first tour guide. Thanks also to my agent, John Pearce, whose support has never flagged, and my editor, Bethany Gibson, whose insightful reading has made this a better book than I thought possible. I'm grateful for the support of the Toronto Arts Council and the Ontario Arts Council.

Many books have been important to the writing of this one: *Eyewitness in Hungary: The Soviet Invasion of 1956*, particularly chapters by Peter Fryer and Dora Scarlett, edited by William Lomax; *The Storyteller: Memory, Secrets, Magic and Lies*, by Anna Porter; *Budapest Exit: A Memoir of Fascism, Communism, and Freedom*, by Csaba Teglas; and *Encounters: A Hungarian Quarterly Reader*, edited by Zsófia Zachár. The most important source for "Now or Never" was *A Student's Diary: Budapest, October 16–November 1, 1956*, by Laszlo Beke. The story of the girl who offers Agnes a candy from her pocket is based on memory recounted on FreedomFighter56.com, an oral history project of The Hungarian American Coalition and Lauer Learning. The Sandor Petofi poem, which was recited during

the revolution, is "Nemzeti Dal" or "The Song of the Nation."
I have used Laszlo Korossy's translation, available on his website
at www.korossy.org/magyar.

After the Russian forces ended the revolution, retaliation for
revolutionary activity was swift and extensive. Between late
1956 and 1959, 35,000 people were charged with political
crimes. Approximately 22,000 were convicted, most for
participating in the revolution or the ensuing "resistance."
Approximately 13,000 prisoners were sent to reopened intern-
ment camps outside of Budapest, and 229 people were executed.
In response to these measures, Hungarians developed what
psychologist Ferenc Marai called a "national amnesia" about
the revolution. This silence and forgetting lasted at least twenty
years (Janos Rainer, "The Reprisals," *Encounters*).

The secret tunnels and underground prisons have never been
found, yet belief in them remains. The inspiration for this book
came originally from Istvan Rev's *Retroactive Justice: Prehistory
of Post-Communism,* in which he analyzes Hungary's attachment
to stories about the secret tunnels. Tibor's two accounts of the
search for prisons under Communist Party Headquarters are
based on witness accounts by Károly G. Oláh and László Papp,
available at FreedomFighter56.com. Gyula's experience in a
deep underground prison is based not on memoirs of prisoners
but on the persistent belief in such prisons.

Ailsa Kay fell in love with Budapest
when she lived there in 2004 and
she returns as often as she can.

Her short fiction has appeared in
literary journals such as *Exile*
and *The New Quarterly*.
She lives in Fergus, Ontario.
Under Budapest is her first novel.

Under Budapest